Dreaming in Norwegian

FRANKIE VALENTE

ISBN:
ISBN-13: 978-1511847353
ISBN-10: 1511847352

For my father,
Dominic Francis Smith

ACKNOWLEDGMENTS

Thank you to my lovely friends and family who have offered their support and encouragement throughout the time it took to write the book. It wasn't the happiest year for me, so it was very much needed and appreciated. Special thanks to Cecilie Johannessen, Nina and Laurie Goodlad and Melanie Hudson for their invaluable contributions to the book.

Thanks to my lovely son, Franklin Smith, for the use of the cover.

Frankie Valente

1

'Hey, you're not supposed to be on that side of the wall; it's a bird sanctuary. Didn't you see the sign?'

Lisa Balfour had been sitting on a deserted beach on an uninhabited island enjoying a few moments of peace and was not happy to see the RSPB warden marching towards her in his pseudo military uniform. He bent down and pick up a length of blue plastic rope and shook it at her. 'Nobody is supposed to cross over this rope.'

Lisa shrugged. 'I didn't know that was a "sign" to say you mustn't go on the beach. It's not exactly what you'd call plain English. I'm leaving now anyway.'

'You could at least take your rubbish home with you,' he replied, pointing to a plastic bottle at her feet.

Lisa was about to protest it wasn't hers, but the warden had already turned away and was gazing up at the Arctic terns, who had a tendency to attack anyone who wandered close to their nesting sites. Lisa picked up the bottle and stuffed it into the deep pocket of her jacket, climbed over the wall and set off over the hill to the boat jetty. The warden marched ahead of her, his eyes peeled for other humans who might dare to be trespassing on the beach.

When Lisa arrived at the jetty, Roland, her archaeology lecturer, and the other students from the field-trip were waiting for her. She took a seat on the boat and immediately felt a tap on her shoulder.

'You OK?' Roland said, leaning in towards her.

'Yeah; sorry I walked off, I needed some quiet time.'

'That's OK. Thanks for coming along and helping me out. I know you've done Mousa Broch to death but I think the first year students have enjoyed it, even if one or two of them aren't taking it seriously. I hope you were using your "quiet time" to think some more about doing a PhD?'

Lisa tugged at the frayed cuff of her shirt then tucked it under the sleeve of her jacket. 'I'm still torn, but time is running out for my grandfather. If I don't record what he did during the war soon, it will be too late. He only started to talk about it after he had his stroke.'

'How old is he?'

'Eighty seven.'

Roland pursed his lips. 'He *was* a young man at the time.'

'Boy; he was only fifteen when he joined the resistance.'

'As I said before, this has great potential. Did you enquire about funding?'

'Yes, I'll find out in a few weeks if I can get a bursary. But even if I don't get the money, I'm tempted to write a book about him anyway.'

'Good for you!'

While they were chatting, the boat pulled away from the jetty and headed back to the mainland. The breeze made Lisa's eyes water. She rummaged in her pockets for a tissue and pulled the plastic bottle out of her pocket and was about to toss it into the bin when she noticed a piece of paper inside. The lid was securely sealed with tape and more intriguingly, there was writing on the paper.

'Hey, did you find a message in a bottle? Let's see!' One of the other students demanded, holding out her hand towards Lisa in an attempt to snatch it from her.

'No, it's just rubbish,' Lisa said, pushing the bottle back inside her pocket. Beside her, Roland chuckled.

Later that evening, after Lisa had put her eighteen month old son, Hansi, to bed she opened the bottle to retrieve the message. It was scrawled on a piece of graph paper, ripped untidily from the pages of an exercise book. The red ink had faded a little but was still legible with effort.

Hello! My name is Joakim Haaland. I live in Norway and I am hoping to find a new friend across the sea. If you find this, write to me and I will write back.

There was an address and it was dated 9th January 2007. Lisa folded the letter up and put it in her desk drawer. She would think about replying another time. After so many years Joakim had probably forgotten all about the message.

2

Lisa ran up the steps to her grandfather's house and opened the front door. She found her mother in the kitchen, muttering about the untidiness.

'Leave that; I'll clear up before I go home,' Lisa said, trying to pre-empt her mother's grumbles.

'He's getting worse. He's not eating properly. This can't go on,' her mother replied.

'I'll make him some dinner too. Stop fretting!'

'It's all very well saying that, but someone has to look after him.'

Lisa left the kitchen and went in search of her grandfather and found him in the lounge, staring out of the window. The television was on but the sound was muted.

'Hello Moffa; how are you today?'

He didn't reply, although Lisa was sure he had heard her. She put her arm around his shoulder and he smiled when Lisa pulled up a chair beside him.

'Seen any interesting birds, Moffa?' Lisa said, noticing the binoculars on her grandfather's lap.

He shook his head. 'I can't see a thing through these. My eye sight is useless these days.'

Lisa picked up the binoculars and cleaned the lens with the hem of her shirt and lifted them to her eyes. It was a complete blur until she adjusted the focus. Then she tried again and watched a robin hopping around underneath the bird-feeder dangling from the washing line. She handed the binoculars back to her grandfather.

'Try that Moffa; your robin's been at the bird-feeder again.'

Moffa tried the binoculars and he laughed when he spotted the bird that had recently taken up residence in the garden.

'I'm not so blind then.'

'Not at all; they were just out of focus.'

'Where's my little man?'

'Hansi's gone to nursery today. I wanted to get you on your own so I could ask you some questions for my project.'

Moffa turned his wheelchair in the direction of the television and reached for the remote control. Lisa sighed.

'How about I make you a sandwich first? Mam said you're not eating properly.'

'Ingrid talks nonsense. Of course I eat; how else would I still be alive?'

Lisa grinned at his belligerence. Her grandfather hated being dependent on other people. His stroke had left him frail and forgetful, but he had regained his speech thankfully, and he could still get around in his new wheelchair. On good days he could get up and walk a short distance with the aid of his stick; but driving was impossible, and this made him miserable.

'Do you want to go for a drive instead? How about I take you up to Lunna Kirk? It's too nice to stay in today.'

Her grandfather turned away from the television and stared at her, as if he sensed a trap, but she had piqued his interest.

'We'll stop at the café at Weisdale on the way if you like. You like it there don't you?'

The Jeremy Kyle Show was starting. Moffa reached for the remote control and snapped it off.

'OK!'

'Great; I'll just tell Mam where I'm taking you.'

Lisa found her mother in the utility room searching through the cupboards.

'What have you lost?'

'Nothing; I was wondering what Dad's done with that old Lalique vase. It's not in the lounge and he says he hasn't broken it, so I thought maybe he had put it somewhere strange. I would hate for it to get broken.'

Lisa shrugged, 'I'm taking him out for a drive. He's not in one of his talkative moods, so maybe he'll cheer up if we go out. It's such a lovely day isn't it?'

'Lisa, why do you insist on bothering him about the past? It's obvious he doesn't want to talk about it. You're upsetting him.'

'Because he won't be here forever, and then I'll never get the chance. I want to get to know him better. Anyway, sometimes he talks when he's in the right mood. I think it helps him. He spends far too much time on his own.'

Her mother slammed the cupboard door shut. 'Just make sure he eats something then. I'm going out with Drew tonight, so I won't be able to come back and cook for him later.'

Lisa raised her eyes to heaven behind her mother's back, before going to help her grandfather get ready. She was surprised to find he had already fetched his jacket and stick. He stood, a little unsteadily in the hall, one hand holding onto the wall for support.

'You're all set then, Moffa?' Lisa said, taking his arm and opening the front door. He winked at her, as if they were conspiring together.

They set off in Lisa's battered Fiat Punto. She switched the radio off in the hope Moffa would talk more, but he seemed content to sit and enjoy the view as they drove along the road from Quarff up to Lunna. As they drove through Lerwick, Moffa stared mournfully at the marina.

'Do you want to stop and look at the boats?'

'Not today thanks. There won't be anyone I know there.'

'Do you miss fishing?'

'I don't miss getting freezing cold; but I do miss going out on the boat.'

'You should go on a fishing trip one day. They run them for tourists in the summer.'

'I'm not a tourist,' he replied, shaking his head, but not taking his eyes away from the harbour.'

They stopped at Bonhoga café in Weisdale. Lisa had chosen this place deliberately, as it was close to a house that had been used as part of the *Shetland Bus* mission during the Second World War. The Norwegian Royal Family had stayed there briefly after fleeing Norway, and she was dying to ask Moffa whether he had met them, but knew from experience any direct questioning would make him clam up.

Lisa ordered tea and cakes while Moffa sat by the window peering down at the stream that flowed alongside the café.

'I'll get my results soon,' she said, as she poured the tea.

Moffa tilted his head to one side. 'Results?'

'For my Masters in Scottish Archaeology.'

'I thought you finished that years ago.'

'That was my degree. I went back to university last year, don't you remember?'

Moffa nodded vaguely and continued to stare out of the window.

'Brown trout,' he said, pointing down at the water.

Lisa only saw the circle of ripples where the fish had submerged beneath the surface again. She grinned at Moffa.

'Hansi loves fish too.'

'Where is he today?'

'At his nursery.'

'You told me already. Where's my brain today?'

'The same place mine is sometimes,' Lisa said, laughing with him.

Moffa bit his cake and chewed thoughtfully for a moment. 'What was Ingrid looking for in the kitchen?'

'That old vase of grandma's, I think. She was worried you broke it.'

'I haven't broken it. I hid it in my wardrobe as I don't want her to take it.'

Lisa put down her cup, spilling some of the tea in her haste.

'Take it?'

'She keeps taking things from the house. She thinks I don't know, but I'm not stupid.'

'Really? I'm sure she wouldn't.' But even as she spoke, Lisa had a feeling perhaps her mother might have helped herself to a few things around the house she thought wouldn't be missed. She wouldn't have considered it stealing; she would say she was de-cluttering.

Moffa watched an elderly woman leaving the café on the arm of a young woman.

'She wants me to go into a home; she says it's all getting too much for her to come in every day to look after me.'

'Oh Moffa, you don't need to go into a home. Tell her there's no need for that.'

'I've tried. But the truth is I don't manage on my own.'

'But can't you get a home help to come in and help you with the shopping and cooking?'

'I don't want a stranger coming into my house and bossing me around. Your mother is bad enough.'

Lisa poured out some more tea, buying time to think before she responded. She had heard her mother complain about looking after Moffa before, which wasn't entirely surprising as her mother had a full-time job and a new boyfriend. For a brief moment she considered offering to move in with her grandfather so that she could help out more.

But Lisa had recently moved into her own brand new housing association home, and was still in the process of decorating it. It had taken ages to get to the top of the waiting list and she had no wish to give up her newly found independence. Added to which, bringing an energetic toddler to live with her grandfather might not be sensible.

'I'll talk to Mam. We'll work something out,' she said.

They left the café and drove up to Lunna Kirk. It was the oldest church still in use in Shetland; the original part of the building had been erected in the Twelfth Century. It was situated a few yards from the beach and in the graveyard was a memorial to Norwegian sailors who had died during the war. Lisa's grandfather had known one of the men and he often used to visit the kirk to pay his respects.

They walked over to the memorial and stood for a moment in silence. On the other side of the wall sheep grazed the grass at the edges of the beach. An otter scampered over the rocks and then splashed into the water and vanished.

Moffa sighed and turned to leave.

'Can we take a quick look inside?' Lisa said, taking his arm.

They made their way slowly across the uneven ground to the entrance. It was bright inside the kirk despite the lights not being on.

Sunlight beamed down onto the altar, highlighting a mass of wild flowers tumbling over the edge of a heavy crystal vase. Petals had dropped onto the purple velvet cloth that was heavily embroidered with gold, adding to its air of faded gothic charm.

Moffa sat down in one of the pews as Lisa wandered around and studied the historic artefacts. She climbed the steps to the pulpit and ran her hand over the ancient bible on the wooden lectern. It was leather bound and embossed with gilt, with an impossibly difficult to read typeface that mimicked the old illuminated bibles from centuries ago. Lisa studied it for a moment. Moffa was sitting with his head bowed, although she doubted he was praying.

'Do you ever wish you could go back to Norway one day?'

Moffa shook his head and lifted his walking stick and tapped it impatiently on the stone floor.

'I'm not fit to travel am I?'

'Maybe not, but if you could would you like to? You must miss it. I've only been there once on a school trip, but it was lovely.'

'It is beautiful; very beautiful. But my memories are not. It's ironic, this stroke makes me forget my neighbour's name and I sometimes forget to eat my dinner, but I never forget what happened all those years ago. Every day I remember. Why can't I forget that the only reason I'm alive today is because I stole my brother's bicycle?'

Lisa had been about to step down from the pulpit, but she froze, not wishing to interrupt him. Moffa was silent for a moment. He held the wooden crook of his walking stick in both hands and shut his eyes.

'I was going to be late for school as I had missed the bus, so I took Jan's bike. He would never let me borrow it, as it was so precious to him, but I didn't care that day. But later on, while I was at school, one of his friends told me Jan was furious with me and was going to "sort me out" when I got home. So instead of going straight home after school, I went to a friend's house, which was even more stupid, because we had a curfew and we weren't supposed to be out after dark. The German soldiers could arrest us. But I was more scared of Jan at the time.'

Moffa paused for a moment. Lisa wanted to go and sit next to him, but she remained where she was, not wishing to kill the moment.

'When it got so late I thought my mother would worry, I knew I had to go home, but I couldn't ride the bike all the way as it would be too noisy, so I hid it in the cemetery and started walking. There were no street lights and not much of a moon, so it was almost pitch black. But as I reached my house I saw German army trucks parked outside. There were soldiers everywhere, so I hid in a neighbour's garden and watched. They dragged my parents and my brother out of our house to one of the trucks. I had no idea why, and part of me wanted to chase after them. I heard my mother screaming and I wanted to run to her, but I was terrified. I knew they would never come home again.'

Lisa's eyes welled, and she quickly brushed the tears away before her grandfather noticed.

'I never went home again either. I waited until the soldiers had gone and then I crept along to the harbour and hid in a fishing boat belonging to my father's friend. It was freezing cold in the boat, and I couldn't stop crying, but by the morning I was so angry I wanted to kill every German that had ever been born.'

'What happened after that?' Lisa said, unable to resist, after a moment of silence.

Moffa rubbed his face with his hands, usually a signal he was tired. To Lisa's surprise he continued with his story.

'Just as it got light my father's friend, Peter, arrived at the boat with his crew. They found me hiding under a tarpaulin. I scared the life out of them, but Peter had heard what happened to my family and he was pleased to see me, although he knew my life was in danger. The Germans were looking for me too.'

'Why would they want you? You were a boy.'

'Peter told me our home was being used as a safe-house for people trying to get out of Norway. We had a large cellar that my father had divided in half and created a hidden entrance to one of the rooms. I didn't know we were hiding people in the cellar; but the Germans found out and that was why my family was arrested. I would have been shot too, to deter any other Norwegians from getting involved in the resistance.'

'Is that what happened to them?'

Moffa nodded. One hand gripped his walking stick and he tapped it on the floor then stood up shakily, holding onto the back of the wooden pew.

Lisa sighed as she stepped down from the pulpit. That would be the end of the story for today.

'I found a letter in a bottle the other day, Moffa. It was from a Norwegian man. He put it in the sea years ago, but I found it on Mousa when I was over there on a field trip.'

'Have you written back to him?'

'Ah, no; I couldn't be bothered, and in any case he's probably forgotten all about it now.'

'All the better to remind him.'

'Do you think?' Lisa said, taking his arm as they left the kirk.

They got back in the car, and Lisa drove up to Lunna House, which had been the original headquarters of the Shetland Bus operation. It was a former Laird's house, hidden away on a remote part of the mainland, but with easy access to the sea.

Lisa parked the car and switched the engine off. It was now a private house and so looking around inside wasn't possible, but Lisa hoped Moffa might be prompted to carry on with his story. This house was where Moffa had spent his first night in Shetland. However, she was disappointed when he sat in glum silence staring into space.

Lisa started the engine again and headed for home. She wondered whether her mother was right; perhaps some things were better left alone.

When they arrived back in Lerwick, Lisa drove to the nursery to pick up her son. Moffa and Hansi adored each other, and Lisa couldn't help laughing when she saw the look on Hansi's face when Moffa spoke to him.

'Hallo mitt oldebarn.'

Hansi struggled in Lisa's arms to reach out to Moffa, as she tried to strap him into his car seat.

'Sit still, Hansi; you can play with Moffa when we get indoors.'

Lisa drove home, listening to Moffa singing in Norwegian to Hansi, who kicked his legs and giggled.

When they got back to Moffa's house she carried Hansi inside and set him down on the floor next to Moffa's chair. Within seconds he had climbed up onto his lap.

Lisa hovered, afraid that Hansi was being a nuisance but Moffa waved her away and she left the room to make some dinner. The impromptu Norwegian lesson resumed.

Lisa made meatballs, as both her grandfather and Hansi loved them, and while everything was simmering on the stove she went back to the lounge to find Hansi snuggled up asleep in Moffa's arms. She walked over to them with the intention of relieving Moffa of the burden, but he silently shooed her away, with a contented smile on his face.

Lisa went back to the kitchen to put the kettle on. She thought back to their discussion about Moffa going into a nursing home. He was such a private person and had clearly had the worst start to his life and she hated the idea of him being bullied into doing something he would hate.

But what could Lisa do to help? She was a single mother with hardly enough money to keep her own house in order. She worked twenty hours a week in a supermarket, studied the rest of the time, and as a consequence had no social life. Hansi's father, Neil, had vanished back home to Australia almost as soon as Lisa discovered she was pregnant. His protestations of undying love and the promise of a new life together in Melbourne were quickly withdrawn.

Lisa served up dinner and carried a plate and some cutlery into the lounge. Moffa had long given up the formality of sitting at the dining table. It was far too much effort.

Lisa set the plate down on the coffee table and then lifted her sleeping son and carried him over to the sofa where he promptly curled up and resumed his nap. They ate their dinner as Hansi slept, with the television news on quietly in the background.

'These are great meatballs; thanks.' Moffa said.

'You're welcome. I'm surprised Hansi hasn't woken up with the smell of food. He must have had a busy day at nursery.'

Moffa pulled a funny face at Hansi, and then his expression changed suddenly, as if he had remembered something sad.

'Moffa, I've been thinking, I might not do the PhD after all. I think Mam's right. I should get a job and start my career and forget about studying. The past is the past, right?'

Her grandfather put his tray down on the coffee table and sat up straight.

'Just because I find it hard to talk about it, doesn't mean you should give up. Give me some time, *min kjære barn*. I will find a way to tell you.'

3

Joakim sat on the decking outside his apartment sipping beer from a bottle. He had finished ordering varnish online for the boat he was renovating. Having completed the last task of his working day he sat with his laptop open beside him, enjoying the evening sunshine. The sun was still high in the sky, and as it reflected on the calm water below his home it was uncomfortably bright. He reached for sunglasses and then logged on to Facebook.

He browsed photos of his sister's new baby. He made the appropriate comments about how cute his new niece was. His sister, Hanne, and her family lived outside Oslo and he hadn't seen them for a few weeks. He was considering when he might drive over and visit when the message icon flashed up in his inbox. He clicked on the message and frowned in concentration as he read it.

Hello Joakim, my name is Lisa Balfour and I live in Shetland. I thought you might like to know that I found your message in the bottle you threw into the sea back in 2007. I found it on an uninhabited island, called Mousa. I expect it has been sitting on the beach for years. Hardly anyone goes to Mousa, just ornithologists and archaeology students mostly. In case you are wondering, I'm one of the archaeology students; at least I was until a few weeks ago. I have just finished my Masters and now I'm about to start a PhD. I will be researching the Shetland Bus Operation. My morfar is Norwegian and he took part in the Shetland Bus, and then he came to live in Shetland after the war. I call him Moffa, as I couldn't pronounce morfar when I was little. It is one of the few Norwegian words I know; isn't that terrible? I should pay more attention to Moffa and then I might learn something useful.

Anyway, you said in your message you were hoping someone would write back to you. So here I am, only I don't do snail-mail, so I thought I would look you up on Facebook. Much more 21st Century, don't you think?

Regards
Lisa

Joakim scratched his head and reread the message. It didn't make much sense, even though he understood English perfectly. He had never put a message in a bottle in his life.

He clicked on Lisa's Facebook profile and studied the photo of her. He wasn't sure whether he would describe her as attractive, given that in her profile photograph she was pulling a face at the camera. He clicked on one of her photo albums which showed more student-style pictures of a young blonde woman. She had a quirky way of dressing and seemed to like to party. The photos didn't match the image conjured up by her message.

A PhD sounded a bit too serious. But yes, she was pretty.

> *Dear Lisa*
>
> *I'm sorry to disappoint you but I am not the man who put the message in the bottle. I would <u>never</u> drop litter in the sea. There must be another Joakim Haaland in Norway, so if you want to contact him you will have to resort to snail-mail. Love that expression! (snegl-post in Norwegian).*
>
> *But since you have told me all about yourself; here's a little about me. I live in Larvik, although I used to live in Oslo. I have never been to Shetland, although two of my friends are sailing there in a couple of weeks for the annual Bergen to Lerwick yacht race.*
>
> *Your Morfar sounds interesting. We studied the Shetland Bus at school, although I don't think anyone in my family was involved. Does your studying mean you will have to come over to Norway one day? There's a great museum in Oslo that has some fascinating artefacts from the war.*
>
> *Anyway; time for another beer. It's Friday night and the sun is shining. I hope you find your Norwegian pen-friend.*
>
> *Regards*
> *Joakim*

Joakim switched off his laptop and took it indoors. He hadn't eaten all day and the beer had made him conscious of the gnawing hunger. He opened the fridge and sighed. There wasn't anything interesting to eat so he grabbed his wallet and a jacket and set off on the short walk to the supermarket.

Joakim lived in an apartment above his workshop. It had its own private mooring and a slipway down to the sea from the workshop. His father had a large boat building business in Oslo and had encouraged Joakim into his new career, investing a sizeable chunk of money into the project.

As Joakim made himself something to eat he thought about the curious message from the Shetlander. He had often thought about taking part in the race from Bergen to Lerwick, and wondered whether it was a good time to attempt it. He decided to contact his friend, Lars, and see if he wanted another crew member. Joakim felt starved of adventure and the company of his good friends. He hadn't seen them for months.

As he ate his dinner he opened up the laptop again and logged onto Facebook to send Lars a message about the race. He noticed he had another message in his inbox. He grinned when he saw it was from Lisa.

Hello Joakim (the wrong Joakim)

Sorry for sending you the message earlier. I should have checked to make sure there was only one Joakim Haaland on Facebook. Turns out there are a few of you. But your profile picture shows you working on a boat so I guessed you must work by the sea, and therefore would have plenty of opportunity to throw bottles (aka rubbish) into the water, but clearly you are more environmentally friendly. Suppose a dolphin had swallowed it? I have a good mind to track down the right Joakim and tell him off.

So anyway, you live in Larvik and strangely enough, I live in Lerwick – what a coincidence.

You should take part in the yacht race if you get a chance. There's always a great party to welcome everyone here. I often help out at the sailing club bar; so if you are ever in Lerwick come along and ask for me. I will give you a free beer.

Goodnight from sunny Lerwick,
Lisa

Joakim noticed Lisa had changed her profile picture to something more sensible. In the new photograph she was standing on a sandy beach with the wind in her hair. She had a lovely smile. He decided that instead of replying to her, he would send a friend request. It would be the only way to find out more about her, without committing himself to responding to her by private message. It would do no harm to make a friend in Shetland. It might be fun to meet her if he ever went there.

4

Lisa sat in the library searching through the newspaper archives for information on her project. She needed to find a unique angle on the Shetland Bus. There were a number of historic accounts of the Norwegian resistance movement; most of them written by men who had taken part in it. They were interesting enough to read, but she needed to examine it from a different perspective in order to make it a worthy subject for her thesis.

Lisa was curious about what motivated people to take part in exceptionally dangerous activities in order to save strangers; albeit fellow countrymen. She decided this was the crux of her research project. It would not be sufficient to simply record information about what had happened; but why. Why had people risked their lives during the war, when it might have been safer to have kept a low profile and endure the Nazi occupation?

She leaned back in her seat, stretching her arms above her head for a moment as she wondered what it had been like to live in Norway during the war. Reading through the newspaper articles from the early 1940s, she had a sense that people in Britain had been fairly optimistic they would win the .war. Naturally, this would have been partly due to propaganda and the optimistic reporting of events. And she guessed many people who had also been alive during the Great War would have been buoyed up by the earlier victory over Germany.

But perhaps this optimism had not been present in Norway. Unlike Britain, they had been invaded by Germany. It would have been difficult to keep one's spirits up during this time.

Her mobile phone vibrated in her pocket and she pulled it out and read a text from her mother and groaned.

You need to go and see your Grandfather tonight as I am out with Drew again.

Ever since her mother had started seeing Drew she had less and less time for Moffa; and Lisa was expected to pick up the slack at short notice. Not that she minded going around to see Moffa, but she resented the way her mother expected her to drop everything at her command.

She sent a one word reply – *fine*.

She put away her notebook and picked up her bag and left the library and drove along to the nursery to collect Hansi.

As usual her son greeted her with a cheery giggle and ran to her immediately. She picked him up and kissed his sticky face and collected his bag from the coat pegs in reception.

'So my darling boy, we are going to have our dinner with Moffa tonight. What would you like to eat? Fish pie? Macaroni cheese? Hmm, what else is in our repertoire? Maybe we should go to the supermarket on the way.'

Hansi replied by pulling Lisa's hair; grasping a handful of it all the way out to the car. Lisa untangled his chubby fingers and strapped him firmly into his car seat. She reached into her pocket and pulled out a scrunchie and pulled her hair back into an untidy ponytail in an attempt to keep it out of reach of her son.

Lisa bought sausages and potatoes in the supermarket, counting out the coins from her purse, wishing she could treat Hansi to something more exciting than bangers and mash. She hoped she would find some vegetables in the freezer at Moffa's. It was all very well her mother asking her to go and cook for her grandfather, but he didn't always have enough in the cupboards to make a decent meal, and Lisa didn't have the money to cook for the three of them on a regular basis; sometimes not even enough to cook for her and Hansi. She hated asking her grandfather for money, even though he was always happy to oblige.

She carried Hansi into Moffa's house and took the groceries into the kitchen before going in search of her grandfather. She found him sitting on the end of his bed, wearing his pyjamas and dressing gown and winding up his old-fashioned alarm clock.

'It's a bit early for bedtime Moffa; aren't you feeling well?'

Moffa shook his head.

'My clock has stopped. What time is it?

'Just after five; I came round to cook you some dinner. Mam's going out tonight.'

'I've had my dinner already. I thought it was time for bed.'

The sun was still streaming in through the gap in the curtains. Lisa knew better than to point out it was still daylight. At this time of year it was light until after midnight.

She headed back to the kitchen which was spotless. There was no way Moffa had eaten anything since her mother visited at lunch time. She hurried back to his room.

'I think you might be hungry enough for some more dinner Moffa, so I'm going to make you and Hansi some sausages and mashed potatoes. You don't need to get dressed again, but maybe you would like to watch some television with Hansi while I cook.'

Moffa reached for his walking stick. He stood; then paused for a moment testing his legs before attempting to walk. Lisa picked up Hansi who had been sat on the floor, playing with the ebony carved wooden elephant Moffa used as a door stop.

Lisa put the television on and settled Hansi down on Moffa's lap. She gave the room a cursory sweep for potential hazards and then retreated to the kitchen. She was about to put the radio on, but then stopped when she heard Moffa talking to Hansi.

As she peeled potatoes Lisa listened to Moffa singing. She walked out to the hall to hear it better. She remembered the tune and as Moffa sang, the words came back to her. It was about a sleeping bear in a cave. She went back to the kitchen, grinning at the sound of

Hansi's giggles, as Moffa pretended to be the grumpy bear that had just woken up.

When dinner was ready, Lisa carried the plates into the lounge. Hansi was sitting on the floor playing with an ancient set of wooden building blocks. Moffa was counting the bricks for Hansi as he stacked them up.

'En, to, tre, fire, fem, seks...oh no!' Moffa said, as the tower collapsed. Hansi giggled and turned to Lisa, his eyes lighting up at the sight of food. He stood up quickly and launched himself at Lisa pulling at the fabric of her jeans as she handed a plate to Moffa.

She put Hansi's plate down on the coffee table and picked him up and carried him on her hip as she fetched the old wooden high chair that had served three generations of children. Moffa had made it for Ingrid nearly sixty years ago, but it was still functional, if not a little worn.

Lisa lifted Hansi into the high chair and put his dish of food in front of him. He dived straight in, picking up a tiny piece of sausage with his fingers and popping it into his mouth, with a smile. He had never been a fussy eater. He was a bonny sturdy little boy; fast to walk; quick to laugh and always curious about his environment. He was a delightful child to spend time with; the only sadness being that his father had never played a part in his life. Then again, Lisa's own father had been absent too; and in both cases Moffa had stepped in and had been the perfect grandfather.

Lisa picked up the spoon to help Hansi eat his potatoes, but he tried to snatch it from her. When she held it out of reach, he screwed up his face to protest. Lisa gave in and handed him the spoon; knowing full well more potato would end up on the floor than in his mouth.

She went back to the kitchen to fetch her own dinner, and then sat on the sofa where she maintained a close eye on Hansi's progress. She noticed Moffa was eating his dinner with enthusiasm; so much for his protestations he had already eaten.

After dinner, Lisa brought Moffa a cup of coffee. She moved one of the sofa cushions to make herself more comfortable and discovered her mother's electronic notebook - she must have forgotten to take it home.

Lisa decided she might as well have a browse on Facebook while Hansi was playing. She opened up the notebook and it whirred back into life as if it hadn't been switched off properly. Ingrid had obviously been looking at eBay before abandoning the notebook. Lisa couldn't resist seeing what her mother had been buying. She had been looking at Lalique vases. One very similar to Moffa's vase was for sale for over £1000.

Lisa put the notebook down and left the room without speaking. She went to her grandfather's bedroom, looked in the wardrobe where she found nothing but clothes neatly hanging on rails, and then got down on her hands and knees and checked under the bed. There was nothing under there other than a couple of pairs of shoes. She got up again and marched back to the lounge.

'Has Mam tidied your room for you today? Or would you like me to do anything?'

'She made my bed for me already, thanks.'

'Has she found the vase yet?' Lisa said, grinning conspiratorially.

Moffa looked blank for a moment; then he shook his head.

'I don't think so. She wouldn't look in my wardrobe.'

Lisa wondered what her mother was playing at. It seemed a little insensitive to take things from the house, even if she would inherit them one day.

Hansi attempted to climb onto Moffa's lap. Moffa's left arm had been weakened by the stroke but he managed to assist the little boy. They giggled together, pulling faces until Hansi rubbed his eyes and buried his face into Moffa's chest. He was exhausted and Lisa knew he would be asleep within moments.

'I had better get our little man home to bed,' Lisa said, as she logged out of the notebook and put it back where she found it, under the cushion.

Moffa pulled Hansi to him, as if he didn't want him to go.

'Do you have to go now? We were having fun.'

Lisa tapped her fingers against her lips, wondering whether she would regret what she had to say.

'Moffa? Would you like me and Hansi to move in with you? That way I could cook you dinner every night. I can tidy up for you too, so Mam doesn't have to.'

Moffa turned his head away as if he hadn't heard her; but Lisa saw him lift his right hand to his eyes as if he was discretely wiping a tear from them. His head dropped until his cheek was pressed against Hansi's face.

'What do you think, Hansi? Do you want to come and stay with your old Pop-pop?'

Hansi wriggled to get off his lap; he wanted to sleep. Lisa picked him up and set him down on the sofa for a moment. He instantly curled up on his side and closed his eyes.

'I wish I could sleep so easily,' Moffa said.

'Me too. So, what do you think of my idea?'

'I would like that. But won't it be hard for you looking after both of us. You have your work, and your study. Aren't you afraid of taking on too much?'

'It's no bother at all. Hansi loves spending time with you; and so do I.'

5

Lisa moved into her grandfather's house the next day. She borrowed a van from a friend and packed up her belongings. Moffa had not used the upstairs of his house for over a year. There were three bedrooms and a bathroom upstairs, so Lisa took the largest one for herself and Hansi, and turned another bedroom into a little sitting room. She stored the furniture and household items she did not need in the loft.

Her mother arrived as Lisa was rearranging the kitchen.

'What's going on here?'

'I think you're right, Moffa can't manage on his own so we're going to live here with him.'

'What? Did my father agree to this?'

'Of course he did. He loves having Hansi here. It's company for him. I think he gets lonely on his own.'

'What about your house? Are you going to get someone to rent it from you while you stay here?'

'No; that would be illegal.'

Her mother shrugged. 'So what, everyone does it. You'd be a fool to give up the tenancy now; they're like gold-dust.'

Lisa set her spice rack firmly down on the kitchen worktop.

'It's too late; I've already given the keys back to the housing association.'

'But what happens when he goes? He's eighty seven already; he won't live forever. What will you do then?'

'Ah, I see. So you're worried you won't be able to get rid of your *sitting tenants*? Don't worry, we'll move out straight away. And by the way, Moffa knows about you taking his stuff. What gives you the right to do that?'

'They were my mother's things. She wanted me to have them and it has nothing to do with you.'

'You're right. It has absolutely nothing to do with me, but it has everything to do with Moffa. They *will* be your things one day; but not right now. Not while he's still alive and wants Grandma's stuff around him.'

'You think you know everything don't you? Well, we'll see how you feel in a few weeks when you're fed up being at his beck and call. And don't think I'll come charging in like the cavalry. You're on your own with this.'

Lisa watched, dumbfounded, as her mother marched into the living room, retrieved her notebook and flounced out of the house without acknowledging her father.

Lisa shut the front door her mother had left open then went to see Moffa who was taking an unusual interest in the garden. He had his back to Lisa, and was fumbling in his pockets for his cotton handkerchief. He blew his nose.

'Did you hear any of that?'

'I heard everything. Why is she like that? What have I ever done to upset her?'

'I don't think it's you, Moffa. She's just as mad with me. Give her some time; she'll calm down. Anyway, how about I make us some lunch and maybe you can carry on with your story about what happened during the war.'

Moffa shook his head, turned his wheelchair around and propelled it towards the kitchen.

'What do we have to eat today? I should give you some money to go shopping.'

'Another time, Moffa; I think there is enough food in the cupboards for today.'

'OK then, but we need to talk about money sometime. I don't want you paying for everything.'

'I'm not exactly broke, you know. I work part-time, and I won't be paying rent from now on, so it's only fair I get the food shopping and help with the other bills.'

'What other bills? Everything is paid for by my pension.'

'Well, all I can say is you must be good at budgeting, as I can't imagine a state pension stretching that far.'

'Who said anything about a state pension?' Moffa said, grinning at Lisa. He swung open the fridge door and frowned.

'No; there's nothing in there I feel like eating. We should go out for lunch. I feel like celebrating.'

Lisa didn't bother to protest. She was happy to see Moffa so enthusiastic and cheerful.

'Are you able to walk far today; or shall we take your wheelchair?'

'I think I might need the chair today. My leg is playing up. Will it fit in your car?'

Lisa pulled a face, as she stared at the chair. She shook her head.

'I don't think so. Well, it might if I take Hansi's seat out first, but that's such a hassle. Maybe we should go out another day, when you're feeling stronger.'

'Nonsense, we'll take a taxi then. I'm eighty seven you know; I may never feel stronger again.'

Lisa phoned the taxi company and asked for a car that was suitable for taking a wheelchair. Then they got ready to go out.

'Let's go to Fjara,' Moffa said. 'I want to go somewhere with a nice view - my treat!'

They took a table by the window and Lisa pushed Moffa's wheelchair into place. As they waited for their food Moffa watched the seals shuffling around on the rocks in the sun. He noticed a fishing boat puttering around in the bay.

'I might see if I can go out fishing for the day. Who cares if people think I'm a tourist.'

'That's a great idea; and I don't think anyone will believe you're a tourist. I'm sure people will remember you. It's not that long since you gave up fishing is it?'

'Over fifteen years.'

'Wow, already? Doesn't time fly.'

The waitress brought over their lunch, steaming bowls of Cullen skink and homemade rosemary bread. Moffa shook out his napkin and put it on his lap.

'This smells good, but your grandmother used to make the best fish soup ever. It's too bad you never got to know her well.'

'I know. Sometimes I find it hard to remember her, but when I smell cinnamon I always think of her.'

Moffa laughed and nodded.

'Yes, cinnamon; she used to put it in her apple cake. She made it at least once a week. It was my favourite.'

'I shall have to try and make it for you one day.'

'Not one day! Never say one day; one day never happens.'

Lisa frowned, her head tilted to the side. 'What do you mean?'

'Don't put things off, thinking they will happen. You have to plan things – do things. Your grandmother used to say we would go to New Zealand one day. She wanted to visit some of her relatives. But it was always "one day" we'll go there for a holiday. But as you know, we never went.'

'I'm sorry. You're right. I will make you an apple cake today. I'll go to the shops before I pick Hansi up from nursery.'

Moffa nodded triumphantly. For a moment Lisa wondered whether she had been manipulated; but he had a point. Lisa was altogether too fond of saying she would do something one day, and it never happening.

'Speaking of not putting things off; we should get back to talking about the war. I want to write down your story as part of the research. But it won't all be about you, Moffa. I will be interviewing people from more recent conflicts too. I have decided the essential question I want to address is why do people risk their lives for others, when they could just as easily keep their heads down and stay safe?'

'That's a good question. But in my case I couldn't keep my head down and stay safe. I was on the run from the Nazis, and I had nowhere to go. Joining the resistance was as much about saving my own life as helping anyone else. It wasn't half as noble as you might think.' Moffa dipped a piece of bread into his soup bowl to mop up the dregs.

'You remember I was telling you about hiding in Peter's boat after my family were arrested?' Moffa pushed his empty bowl away. Lisa nodded, and prayed the waitress wouldn't interrupt them for a little while. She wished she had a way of recording the story.

'Well, anyway, I discovered Peter was not simply a fisherman. He was part of the resistance; in fact he was one of the first volunteers for the Shetland Bus. He explained to me all about my parents' involvement; how they kept refugees hidden in our house until it was safe to get to one of the fishing boats and to make their way across to Shetland. He was devastated by what had happened to my family; not least because he and my father were best friends, but also because he felt anxious about his own safety. Nobody could be sure whether or not my parents and my brother had been tortured into telling them about who else was involved'

Moffa took a sip of water and stared out the window at the sea for a moment.

'I had wondered why Peter and my father hadn't seen each other for a while. It turns out they had avoided being seen together so that if the Germans were watching they would not know who else might be involved. Peter had come to his boat that morning with the intention of leaving the town for a bit. His wife and children had already gone up north to stay with family. He was terrified he would be arrested next.'

'So what happened?' Lisa said.

'Peter took me with him. He could hardly do anything else. He gave me some old oilskins to wear so I looked like a fisherman too. Then we set out to sea. We fished, or at least pretended to. And we kept watch for patrol boats, and in the middle of the following night we came across another fishing boat, only this one wasn't out fishing either. Peter said I had to get on the other boat, which was heading for Shetland. He wished me luck and I had a feeling I would never see him again.'

The waitress came along and cleared the table and asked if they wanted anything else. Moffa asked for some coffee.

'That was the first time I had been to Shetland; in fact it was the first time I had been out of Norway. I didn't speak a word of English, but I understood a bit of Russian and German. I was homesick and I missed my family, but I was relieved to be somewhere relatively safe. I stayed with a Shetland family for a little while. That was how I first met your grandmother. She lived next door and she was friendly to me; showing me around the place and looking after me, teaching me some English. I was a bit lost back then.'

'I'm not surprised,' Lisa said, then regretted her interruption, as Moffa picked up his coffee and sipped it as he stared out of the window in silence.

'But after a few weeks I decided to volunteer to go back to Norway to do what I could to help. It took a lot of persuasion on my part, because I was so young, but I managed to argue that my youth might be of use, since I might be able to run errands and pass on messages with less chance of being captured. So that was how it started. I had a little bit of training first, and then I sailed back to Norway; up to Ålesund, where I had never been before. I had new papers, a new identity, and to all intents and purposes, a new family. I was now the son of a fisherman and I became known as Peter Andersen, instead of Edvard Christiansen. I chose this name after my father's friend. We had just found out he had been captured.'

'Oh, how awful. Did you find out what had happened to him and his family?'

'His wife and children were safe, but ...'

Moffa looked up at the clock and reached into his jacket pocket for his wallet. 'It's time to go.'

Later that afternoon Lisa collected Hansi from nursery and stopped off at the supermarket on her way home. She went to the cashpoint first to check her bank balance, instantly more relaxed when she saw her child benefit had been paid in. She hadn't been entirely honest with Moffa about her finances, as she hadn't wanted to seem like a burden. Lisa earned a pittance on the check-out of the supermarket, and Hansi's nursery fees took up much of her earnings. The rest of her income came from child benefit and tax credits, which gave her just enough to keep them alive. She had been looking forward to the boost in income from her PhD bursary. It would be a comparative fortune to what she was used to. However, since she would have to cut down her hours at the supermarket to look after her grandfather she would be no better off for a while. Still she now had £80 in her account – enough for the next few days.

Back at the house Lisa discovered Moffa had a visitor. He seemed vaguely familiar but Lisa couldn't remember his name. She offered to make him some tea but the man declined. He stood up and shook hands with Moffa and said goodbye. Lisa went back to the kitchen to put the groceries away, before Hansi had a chance to rummage around in the shopping bags.

'Who was that man?' Lisa asked Moffa, when she brought him a cup of coffee.

'Mr Jamieson.'

'The solicitor?'

'Er, yes. He comes to see me every so often; he manages my affairs.' Moffa picked up the remote control and switched on the television.

'Oh!' Lisa replied, wandering back to the kitchen. She wondered what affairs Moffa needed managing, but it wasn't her place to ask.

She found a recipe for Norwegian apple cake online and started peeling some cooking apples, while the pack of butter softened in a bowl on top of the stove.

She listened for signs that Hansi was getting up to mischief and checked on him frequently, but he seemed content to sit with his great-grandfather watching the television.

While the cake was in the oven and Hansi was eating baked beans on toast for his tea, Lisa switched on her laptop to see what was happening on Facebook.

There was a personal message from Joakim. She hadn't heard from him for a few days so she was intrigued.

Dear Lisa, I have been asked to join the crew of a yacht taking part in the Bergen to Lerwick race next week. It will be my first time in Shetland so I hope you can come along to meet us. I would love to hear about your Shetland Bus project – and you can tell me where all the best places to visit in Shetland are. We will be staying for a few days before we go back. Joakim.

'Moffa, do you remember me telling you about that message in the bottle I found. Well I tried to contact the man, only I got the wrong one, but he seemed nice and now we're friends on Facebook; anyway, he is coming over to Shetland next week for the yacht race. He wants to meet me.'

Moffa smiled, although he was only half listening to her. He had a tendency to glaze over at talk of things like Facebook and the internet.

Lisa glanced at Hansi, who was picking up baked beans with his fingers. She was tempted to insist on feeding him with a spoon, but knew a battle would break out. She left him to it; he wasn't going to waste away with hunger.

She thought of Joakim and scowled. Who on earth could she get to babysit while she went to meet him? Moffa could not manage on his own with Hansi, and her mother would be working. Even though it was hardly a date, she didn't think she could take Hansi with her. The only way she would be able to meet Joakim without Hansi was during the middle of the day while he was at nursery. She had to hope their yacht was one of the first to arrive, as the winner usually crossed the finishing line around mid-day.

Lisa went out to the garden to take in some washing she had hung out that morning. She noticed the next door neighbour was in her garden. Lisa bundled the sheets and towels into the basket and then went across to say hello to Margaret.

'Eddie told me you and Hansi were coming to stay with him. He's delighted. What fun it must be for him to have a little boy in the house.'

'They seem to enjoy each other's company at the moment. I hope Hansi doesn't wear him out.'

'I don't think there's much danger of that. I think you're the one who will be worn out first,' Margaret said. 'Eddie tells me you're going to study for a PhD. My heavens, he's awful proud of you. And with good reason my dear. What a lot of work to take on, and with a toddler and your grandfather to look after. Well, I expect Ingrid will still come along and help too, won't she?'

Lisa smiled, but Margaret could see she had touched a nerve.

'Well do let me know if there is anything I can do to help, won't you? I'm always happy to babysit Hansi anytime, or I can sit with Eddie if you're busy with your studies. We often play cards together.'

'Thank you. That's so kind of you, Margaret. I might take you up on that offer one day. We're getting settled in now; I'm still unpacking, but I'll invite you around for tea with us; next week in fact,' Lisa added quickly, remembering her recent conversation with Moffa.

Lisa carried the linen basket indoors and put it in the utility room. The kitchen was filled with the scent of apples and cinnamon. She took the cake out of the oven and tested it with a knife. It was cooked to perfection. She set it down on a cooling rack and then went to see what was happening in the lounge. Moffa had managed to get out of his wheelchair and was sitting on the sofa with Hansi, flicking through a picture book.

'The cake is done; it's cooling.'

'It smells good. *Den eplekake lukter godt,* Hansi?'

Hansi climbed down from the sofa, sensing food was on offer. Lisa rolled her eyes at Moffa as she picked Hansi up. 'Neither one of you wants to wait until it's cold, eh?'

'Why wait? I'm eighty seven already!' Moffa shrugged and lifted his hands in the air.

Lisa laughed and shook her head.

'Eighty seven; you'll be here until you're a hundred and seven.'

'Well, just in case, I might have a little slice of cake now, with some coffee, please.

6

While Hansi was fast asleep in his cot, Lisa decided to write back to Joakim. She chose not to mention the presence of a small child in her life; it didn't seem appropriate. Lisa had never allowed any photographs of Hansi to appear on Facebook and she never mentioned she had a child. This was deliberate as she still had friends in common with Hansi's father and she refused to allow him such easy access to news of his son. As far as Lisa was concerned if he wanted to know how Hansi was doing then he had to pick up the phone or write to Lisa directly. She did not want him to simply be able to access Facebook for progress reports. So far, Neil had never bothered to find out.

Lisa put all thoughts of Neil out of her head as she logged on to Facebook.

Dear Joakim. It would be lovely to meet after the race. What's the name of your boat? I'll come down to the harbour when it arrives. There's a website that tracks the progress of the race, so I can easily look out for your arrival. There will be a party at the boating club that night, if you and your friends want to come along. A local band will be playing and they're really good, if you like traditional Shetland music.

See you next week! Lisa

Lisa dithered over the message for a moment, typing an *X* after her name before deleting it again. She did not want to send any premature messages of affection. She caught up with some of her other Facebook friends and within a few minutes Joakim replied.

Our boat is called "Solbritt". The sails are blue and yellow, with a royal blue spinnaker; in case you can see us before we reach the harbour. My friends are Lars and Anders. We all like traditional music. Anders plays the banjo and Lars plays a mandolin and I'm sure they will bring their instruments along on the journey. I'm looking forward to this now. It will be an adventure. My friends are very competitive. They came second in the race two years ago and they're looking for a win this year.

Over the next few days Lisa and Hansi settled into their new home. She went through the formalities of changing her address. Just occasionally she stopped to think about whether it had been sensible giving up her old home. She saw it advertised in the *Shetland Times* and had a tiny twinge of anxiety.

'I'm so happy you're here,' Moffa said, as Lisa sat reading the newspaper. 'My little man is happy too,' he continued, pointing at Hansi who had fallen asleep on the sofa after his lunch.

'He's very happy. Although I'm worried he'll end up speaking Norwegian and I won't be able to understand him.'

Moffa laughed. 'Nonsense, you understand fine. You're just too lazy to try and speak it yourself.'

'But it's so hard. I remember some of the songs you taught me, but I could never have a proper conversation with anyone in Norwegian. In any case all the Norwegians I know all speak perfect English.'

'Bah!' Moffa said, shaking his head with exasperation. 'Is there any more apple cake left?'

'No, but I made a plum cake this morning.'

'Plum cake? Your grandmother used to make plum cake too.'

'I know. I found her recipe cards in the cupboard.'

'You're an angel sent down from heaven.'

'I didn't think you believed in all that, Moffa.'

'What? Nonsense! Of course there's a heaven; and angels. As for the rest - I'm not so sure.'

Lisa put down the paper and went out to the kitchen to make some coffee to go with the cake. It was so easy to keep Moffa happy. She waited for the kettle to boil and saw Margaret in her garden, dead-heading some flowers. Lisa stepped outside.

'Hi Margaret; I'm making some coffee and wondered if you would like to come over. I made my grandmother's plum cake this morning.'

Margaret pulled off her gardening gloves.

'That would be lovely. Let me go and wash my hands; I'll come over in a minute.'

Lisa went back to the kitchen feeling a little guilty. She wanted to ask Margaret if she would babysit on Friday evening, and wondered if she would feel ambushed. Still, she thought, she needed to get to know her neighbour better if she was going to live here for a few years.

7

Joakim packed his bag, already regretting his impetuous decision to sail to Shetland. But he couldn't let his friends down now; although he wasn't entirely sure he might not let them down anyway. It had been nearly three years since he had been to sea - and with good reason.

It was a long drive from Larvik to Bergen and he needed to make sure he remembered everything. In his youth he had prided himself on travelling light, but now he would never be so carefree again. It was hard to travel light when one of your essential items to pack was a spare prosthetic limb.

As he put his spare prosthesis into his bag he thought about Lisa and wondered whether he should have warned her he was disabled. Then he dismissed the idea; it wasn't like they were going on a date.

He zipped up the bag then sat down on his bed in despair. It had been two years since his girlfriend, Astrid, had left. She had stuck by him after his injury, and all through his recovery; but he had asked her to leave after constant arguments about his mood swings and his inability to sleep at night.

Two years on, he was almost back to his normal self; apart from his confidence, which appeared to have been amputated along with his leg.

He reached for his laptop and logged on to Facebook, wondering whether Lisa was online. She seemed to spend most of her evenings online, and they had got into the habit of exchanging increasingly flirtatious banter. He saw the little green dot beside her name and noticed she had updated her status.

It was a photograph of her holding up a fishing line with four shiny black and silver fish attached. Next to her was an old man who was sitting down in a small fishing boat, smiling happily at the camera. Lisa had written a caption "mackerel for tea – after successful fishing trip with Moffa."

Joakim clicked on Lisa's name and sent her a personal message: *Great photo of the fish; looks like your grandfather had a great time.*

A moment later Lisa replied: *He had the best time ever! I've been trying to get him out in a boat since his stroke. It was the perfect weather today so I managed to persuade him at last. We saw some dolphins too – magic.*

Did you get photos of the dolphins?

Sadly no; they were too fast for me, by the time I got my camera out they had gone.

Do you get Orcas in Shetland?

Sometimes. I have seen them twice.

We used to see them a lot when I was in the Coastguard Service.

Wow, I didn't realise you had been in the Coastguard. What a career change you've had, although I guess it's still all about boats.

Joakim realised he had the perfect chance to explain about his injury. His fingers hovered over the keyboard for a moment. The cursor was flashing to indicate Lisa was typing him another message.

Moffa told me the Coastguard Service is part of the military in Norway and you probably did your national service with them. Is that right?

Yes I did. Only I signed on for a few years afterwards as I enjoyed it. It was a great place to work as they let me have time off to compete in skiing competitions.

Joakim pressed send - before he had time to delete the sentence. Instead of letting Lisa know he was disabled he was boasting about his sporting achievements. What an idiot, he thought.

I've never been skiing before, although I've always wanted to try. We don't get enough snow for that kind of thing. Tell me you didn't do that mad ski-jumping. I hate heights. I can't bear to watch it on TV.

No, that wasn't my sport; although I did give it a try. I never used to mind heights, but I don't like them so much now. I used to do slalom racing. I was picked for the Norwegian team for the Winter Olympics, although I never got a chance to compete, due to an injury.

There, he had said it. Or at least, he had hinted at it.

Oh you poor thing. Can't you have another go next time? You're not too old for it now are you?

Joakim sighed; no he was not too old. He was about to explain why he no longer competed but he was interrupted by another message from Lisa.

Got to go – speak again soon, can't wait to meet you on Friday or whenever you finally get to Shetland – wind forecast is not great is it?

The green dot disappeared beside her name indicating she had logged off. He decided not to tell her while she wasn't online. Or perhaps he wouldn't tell her. Why should he? They were just friends. He had no expectations of anything else and she hadn't given any indication she expected anything from their meeting.

Joakim finished packing his bag and carried it out to the car, then set off on the drive to Bergen. It was nearly midnight but the sun had only just set. He loved driving at night in the summer; the roads were empty and the landscape was so beautiful in the soft twilight with the birds still singing in the trees.

Nowadays Joakim was always happiest in his car. On the road, he was just another young man in a car; although he felt sure he wouldn't have been driving a Volvo estate if he hadn't lost his leg. A red sports car pulled out of a junction ahead of him, forcing him to slow down. He frowned at the car as it sped away. That would have been his kind of car once upon a time.

8

Lisa sat on the edge of her bed. Hansi had
woken after a bad dream and was finding it
hard to settle. He gripped her fingers and she
was stuck; every time she tried to disengage
her hand, he woke and started to whimper.
Since Hansi hardly ever cried, Lisa was a little
concerned. She hoped he wasn't coming down
with something.

Lisa had confided in Moffa that she was
going to meet the young Norwegian man she
had met online. Moffa had narrowed his eyes
at her and shook his head. But a little while
later he had reached for his wallet and taken
out some money and handed it to her.

'Buy yourself something nice to wear.
Stop looking like a student all the time.'

'But I am a student,' Lisa replied. She
waved away the money.

Moffa had shrugged and refused to put it
away. 'I know you spend everything you have
on Hansi, it's time you let someone look after
you occasionally.'

Lisa wondered what she should buy with
the money. It was hopeless arguing with
Moffa, and anyway, he would demand proof

she had spent the money on herself. There was no denying she needed some new clothes.

She pulled at a loose thread from the frayed knee of her jeans. They had not been ripped through any misguided attempt at a fashion statement. She had torn them by accident on a barbed wire fence when she was out walking.

But she wasn't sure she wanted to go to the effort of buying something new to wear just to meet Joakim. She felt uncomfortable at the idea of making a special effort; that was the way to get hurt.

Neil had broken her heart when he returned to Australia within a few days of Lisa telling him she was pregnant. He claimed it had always been his intention to go home; he protested his visa would not allow him to stay longer, but he hadn't asked her to go with him. He had not called or written, and in return Lisa had not told him when Hansi was born. She imagined Neil would have heard about his son from mutual friends, but she did not know for sure. Lisa tried not to think about their time together in Edinburgh. They had met while she was in her final year at University. She had shared a flat in the city with two other students and one of her flatmates had introduced her to Neil. It had been love at first sight; at least for Lisa. She had thought it was mutual, but now it seemed like Neil had simply thought of Lisa as another adventure in his gap year.

Neil left Scotland on the afternoon of Lisa's final exam; on the day she had anticipated celebrating the end of her degree.

Instead she had sat in her flat in despair and disbelief, and within the week had packed up all her belongings and returned to Shetland.

Lisa had not heard a single word from Neil since his text from the airport saying goodbye. If it wasn't for Hansi she could almost imagine their six-month romance had never happened. But Neil had left her with something else besides Hansi; a deep distrust of relationships.

But that was fine. Lisa was not looking for a relationship. As she thought about meeting Joakim, she reminded herself he too lived in another country; it would not be wise to get too close.

9

Joakim arrived in Bergen in the early hours of the morning and went straight to bed at his friend's apartment, sleeping almost until lunch time. Lars woke him up with a mug of strong black coffee and a cinnamon scented pastry. Joakim opened one eye and pulled the sheet over his head and groaned.

'Did you sleep ok?'

'Yes, but not enough.'

'You can catch up tonight. We should go down to the boat and make sure we have everything.'

Joakim looked through the open bedroom door into the lounge and saw Lars' wife, Anita, sitting on the floor with their two year old daughter, Freya.

'OK, give me a few minutes,' Joakim replied, tapping his leg and reaching down to the floor for his prosthetic limb.

'Yeah, sure. Take your time. There are clean towels and stuff in the bathroom.'

An hour later they arrived at the yacht. Joakim was relieved to see the boat was berthed at a jetty that gave almost level access to the deck. He climbed aboard without difficulty and then held his hand out to Anita who had brought Freya along. The little girl wore a red life jacket and was clearly used to being aboard the boat. She opened the door to the cabin and sat down on one of the seats and immediately reached up to the shelf behind the seat and found a doll she had left there. She sat with the doll on her lap and chatted away to it in a curious mixture of English and Norwegian.

Joakim inspected the boat, which he had not seen since it had left his boatyard a year ago. It was the first boat he had refurbished since taking up his new profession. He sat down on a seat opposite Freya and smiled with pride, both in the boat and his achievement in being able to sit in it without too much stress.

Lars passed bags of groceries over to Anita and went back to the car for more. Joakim jumped up to help but Anita shooed him away.

'You stay there and watch Freya, she's a devil near the water; no fear at all.'

Joakim smiled, knowing Anita was simply being tactful in suggesting he was better placed to watch the child than to lift things into the boat. It was unnecessary as he could have managed perfectly, but he sat and watched as Anita unpacked the bags and put things into cupboards in the small galley kitchen. She worked quickly and efficiently, and had stowed everything away before Lars appeared with more bags.

'Have you been far in the boat this year?' Joakim asked Lars.

'Yeah, we took it up to Ålesund a few weeks ago – remember that week in May when the weather was really great?'

Joakim nodded.

'How does she handle at sea?'

'Very well; not that we have seen any rough weather yet, but it's been great so far,' Anita added, looking at Lars for agreement.

'We're hoping to sail around to Larvik later in the summer, and maybe even to Oslo.'

Joakim grinned at his friend. He watched Lars hand Anita the last tin to put away and then put his arm casually around her shoulders. They were a great couple. They had met in Peru six years ago while they were both back-packing around South America. Anita had moved to Norway a year later and had settled in well, working as an editor for a British publishing company. The wonders of the internet meant she could work from home in Norway, as easily as from an office in London. Lars was now working as a translator and interpreter. Apart from his native Norwegian, he was also fluent in English and Spanish.

'Did you hear Astrid got married a few weeks ago?' Lars said, as he sat next to Freya and put his arm around her.

'Yes, she invited me, but I didn't go. That would have been awkward.'

Joakim stared down at his feet, feeling an itching sensation in his left foot; the foot he no longer had. For some peculiar reason his phantom feelings would erupt at the first sign of emotional stress. He had learned to ignore it, even though all he wanted to do was to kick off his shoe and scratch the itch. He shut his eyes for a moment and the first memory that came into his head was kissing Astrid after winning his gold medal at the National Ski Championship five years ago. He had asked her to marry him later that night when they were celebrating in the hotel.

'So, do you think you have everything you need for the journey?' Anita said, as she rifled through the cupboards.

'We have fuel, water, food, all the safety gear, lifeboat, lifejackets, flares, radio transmitter, and spare sails. Yeah, I think we're good to go, don't you, Joakim?'

'Er, yeah, sounds good,' Joakim replied to Lars, even though he hadn't been listening. 'When will Anders arrive?'

'Tonight! We're cooking dinner for you guys at our place. Saves getting a babysitter for Freya,' Anita said. 'It will be nice to catch up with you both. I'm only jealous I can't go too.'

'Why can't you? There's enough room.'

Anita nodded in Freya's direction.

'It's one thing going out for a nice sail on a sunny day with her, but not in race conditions. You know what Lars and Anders are like. They want to win. We would only get in the way.'

Joakim laughed and pulled a face at Lars.

'I hope I don't get in their way too. I'm a bit of a liability at the moment.'

'Don't be soft. If you can do up this boat, then I'm sure you're up to sailing her.'

Joakim shrugged.

'Anyway, is there anything else you need to do here, or can we go home? Freya will need an afternoon nap soon.'

10

On the morning of the race Lisa woke early.
Sunshine streamed through the curtains,
shining a spotlight on Hansi as he slept
soundly in his cot. It was unusual to wake up
before her son; it was normally his cries for
attention that acted as an early morning
alarm.

She sat up and reached up to the
window and lowered the black-out blind until
it created a shadow over Hansi. She didn't
want to block out the sun entirely as she loved
waking up to a sunny day, but it was only a
little after five. She snuggled down under the
duvet and shut her eyes for a moment, and
tried to go back to sleep, but it was no use.

She opened her eyes again and stared at
an oil painting on the wall. The painting
belonged to her grandfather. It depicted a
white wooden church close to the seashore,
with snow-capped mountains in the
background. It was so quintessentially
Norwegian it could have been a postcard.

Lisa thought of Joakim and felt a flutter.
Margaret had kindly agreed to babysit Hansi
in the afternoon and had said she would
happily put him to bed that night and stay in
the house with Moffa until Lisa came home.

Margaret was in the habit of coming over to the house to see Moffa and had always got on well with Hansi. She had three grandchildren and often babysat for them, so Lisa felt fairly relaxed about being able to go out and meet Joakim.

Although she told herself it was not a date, it was in fact the first time she had gone to meet a man since she had split up with Neil.

Hansi turned over in his sleep and then a moment later he sat up. It was like watching a Jack-in-the-box. One moment he was dead to the world and the next he was springing to his feet and attempting to hurl himself over the bars of the cot. Lisa didn't think it would be long before he managed to climb out and escape. She got out of bed and picked him up, hoping he would settle for a cuddle in her bed before breakfast.

Surprisingly, Hansi was content to snuggle up to Lisa and a few minutes later he dozed off beside her, his hands clutching her pyjama top, anchoring her to the bed.

Lisa heard movement downstairs and realised Moffa had got up. He was always an earlier riser, even long after retirement when he had no need to get up at the crack of dawn. Lisa could not imagine being like that herself. She constantly craved more sleep and her night time fantasies were of a lie-in; alone.

She released herself from Hansi and snuck out to the bathroom and took the fastest ever shower and got back to the bedroom in time to see Hansi sit up and look around in sleepy wonder. Then he snapped to attention and climbed off the bed and launched himself at Lisa's legs.

'Hey there, little man, how are you today? Shall we get you changed out of that nasty nappy and get some breakfast?'

'Pop Pop!' Hansi replied, struggling to free himself from Lisa's arms.

'You can see Pop Pop in a minute. We have to get you dressed first. Pooey; you're one stinky boy!'

Lisa held him at arm's length and pulled a face at him, wrinkling her nose in exaggerated disgust. He giggled, and allowed himself to be disrobed and changed; only squirming around on the changing table when Lisa tried to fasten on a clean nappy.

When Hansi was dressed in a pair of pale blue jeans and a red tee-shirt Lisa carried him downstairs to the lounge and put him in his playpen while she went to fetch his breakfast. As usual he protested loudly as she left the room, but Lisa ignored him. She couldn't make breakfast while he wandered around underfoot, especially while Moffa was in the kitchen too. One of them was bound to trip the other up eventually.

'*God morgen,* Moffa!'

Moffa was sat at the breakfast bar, wearing his old dressing gown. Lisa frowned. It was unlike Moffa not to be dressed already.

'Are you alright?'

'*Ja, ja... nei.*'

'Oh, what's wrong?'

'I'm tired. I couldn't sleep last night.'

'Maybe you should go back to bed then.'

'But it's morning.'

'So? What difference does that make? Why don't I make you some tea and some French toast and then you can go back and have a little sleep again. I'm going to work this morning and Hansi is going to the nursery and Margaret is looking after him for me later.'

Moffa stared at Lisa, taking time to absorb what she had said. He nodded as if he was in agreement with her suggestion, although Lisa wasn't sure he would go back to bed. He was such a creature of habit.

'What kept you awake?' Lisa opened the fridge to get the box of eggs. She quickly cracked three eggs into a mixing bowl and whisked them as she waited for Moffa to reply.

'Your grandmother.'

Lisa's first thought was Moffa had finally fallen prey to Alzheimer's. She didn't know what to say.

'Twenty years ago today.'

'Of course,' Lisa replied, relieved to know Moffa wasn't losing his mind, and feeling slightly ashamed she hadn't remembered the significance of the date. 'Shall we take some flowers to her grave?'

Moffa shook his head.

'Nei, nei; what good would that do?'

'Well?' Lisa shrugged. 'I don't know.'

'Maybe you're right. I think I will go back to bed. I'm not hungry though. I won't have my breakfast yet.' He stood up and shuffled back to his downstairs bedroom and shut the door.

Lisa carried on making the French toast since Hansi would still appreciate it. She sprinkled a slice with icing sugar and a drizzle of raspberry jam and then cut it into cubes for her son. She took the bowl into the lounge and then lifted her son into his high chair. He started to protest at the indignity, craning his head in the direction of the door looking for Moffa, but when he saw his breakfast his eyes lit up and he was sufficiently distracted by the food to give up his fight.

Lisa watched him eat while she drank her cup of tea. She felt guilty at the thought of going to work and leaving Moffa on his own, when he was so unhappy. She wondered about ringing her mother and reminding her what day it was in the hope of prompting her to visit. She hadn't visited since Lisa had moved in, although she had rung a couple of times to speak to Moffa while Lisa was at work.

Lisa decided not to ring her mother; she would obviously know what day it was, so it was up to her to decide whether or not to visit her father.

The morning dragged at the supermarket. Instead of working on the tills Lisa had been asked to put out produce in the fruit and vegetable section, to cover for one of her absent colleagues. It was her least favourite job. Ever since she had picked up a box of bananas and a huge spider had crawled over her hand she had been reluctant to work with any exotic fruit. But she wasn't in a position to argue.

During her fifteen minute tea-break she checked her phone for messages, hoping she might hear from Joakim, although this was unlikely since he would be at sea for a few more hours. There was a text from her lecturer informing her that the results were out for her Masters.

'Oh shit!' Lisa said, to one of her colleagues. 'I need to get to a computer and check my emails. The results are out. I forgot it would be today.'

'Good luck with that!' Ben said sarcastically, acknowledging the fact that Lisa would not be allowed to use one of the computers in the office to check for a personal email. 'You should ask Helen. She has an iPhone – she could access your emails.'

Lisa was too impatient and decided to ring the lecturer instead. With less than a minute of her break left she received the news she had got a distinction.

She hurried back to the shop floor, with a big grin on her face. She resumed sorting out the salad display, almost on the point of bursting into song.

'Someone's happy!'

Lisa turned to see her mother behind her.

'I got my results. I got a distinction.'

'Oh, well done. Does this mean you're going to go off and get a better job then?'

'What do you mean go off? I'm not going anywhere. Anyway, I've told you before I'm going to study for a PhD.'

'For God's sake Lisa, what are you trying to prove? Isn't it time you concentrated on looking after your son. Being an eternal student and slaving away in a supermarket is not the best way of doing that.'

Lisa turned her back on her mother and continued to stack up bags of salad leaves. She heard her mother sigh and start to walk away.

'Moffa's feeling a bit down today. He reminded me that it was twenty years ago that Gran died. Perhaps you should go and see him?'

Ingrid walked away without saying another word.

Hansi fell asleep in the car on the way home from nursery and Lisa had to carry him indoors, still slumbering. She put him down on the sofa and pulled a crocheted blanket over him. The multi-coloured blanket had been made by her grandmother and it always adorned the back of the sofa. Lisa ran her hand over the blanket, smiling at the memory of her grandmother. She went in search of Moffa and found him sitting in his bedroom.

He was sat on his bed flicking through a photo album. He had at least got himself dressed, but he seemed even more miserable than earlier.

Lisa sat down and leaned in to see the photos.

'I love that one of you and Grandma at Mam's christening. Grandma always had such nice outfits, didn't she?'

'I never really noticed what she wore at the time. But you're right; she used to wear some lovely frocks. She made them all herself; so talented.'

'She used to make me dresses too, but I never liked wearing them much when I was little. But I wish she was here now to teach me how to sew. And I would love to do my hair like she used to do hers in that photo. That's back in fashion now, that retro look.'

Moffa shook his head and laughed.

'Retro? Your grandmother would laugh if she could hear you. Ah well, at least I taught you how to fish.'

'And how to change the wheel on my car and where to put the oil and water. Useful skills Moffa; I don't know what I would do without you.'

'Humph!' Moffa put down the photograph album and stood up. He leaned heavily on his walking stick then straightened with a determined grimace and headed for the kitchen.

'What do you want for lunch, Moffa? Hansi's asleep at the moment so I was going to cook something for him to eat later. I'm going out soon, and Margaret's coming round to help you take care of Hansi.'

'Ah yes, you're going to meet your Norwegian friend.' Moffa's eyes glinted wickedly. He hummed the wedding march and chuckled when Lisa put her hands on her hips and shook her head at him.

'For goodness sake Moffa, it's not a date. I can hardly start up a romance with someone who lives in Norway can I?'

'That didn't stop you getting involved with that Australian man. At least Norway is closer.'

'That's different; Neil was living in the same city as me at the time. I had no idea he was going to go home so quickly.'

'His loss!'

'Anyway, I left some shopping in the car. I'll go and fetch it.'

When Lisa returned, laden down with carrier bags she heard Moffa talking to Hansi in the lounge. She sighed; she was sure Hansi needed a longer nap, and he was bound to get up to mischief later if he was tired.

Lisa concentrated on making sure Hansi and Moffa had enough to eat and there were enough toys around to keep Hansi entertained while she was out. She checked online to see how the yacht race was doing and saw Solbritt was neck and neck for second place, and that the winner had already crossed the finishing line.

Her phone bleeped with a text.

We are nearly in Lerwick, but we can't win now. Fighting for second place. See you soon.

Lisa hurried upstairs to her room and opened the wardrobe. She frowned at the lack of options she had. The only dress she owned was an old bridesmaid's dress. The only skirt was a denim mini-skirt that was obstinately splattered in paint after an incident with Hansi whilst trying to paint his bedroom in her old house. Despite Moffa giving her some money to buy herself something new, she simply hadn't had the time.

She thought of the photo she had seen; of her grandmother looking beautiful in a Dior inspired dress with sticky-out petticoats and a tight bodice. Lisa wished she was half as elegant.

She took out her battered jeans and a red gingham shirt and threw them on the bed in disgust.

'Jesus! I shall look like I'm about to go line-dancing. All I need is some cowboy boots; yee hah!'

Lisa flicked through the rail of tee-shirts and shirts looking in vain for something prettier. Moffa was right, her wardrobe was in need of updating, but there was no time.

She got dressed and then wondered whether to put on any make-up or whether to do something with her hair. She settled for mascara and lip-gloss, which was pretty much all the make-up she possessed anyway. Her hair was clean, as she had washed it that morning, but it was limp from wearing her uniform cap at work. She brushed it out and then decided to braid it into a fishtail plait.

She put on a pair of brown leather sandals and then stood in front of the mirror. She wanted to cry; she was so drab and dowdy.

She went downstairs to find Hansi and Moffa. They were watching cartoons and they both grinned at her.

'I should have taken your advice and gone shopping for something new to wear, but I didn't have time.'

'It doesn't matter. You look lovely anyway.'

'Thanks, Moffa. Shall I go and get Margaret? I had better go in a minute. Their boat is about to reach Lerwick, and I said I would meet them on arrival. We're going to go to the Boating Club for a drink, and maybe stay for the party. Who knows?'

Lisa drove into Lerwick and parked her car near the harbour. She got out of the car, locked it, and then unlocked it again and reached in for a Fair Isle cardigan she had left on the back seat. It was cooler than she had anticipated. The cardigan was a bright mixture of blues, greens and pinks. It clashed alarmingly with the red gingham shirt, but Lisa was beyond caring now. She pulled on the cardigan and headed towards the harbour, scanning the boats for Norwegian flags.

11

Joakim sat in the cabin of his friend's boat and composed a text to Lisa.

We've arrived. We came third. A bit disappointing, but a great race. Looking forward to seeing you. Lars and Anders have gone to have a look around the town. I'm still on the boat, if you can find it.

Joakim had wanted to go ashore with his friends, but he thought he ought to wait for Lisa. He stepped out of the cabin and stood on the deck looking at the row of grey stone buildings parallel to the harbour. He watched a bus drive along the esplanade and saw a group of teenage boys walking past, ogling the boats. They stopped to watch as one of the race competitors negotiated its way into the small-boat harbour and tied up.

He scanned the street for Lisa, not sure what he was looking for. All he knew was she had long blonde hair, although that might not be the case now. For all he knew she might have cut her hair or even coloured it. He watched a young woman walking along the street with a scary shade of bright blue hair. He was slightly relieved when she walked past the boats and crossed the road and disappeared inside a shop.

Then he saw a blonde woman walking towards the harbour. She wore jeans and a Fair Isle cardigan. He thought it might be Lisa, but she didn't seem to be heading towards the boats. He watched as she stopped to speak to an elderly woman. They talked for a while, and then the younger woman put her hands to her face, tipped her head back and laughed. Joakim couldn't hear their conversation but the sound of her laughter drifted across on the breeze. He saw the woman hug her older friend and then they parted.

She looked straight at him. He froze, feeling slightly guilty for staring at her. He was about to turn away when she lifted a hand in greeting.

Joakim wasn't sure whether to climb up and meet her on the quay, but he wasn't sure he wanted to attempt to use the ladder yet. Before he had the chance to try, Lisa had reached the quay side.

'Joakim?'

'Ja! You must be Lisa.'

Lisa grinned. 'Is this the boat you renovated? It's lovely. Can I have a look?'

Before Joakim could reply Lisa was climbing down the ladder. He offered her his hand as she stepped aboard.

Lisa sat down on the bench and surveyed the boat. She stared up at the mast and then at Joakim who was still standing up. Neither spoke for a moment.

'Can I get you a drink? A beer?'

'Ah, no thanks; I have to drive home later. But don't let me stop you. I bet you need a drink after such a long journey. How was it?'

'It was good, thanks; a bit rough for a while, but not too bad.'

'So, this is your first time in Shetland? What do you think?'

Joakim shrugged. 'I've only seen the coast so far and this little view of Lerwick from the boat. But it looks nice.'

'Well perhaps I could show you around Lerwick; or do you want to wait for your friends?'

'They'll be fine on their own. We agreed to meet at the Boating Club later.'

Joakim glanced into the cabin, wondering whether he should offer her some coffee. He was at a loss of what to say to her now she was here.

'Show me what you did to this boat,' Lisa said, filling the silence at last.

He gestured for her to follow him into the cabin.

'I did all the woodwork. I made new lockers, new doors, and new bunks and rewired the cabin so there's better lighting and heating.'

Lisa ran her hand over a varnished wood cabinet. She sat down on one of the seats inside the cabin and gazed around at the revamped interior.

'This is amazing. My grandfather would love this boat.'

Joakim sat opposite Lisa and smiled.

'He is welcome to come and see it before we go.'

Lisa didn't reply and Joakim started to feel uneasy being in the cabin alone with her. She was quieter than he had expected. Her

Facebook messages had been chatty and friendly. In real life she was shy. She also seemed much younger than twenty six. In fact she could easily pass for a teenager. He wondered whether she had lied about her age.

She was pretty though, with a fresh-faced innocence, exaggerated by the fact she was wearing her hair in a plait. Her clothes lacked any attempt at glamour or sophistication, which he found refreshing. He had been vain enough to think she would have made a particular effort with her appearance. His ex-girlfriend had never gone anywhere without wearing make-up; even on the ski-slopes.

'Well you won't see much of Shetland sitting here, do you want to have a look at Lerwick? I can show you where all the best shops, cafés and pubs are.'

Joakim nodded, although he didn't feel up to walking far. His prosthetic leg had started to feel extremely uncomfortable during the voyage. The rough sea and the effort needed to counterbalance the rocking movement of the waves had made his leg ache. He also seemed to have developed a large blister on his stump, after getting drenched in sea-spray. However, he did not want to say anything to Lisa about his injury; at least not yet.

Lisa stepped out of the cabin and within seconds had climbed the ladder leading up to the quay. Joakim grabbed his wallet and his jacket and closed the cabin door and then frowned at the ladder. The rungs were narrow and looked wet from where they had recently been covered by the tide.

He grabbed hold of the handrail and tested his good leg on the first rung. Lisa had her back to him, and was fiddling with her phone.

Joakim gritted his teeth against the discomfort and struggled up the ladder, knowing everything would feel much better once he was on dry land. He made it to the top of the ladder without any drama and stood beside Lisa while she finished her text.

'Sorry; just checking up on Moffa!'

'No problem, so where is the best place to get a cup of coffee here?' Joakim smiled at Lisa, the relief from his successful ascent to the quay had made him relax a little.

Lisa grinned and pointed in the direction of a café across the road from the harbour. There were tables and chairs outside, with a few people enjoying the sunshine along with their afternoon tea.

12

Lisa sipped her cappuccino and studied at her new companion. He was her idea of a stereotypical Norwegian, with his naturally fair hair, which was cropped short, exposing his tanned face. His eyes were the blue of a deep fjord; glacial in their coldness when he wasn't smiling, but radiating warmth when he did. But for such a drop-dead gorgeous man he seemed remarkably ill at ease. Lisa watched as he rubbed his hand over his left knee. She couldn't tell whether it was a nervous gesture or whether he was uncomfortable.

'Joakim!'

Joakim lifted his hand to greet two young men who were walking towards them.

Lars and Anders sat down at the table after Joakim had introduced them to Lisa.

'Look what I bought Freya,' Lars said, taking out a Fair Isle cardigan from a brown paper carrier bag. 'That's my daughter; she's two,' he added for Lisa's benefit.

Lisa plucked at the label. 'That was knitted by my late grandmother's best friend; it's beautiful. I hope she likes it.'

Lars showed her some gloves. 'I bought these for my wife. I might go back and buy her a jumper too, but it is so hard to buy clothes for Anita. I never get it right.'

Anders laughed sympathetically.

Their conversation turned to the competition. Lisa was gratified they carried on talking in English. She was impressed at their fluency and commented on it.

'My wife's English. I speak it most of the time at home,' Lars said, 'although I'm teaching Freya to speak Norwegian.'

'That's cool. I live with my Norwegian grandfather. He used to teach me songs when I was little. I've learned a few words, but I never have the confidence to try speaking it, and not much opportunity either, apart from talking to my Morfar.'

Lisa had been on the point of saying she had a son, but for some reason she shied away from talking about Hansi. She was always cautious about mentioning her son; not because this might be a deal-breaker for a new relationship, but she found people judged her differently, and less favourably, when they discovered she was a single parent.

'Ah yes, your Morfar took part in the Shetland Bus; Joakim told us about him. There can't be many men like him left now.' Lars said.

'Not many at all; that's one of the reasons I'm about to start my PhD this year, on the Shetland Bus. I want to capture the stories before it's too late.'

'A PhD? Wow, you don't look old enough.' Anders said, and then pulled a face as if it had occurred to him he might have been rude.

'I'm twenty six, so that's pretty old to still be studying. My mother thinks I should stop now and get a proper job.'

'No, no; don't do that. This is such an important subject to study. I think a lot of people in Norway would be interested in your grandfather,' Lars said.

Joakim nodded. 'So what if you are thirty when you start your career. Age is just a number. You should do what makes you happy, because you never know what's ahead of you.'

'So where is this Boating Club – I hear there is live music there?' Anders said, after a brief silence.

Lisa pointed. 'It's down that road; not far. Do you want to go there now?'

'Yeah, sure! We have to experience the local culture,' Anders said, as the other two laughed.

'Ha! You mean you have to experience the cheap alcohol!' Lisa replied.

'And that!'

Joakim drained the last of his coffee then put his hand on the slightly wobbly table to stand. Lisa noticed Lars was watching Joakim with concern and as Joakim began to walk away from the café, she saw he had a limp. She remembered what he had said about not being able to take part in the winter Olympics. She realised he must have had a fairly serious accident.

Anders walked beside Lisa and started a conversation about life in Shetland. As they talked Lisa forgot about Joakim for a moment. He walked behind her with Lars and the one time she stopped and looked around as they crossed the road Joakim had paused at the window of the bookshop.

When they arrived at the Boating Club they found a table overlooking the harbour. The yacht race was still in progress and so the club house was not as full as Lisa expected. Norwegians and Shetlanders, as well as a couple of Swedes were sitting around talking and drinking. There was laughter and animated discussions about the race. It was hard to tell which nationality the sailors were. They all wore varieties of marine clothing; bright coloured *Musto* tops, *Helly Hansen* jackets and the ubiquitous leather deck shoes.

Lisa had always been drawn to men who spent most of their time outdoors. Despite the fact that she spent many hours locked away with her books and her computer, she was an outdoorsy kind of girl. She had spent many hours of her childhood on her grandfather's fishing boat, before he had retired. She prided herself on her ability to fish, and to navigate a boat around the inshore waters of Shetland.

A group of local musicians piled into the bar and started to set up in the makeshift stage area. A few minutes later they began their first set. The music was not so loud that it was impossible to carry on a conversation.

Lisa stared at Joakim as he talked to Anders about the race. They were looking at the live results on an iPad, waiting for someone they knew to cross the finishing line. Lisa felt a little superfluous to the conversation and she wondered whether she should go home. Joakim hadn't said much to her since they had arrived at the club and she had the impression he was not entirely impressed with her. She was glad she had not gone to any special effort. It had been nice to meet him, but there was no spark between them. She saw him staring out of the window as if he would rather have been outside.

She sipped her coke and decided that she would leave before the next round of drinks was bought. She turned her attention to the band. She knew most of the musicians and she grinned at one of the young women playing the fiddle. Angela wore a red mini dress, black lacy tights and black Dr Marten boots. Her long shiny brown hair hung down her back and she seemed to mesmerise some of the audience with her quirky beauty.

'I wish I could play the fiddle,' Joakim said, when one of the songs ended. 'Do you play any instruments, Lisa?'

'Nah, not really. I did have fiddle lessons when I was younger, but I didn't have the patience for all the practising. I wish I had stuck to it now though. What about you?'

'I play the guitar! Badly, I don't have much patience for practising either. I was too much into sport.'

'Skiing?' Lisa said.

'Skiing, ice-hockey, football, running – all sports.'

'Wow, you must be fit then.'

Joakim chewed his lip and nodded, but seemed more interested in what was happening outside. Two yachts were sailing past on the way to the line. A Norwegian flag fluttered from the mast of the yacht in front and there was a little cheer from the Norwegians when it crossed the line in front of the Shetland boat.

'Can we get food in here?' Anders said to Lisa.

'Yes, I think I heard someone say there would be a buffet upstairs. I'll go and ask for you.'

Lisa hurried away from the table, eager to get away from them for a moment. She was finding it hard to mask her disappointment in Joakim. He was nowhere near as friendly as he had seemed online. She wondered whether he had a girlfriend. His friends had talked about their wives openly. Joakim was thirty and *fit*, it would be odd if he was still single.

Lisa went upstairs and discovered the buffet would be ready in about twenty minutes. She decided she would leave then. It would be a good opportunity to make her excuses and go home.

She went downstairs and decided to visit the bathroom first. As she passed the door to the men's toilets the door opened and a man walked out. Before the door shut behind him Lisa heard two men arguing in Norwegian.

When she went back to the bar she found Lars sitting on his own; he looked a little embarrassed.

'The food will be ready in about twenty minutes.'

'That's good; I'm starving now. We were so busy this morning trying to get across the line we didn't have much breakfast, and we haven't had lunch either.' He rubbed his stomach and pulled a face as if he was in pain.

Lisa laughed. She reached for her drink and finished it.

'Can I get you another drink?' Lars said, reaching for her empty glass.

'Oh, no; I think I'll go soon. I'm sure you don't need me hanging around with you all afternoon.'

'Don't go yet. Joakim's been looking forward to meeting you. It's all he's talked about.'

Lisa tilted her head to one side. 'Well, I don't think I'm what he expected as he doesn't seem happy.'

'Oh, that's not the reason. He...well, it's not for me to tell you. But give him a chance. He's a nice guy, but he's been through a tough experience.'

'Has he been married?'

'No, in fact his ex-fiancé got married a few weeks ago.'

'I see.' Lisa smiled. So that explains it, she thought.

Anders and Joakim came back to the table and sat down. Joakim grimaced and grasped his leg.

'*Gjør det vondt?*' Lars said.

'Ja. But it's ok.'

Lisa worked out what Lars had said to Joakim. "Does it hurt?"

'Who would like another drink?' Anders said, picking up the empty glasses.

Lisa shook her head. She was still inclined to go home. Joakim's friends were the only ones making her feel welcome. Joakim sat hunched over in his seat looking fed up. Lisa stood up to go.

'It was nice to meet you all. I hope you enjoy yourselves in Shetland,' she said.

Joakim looked up and nodded blankly. He seemed to be in a dark world of his own.

Lars frowned at Joakim and said something in Norwegian to him that Lisa didn't understand. She walked out of the Boating Club, humiliated. She glanced at her watch. She didn't have to get home for ages so she decided she would go to the supermarket and get something nice for dinner. She craved chocolate, and wine; lots of wine. She had only walked a short distance when she heard someone running behind her.

'Lisa! Wait!'

She sighed when she saw Lars and stuffed her hands into the pockets of her jeans, but waited for him to catch up.

Lars led her over to a bench on the pier and they sat down.

'I'm sorry about Joakim. He's not usually like this, but he is in a lot of pain.'

'About his ex-fiancé; yes I know.'

Lars laughed. 'Not that kind of pain.'

'What kind of pain then?'

'His leg is hurting. I know he hasn't told you about his injury, and it isn't my place to tell you, but I wanted to explain.'

'Oh, he told me he got injured before the Olympics. I didn't realise it was still troubling him.'

Lars pulled off his baseball cap and ran his fingers through his hair for a moment and then put the cap back on.

'He lost part of his leg. He can never ski again. It was awful for him.'

'What?' Lisa said, 'Oh my God, why didn't he say? I thought he had just broken it or something.'

'He doesn't like to talk about it much. And normally it isn't a problem for him. He has a prosthetic limb and most of the time he gets around fine without any bother, but the sailing seems to have made it hurt. You know; trying to stand when the boat is rolling. It can be hard with two normal legs can't it?'

Lisa shrugged.

'What can I do to help? Does he need to see a doctor? Should we take him to the hospital?'

'No, he only needs to rest it. We'll take him back to the boat so he can have a sleep. If he takes the prosthetic off for a bit it will feel better soon enough.'

'Oh, right. That seems sensible. What a shame he won't get to see much of Shetland while he is here then.'

Lars shrugged. 'Yeah, he was looking forward to that.'

Lisa stared down at her feet for a moment and then had an idea.

'Do you think he would be OK if I drove him around the place? Would he be alright sitting in a car? He could take his leg off; I don't care. We have a wheelchair in the house, if that would help.'

'So it doesn't bother you – his injury?'

'No; why should it?'

Lars put his arm around Lisa's shoulders and hugged her.

'I knew it wouldn't, but he thought you would be put off.'

They walked back to the Boating Club and found Anders and Joakim deep in conversation. Anders nudged Joakim and nodded in Lisa's direction. Joakim smiled cautiously.

'I'm going to take you on a magical mystery tour of Shetland,' Lisa said. 'If you want to, that is? I'll go and get my car and pick you up outside in about five minutes.'

Joakim grinned. 'Ja; that would be great Lisa.'

13

Lisa parked her car outside the Boating Club and before she had switched off the engine Joakim appeared at the door. He got in the front seat and they waved goodbye to Lars who stood in the doorway of the club.

'I'm sorry, I should have warned you,' Joakim said, as Lisa put the car in gear and set off.

'That's OK. We all have things we don't go shouting about straight away. It's no big deal.'

'Well, it's a big deal to me.'

'Um, yeah, of course; but you know what I mean.'

Joakim grinned.

'So what happened then?'

'It's a long story,' he said.

'In that case I know where I'm going to take you. It should give us at least a couple of hours; that long enough?'

Joakim recounted the story of how he had lost his leg while he was working for the Coastguard. Lisa listened as she drove, sometimes finding it hard to concentrate on the road, as he explained how his vessel had been chasing a suspected drug smuggler along the Norwegian coastline. They had brought the small fishing boat to a halt and attempted to board it. Then someone had opened fire on them and Joakim had been shot in the legs. The fishing boat had tried to take off again and outrun the Coastguard vessel but they had eventually caught them again and this time the drug smugglers had been arrested. Meanwhile Joakim had been airlifted to hospital for treatment.

Joakim had surgery to remove four high velocity bullets which had fractured the bones in his left leg, and damaged tissue in the right leg too. He had lost a lot of blood but the surgeons were confident he would recover from the injury. However, a month later when the wounds would not heal and a life-threatening infection had set in, the surgeon decided it was necessary to remove his lower left leg.

'I had already missed the Olympics by then and I don't think I cared what they did to me; to be honest I was kind of out of it on morphine and antibiotics.'

'Really? There wasn't any more that could be done for you?'

Joakim shrugged. 'I don't know; maybe a different surgeon, a different hospital? Perhaps someone else would have treated it differently. All I knew was the infection was starting to spread and they thought it was best to take radical action.'

'That's awful. So did you have to leave the Coastguard then?'

'Of course. I was offered a desk job and I nearly took it, but my Dad persuaded me not to. He got me set up working with boats instead.'

'What happened to the drug smugglers? I hope they're still in prison.'

'I think most of them are. The one who shot me is dead though.'

'Good! Bastard!'

Joakim shook his head.

'It wasn't so good; Anders nearly lost his job over it. He was the one who shot him. And of course there was an investigation, and he was accused of shooting the man as an act of revenge, not self-defence. Luckily he was cleared of the charge, but he left the Coastguard not long after.'

Lisa stopped the car next to Eshaness Lighthouse and switched off the engine.

The lighthouse was perched precariously on the edge of the high cliffs. In the distance a sea stack emerged from a shroud of sea mist. Sea birds circled over the water, dive-bombing for fish, and screeching to each other.

'Nice view.'

'It is kind of dramatic here. I like going for walks along the cliffs, but I guess you wouldn't want to do that now.'

'I can at least get out of the car; I would like to see the cliffs.'

They walked the short distance across the grass to the edge. Gannets swirled below them and a couple of puffins crouched down in the grass next to their burrows.

Joakim sat down on a rock and stretched his legs out. He held his left leg and Lisa noticed a flicker of pain in his face.

'Would it help if you took it off for a while?'

Joakim nodded.

'Do you have any plans for this evening?'

'No.'

'Well how about coming back to my grandfather's house. I can cook you some dinner. You can take your leg off; nobody will care. Moffa would love to meet you I'm sure.'

Joakim didn't reply.

'I'm not that bad a cook!' Lisa said, grinning at him.

'OK then. But I need to stop at the boat and get something first.'

'Sure, no problem.'

They drove back to Lerwick, talking all the way.

'The Norwegian Royal Family stayed at this house during the war,' Lisa said, as she slowed down past a large dwelling surrounded by mature trees. There were no other cars on the road so Lisa paused by the gate and they looked into the garden.

'It could almost be Norway here, with all these trees,' Joakim said.

'I wish I could take Moffa back to Norway for a holiday. But he isn't up to travelling these days. I have this feeling that as time goes by he is getting more and more homesick. He doesn't talk much about his childhood, but I know he thinks about it.'

'How long has he lived here?'

'He moved here permanently after the war. He started to tell me the story about how he got caught up in the Shetland Bus; but he gets tired when he talks about it. I don't like to push him, although I would love to find out more. I start my PhD in September so I will have to make an effort to get him talking, and to record it if I can. I also want to talk to anyone else still alive if that's possible.'

'I can't imagine many are left now.'

'No – I think it is only because Moffa was so young at the time. Most of his associates would have been a lot older than him. But I'm going to widen my study to include people in modern day conflicts that've helped others to escape from warzones. I'm curious about what drives people to risk their lives for others.'

'That sounds interesting. I often wonder the same thing. I didn't think joining the Coastguard Service would be putting my life at risk. I wonder whether I would have done something different if I had known. And it's not as if I was saving a life at the time.'

'But you saved lives during your career didn't you?'

'Ja, we did.' Joakim smiled. 'We rescued a little boat with two boys in it once. Their engine had broken down and they were caught up in some bad weather. It was a great feeling when we radioed through to base to say we had them safe and well. Their mother gave me a big hug when we got them back to shore. It made my day.'

'I bet!'

Lisa drove into Lerwick and stopped her car close to the harbour.

'I'll be back in a moment,' Joakim said, as he got out.

Lisa watched him limp across to where his boat was berthed. He stood at the edge, talking to someone on the boat below him. A moment later Anders appeared beside him and they both looked over at the car. Anders waved at Lisa. The men stood and talked for a moment and then Lars emerged from the boat carrying a red canvas holdall. He passed it up to Joakim.

A moment later Joakim open the door and slung his bag into the back seat.

'Is this your car?'

'Yes, why?' Lisa said, as she started the engine.

'You have a baby seat in the back. Do you have a baby?'

'Yes I do. I have a little boy called Hansi,' she said, trying not to sound apologetic.

'Hansi? Cool name. How old is he?'

'About eighteen months.'

Lisa waited for him to ask another question, but he didn't. She drove back to Moffa's house and parked on the drive. Hansi appeared at the window, standing on the sofa.

'There's my little man,' Lisa said. 'I couldn't keep him a secret for long.'

'Why the secret; kids are great?'

Lisa got out of the car and led the way into the house.

Margaret appeared in the hallway with Hansi.

'You're back early!' Margaret said, letting go of Hansi's hand and laughing as he launched himself at Lisa.

'Margaret, this is Joakim. He sailed over from Norway. His boat came third in the race.'

'Pleased to meet you, Joakim. Well, if you're back, I will leave you to it, Lisa. Hansi was asking about his tea, I was about to make him something.'

'Thanks so much for looking after him.'

'Your grandfather did most of the entertaining.'

'I bet he did!'

Margaret left and Lisa picked up Hansi and introduced him to Joakim. Hansi seemed unimpressed and squirmed to get down again. He toddled back to the lounge and Lisa indicated to Joakim to follow her.

'Moffa; I brought someone to meet you. This is Joakim Haaland.'

Moffa was sitting in his arm chair and he stood up and reached out to shake hands with Joakim, looking surprised and delighted.

They greeted each other in Norwegian. He laughed as he sat down and gestured for Joakim to sit down. Moffa snapped off the television and gave Joakim his full attention.

'*Kaffe? Eplekake?* I'm going to make something to eat for Hansi and then cook some dinner for us.'

Moffa nodded enthusiastically, almost waving Lisa away so he could continue his conversation with Joakim.

'I would love some coffee and apple cake,' Joakim said.

Lisa led Hansi out to the kitchen and set him down in his high-chair. She made him fish fingers and baked beans and while he was eating, she thought about what to cook for Joakim. She hadn't been prepared to cook for a guest so she was at the mercy at what was in the fridge. She carried coffee and apple cake into the lounge and found the men in animated conversation. Lisa set the tray on the coffee table.

'Didn't you want to take your leg off? You can stretch out on the sofa if you want. Make yourself at home.'

Moffa frowned, confused by what she had said.

'Joakim lost his leg a few years ago. His prosthesis is bugging him. I said he should take it off and rest his leg for a bit. We don't mind, do we?'

Moffa shook his head.

Joakim looked embarrassed, but as Lisa left the room he unzipped the leg of his tracksuit trousers.

Hansi finished eating and was now covered in flakes of fish and baked bean sauce. Lisa carried him upstairs to clean him up. He rubbed his eyes and snuggled against her, and she decided it was time for bed. Hansi kept strange hours. As hard as Lisa tried to get him into some kind of routine the more Hansi resisted. He slept when he was tired and he stayed awake when he wasn't, regardless of what time it was.

His eyes started to shut even as she brushed his teeth. She quickly changed his nappy and put him in his pyjamas, his limbs heavy, and for once not wriggling. Lisa set him down in his cot and he turned over immediately into his favoured sleeping position, on his tummy.

An hour later Lisa served up shepherd's pie for dinner. They ate in the lounge with their plates on their laps. Joakim was sitting with his legs up on the sofa so Lisa sat on the remaining armchair. While they ate Moffa carried on his conversation with Joakim. They spoke in Norwegian, but Lisa didn't mind. She appreciated Moffa rarely got to speak in his native language. She listened, although she was only able to pick out a few words. She discerned they were talking about the places they had grown up in, about politics and the landscape.

As Lisa took their plates away Joakim reached into his bag and took out a bottle and handed it to Moffa.

'Oh boy, I haven't had this in years. Lisa, get us some proper glasses; they're in the kitchen. We are having something special.'

'What is it?' Lisa said, as she leaned over her grandfather's shoulder to examine the bottle.

'Akevit, or aquavit, as it is known here. It's our equivalent of whisky I suppose, although it is closer to vodka.'

'It doesn't look like vodka,' Lisa said, as she lifted the bottle and studied the golden yellow contents.

'It doesn't taste like either of them,' Joakim said, grinning at Lisa.

'Well, I had better not have any as I have to drive Joakim back to the boat later.'

'You don't have to go back to the boat tonight do you? Why don't you stay here, Lisa can take you back in the morning.' Moffa said.

Joakim shook his head. 'No, it's OK; I don't want to be an inconvenience.'

Moffa's face fell. There was no doubt he was enjoying Joakim's company.

'It's no trouble having you here at all. There's a spare room upstairs, or you could sleep on the sofa. There's a downstairs bathroom so you wouldn't disturb anyone.'

Moffa nodded vigorously in agreement.

'Well OK, if you're sure.'

Lisa fetched Moffa's traditional aquavit glasses from the kitchen and set them on the coffee table.

'Shall I get some ice? Do you have it with lemonade or tonic?'

Moffa and Joakim laughed conspiratorially.

'What?' Lisa said.

'We drink this on its own in Norway. No ice, no mixers, but sometimes with a glass of beer on the side.'

'Oh, well we don't have any beer in the house.'

Lisa sipped it and wrinkled her nose. It smelled and tasted a little medicinal and she wasn't sure she liked it. But Moffa leaned back in his chair with a contented smile on his face. He shut his eyes and Lisa knew he was back in Norway, at least for a moment.

She left the men talking. Moffa had reverted back to Norwegian as if Lisa wasn't even in the room. She hadn't seen him so happy in ages. She went back to the kitchen and washed up; then went upstairs to check on Hansi who was still sleeping.

When she returned to the lounge Moffa was talking quietly and Joakim was leaning forward, listening intently. Lisa stood by the door not wishing to intrude on them. Joakim glanced up and gestured for her to come and sit with them. Moffa continued to speak, as if he was in a trance.

She sat next to Joakim and reached for her glass. She took another sip and this time it tasted sweeter. She inhaled the spicy fragrance. It was warming and pleasant. Moffa was talking about the war. She was about to butt in and ask him to talk in English, but she didn't want to kill the moment.

'Excuse me Lisa, I need to use the bathroom,' Joakim said, when Moffa had paused to refill their glasses.

'Oh, right; let me show you where it is.'

'I need to put my leg back on first,' Joakim said, reaching down for it.

Lisa stood up to give him some space.

'You could use my grandfather's wheelchair. It's out in the hall. Save you putting that on again, if it is uncomfortable.'

Joakim shook his head, but almost immediately changed his mind. 'I think I might borrow the chair, if that's alright?'

Lisa brought the wheelchair into the lounge and set the brake on and then walked out to the kitchen.

She put the kettle on to make some coffee and gazed out of the kitchen window. It was almost ten thirty and the sun was setting. The sky was pink over the sea. The kitchen window had been left open and Lisa heard birds twittering on the roof of the house. Whilst Shetland did not get hot sunny days often, the long summer days, the "simmer dim" in local dialect, more than made up for it.

'Lisa?'

Joakim appeared at the kitchen door in the wheelchair.

'Hi,' she said, 'I was going to make some coffee; would you like some?'

'Yes please. I'm sorry I haven't had a chance to talk to you this evening. You must be bored listening to us speaking in Norwegian.'

'Not at all, my grandfather's enjoying himself. Thanks for listening to him. I only wish he would tell me more about his life.'

'He has some fascinating stories to tell. But I think he's getting tired now. Maybe I shouldn't have given him the alcohol.'

Lisa smiled. 'He hardly ever drinks. I'm sure it won't do him any harm. I'll see if he wants some coffee before he goes to bed.'

Joakim propelled the chair back to the lounge. Lisa followed him and they found Moffa sitting quietly, staring out of the window.

'Would you like some coffee, Moffa?'

He shook his head. 'I think I had better go to bed, this drink has gone to my head.'

He stood, a little unsteadily. Lisa took his arm and led him out to his bedroom where he sat down heavily on the bed.

'He's a nice boy, Lisa. I've had a lovely evening. But I will leave you two to talk.'

'You sure you're OK? Do you need anything?'

Moffa waved her away. Lisa kissed him goodnight and returned to the kitchen to make coffee.

Joakim was sitting in the wheelchair reading *The Shetland Times*. He put the newspaper down when Lisa appeared with two mugs of coffee. She sat down in the armchair Moffa had vacated.

'It's a lovely evening isn't it? I would love to go outside for a while. Would that be OK?'

'Of course!' Lisa replied. She walked over to the French doors and opened them. Joakim wheeled his chair out onto the decking and over to a wooden bench. Lisa fetched their coffee and when she went outside, Joakim was sitting on the bench admiring the view.

She sat beside him gazed up at the hills. A curlew took flight behind them, pleepsing as it soared overhead.

'I always loved this view as a child. You can't see it from here, but there is a little bit of beach between those two hills.'

'I can hear the sea, it can't be far away.'

'You can see it from the kitchen window; it is close enough to walk to.'

'It's perfect. I live in an apartment above my workshop. It's right on the edge of the water. In the summer it's beautiful, but sometimes in the winter it can be bleak.'

Lisa shivered. The air was cool despite the glorious sunset. She went inside and grabbed the crocheted blanket from the back of the sofa and brought it outside. She spread it over their legs as she sat down, and then pulled her half of it over her shoulders.

'I sit out here a lot. Moffa goes to bed early, and obviously Hansi does too, so I come out here on my own. It is perfect on a night like this.'

'It's lovely. I can't imagine living somewhere without a nice view. How long have you lived with your grandfather?'

'A few weeks; I had my own place, but Moffa wasn't managing on his own. My mother and I used to take it in turns to come in and make sure he was OK, but for some reason my mother and Moffa don't seem to get on and it was making him miserable. So I decided to move in with him. Unfortunately, now my mother hardly ever helps out; but Moffa is happy, and so is Hansi. And as you can see this is a lovely place to live.'

'It's a shame about your mother. But after what your grandfather said to me this evening, I think I can understand why they fell out.'

Lisa had been staring dreamily into the distance, but she snapped to attention. 'What? What did he tell you?' She sat up straight and pulled the blanket down as if she was about to stand up.

'Ah, maybe I shouldn't have said anything. He wasn't sure if you knew; but he didn't want to be a disappointment to you.'

'How on earth can he be a disappointment to me? What could he have said or done that would upset me?'

Joakim reached for Lisa's hand and squeezed it briefly before letting go. 'I can't imagine you would be upset, but it might be a bit of a surprise.'

'Tell me!'

Joakim leaned forward and set his mug down.

'Just after the war Edvard was seeing a young woman, Lisbet. He had helped rescue her and her family and they became close. He didn't have any of his own family left, so he moved to Oslo and lived with them for a while. Everything was fine for a little while, but a year after the war ended Edvard started to become depressed. I suppose that's only natural after what he had been through. He started to become paranoid about the people who had betrayed his family to the Nazis. He couldn't sleep, he felt angry all the time, and he fell out with Lisbet because he was so argumentative. He decided to leave Norway, so he travelled to Sweden and then across to Denmark. He didn't say goodbye to Lisbet and didn't tell anyone where he was going. But he couldn't settle anywhere for long and eventually he made his way back to Shetland and found your grandmother, who he had met during the war. Edvard felt safer and happier in Shetland and a few years later he married your grandmother. Well, you know how that ended don't you?'

Lisa nodded.

'What Edvard didn't know was Lisbet was pregnant when he left Norway. And since he didn't contact her again he never found out. Lisbet had no idea where he had gone to. She tracked him as far as Sweden but she had no idea where he ended up. She believed he had gone to America to find some cousins.'

'Crumbs! Poor woman; that must have been dreadful for her. How did Moffa find this out – and when?'

'A few years ago one of the other Norwegians who had been involved in the resistance died, here in Shetland. A few dignitaries came over for the funeral and Edvard attended it too. He met someone from Ålesund who knew Lisbet and that's how he found out he had another daughter. Her name is Karen.'

'Oh, Christ! So this is why my mother is mad at him. She has an older sister. I wonder why she didn't tell me.'

'What would you have done if she had told you?'

'Well, I would have wanted to meet this woman. She's my aunt.'

'Exactly. Your mother knows Moffa wants to meet her too but she seems to feel threatened by it. She has tried to discourage him from getting in touch; she thinks it would be upsetting for everyone.'

'You mean she's worried she might have to share the inheritance – this house?'

Joakim shrugged, but it confirmed what Lisa suspected.

'Poor Moffa. He's not really well enough to travel, but he ought to meet his daughter before it's too late. Maybe we can persuade Karen to come over to Shetland. Is her mother still alive too?'

'Edvard doesn't know. He hasn't tried to contact them. He feels too bad about what happened. He doesn't think they would want to see him.'

'We could Google them and find out. I'll ring them.'

Joakim shifted uncomfortably and pulled a face.

'I'm not sure a long distance phone call is the way to go. The surprise might not go down well. It would be better to meet them and see how they feel about seeing your grandfather. We don't know what Lisbet has said to Karen, or her family. She may have got married and kept it a secret.'

'You're right, but nipping across to Norway is not exactly something you can do quickly.'

Joakim raised an eyebrow and grinned at her. 'Well I'm here, and it wasn't too much bother.'

'Unlike you, I don't have access to a yacht, and I can't afford to fly there, and I have a little boy I would have to bring with me.' Lisa sighed. She wanted to meet this extended family of hers. She was curious about her aunt and whether or not she had any Norwegian cousins. Her family had been disappointingly small, without any brothers or sisters and no aunts or uncles; and a largely absent father. Her son was growing up in an equally small family. It was exciting to think there were other people in the world she was related to.

'But theoretically it is still possible to fly there isn't it? I was thinking of flying to Bergen instead of going back on the boat. Come with me.'

Lisa shook her head slowly.

'I would love to, but I can't afford it. Even if I could afford the flights, I would have to hire a car and stay in hotels and stuff. It would be impossible.'

'That's a shame. It might be good for your research to interview someone who had been rescued by your grandfather – if she is still alive.'

Lisa flung the blanket aside and stood up.

'You know what, that would be nice, but you don't get it, do you? I simply don't have the money.' Lisa hurried inside the house and rushed upstairs. She stopped at her bedroom door and listened to the gentle snores coming from the cot. She wanted to throw herself down on her bed and cry. The humiliation was too great. She was a failure, who could no more dream of flying over to Norway on a mission to reconcile her grandfather to his family, than fly to the moon. Clearly Joakim inhabited another world where jetting off to another country on a whim was a casual thing.

She remembered her manners and went downstairs to her guest. She found him back in the wheelchair closing the French doors and locking them.

'It's getting cold out there now,' Joakim said.

'Listen, I'm sorry, I was rude to you. It's just …'

'Don't apologise. I know it can't be easy on your own.'

Lisa slumped down on the sofa with her head in her hands. 'It must have been harder for Lisbet in those days.'

'I'm sure it was. Anyway, I've been thinking. If we flew over to Bergen I could drive you to wherever your aunt lives. Edvard thinks she lives somewhere near Ålesund which is about seven or eight hours drive from Bergen. It's a beautiful drive in the summer. I would be happy to take a little extra holiday. It would be fun.'

Lisa felt tears prick her eyes. Joakim was being so kind to her, but it would still be impossible. She had less than £100 in her bank account. She didn't have a credit card or any savings. She had just enough money to put petrol in her car and buy her share of the groceries for the week before she got paid again.

'Maybe next summer I can come over. I'll have got my PhD funding by then.'

'You're right. There's always next year.' Joakim said, as he stepped out of the wheelchair and eased himself down on the sofa next to Lisa. He put his arm around her shoulders and hugged her.

Lisa bit her lip and hoped her grandfather would still be around next summer.

14

Joakim pummelled the pillow into shape and tried to sleep. The sofa was comfortable but he was still wide awake and forced to listen to the birds outside, and the ticking of a large carriage clock on the mantelpiece. This trip to Shetland had not turned out as expected. He had imagined meeting Lisa and having a few drinks in the Boating Club; maybe even some harmless flirting with her. He had not expected to become embroiled in a family drama. And he had not expected Lisa to be a serious, hard-working, single mother. The photos and commentary on Facebook had showed a different side to her. Then again, he probably wasn't what Lisa had expected either.He thought about what Edvard had told him about his daughter. It was clear he felt time was running out for him and he wanted to make his peace with her, and perhaps even her mother, before he died. He hadn't asked Joakim for his help and yet Joakim felt an obligation. This man had risked his life for so many Norwegians. He had lost all of his family through an act of treachery and he deserved help now.

Joakim appreciated it would be easy to slip away and return to Norway and keep out of the drama. It would not serve any purpose to get involved. Lisa was a lovely girl, but she wasn't interested in him romantically. She had her hands full caring for her son and grandfather, as well as trying to study. There was no future for him with her. And yet, he sensed he had gained a true friend. He was surprised how unaffected she had been by his disability. She simply treated the situation with pragmatism and tact.

He thought about Edvard; such an interesting character. Joakim, along with every other Norwegian, had learned about the heroics of the Shetland Bus men, at school. He had never met anyone involved before, and he had been fascinated by the little Edvard had shared with him about his exploits during the war. He would love to spend more time with him and he could understand why Lisa was inspired to research the subject.

However, what struck him was how sad Edvard was not to be able to meet his daughter. Edvard had so many regrets. The guilt he felt at leaving a young woman behind who had been pregnant haunted him every day since he had found out. This had been exacerbated when Lisa had been abandoned when she was pregnant. He knew Lisa had had an easier time of it than Lisbet had; obviously there was less social stigma affecting Lisa. However, she had still struggled with finances, and her social life was non-existent compared with most young women.

Edvard had tried to visit Norway a couple of years ago, but he had been unwell, and now, since his stroke, he did not feel confident about travelling. He also didn't know what kind of reception he would get from Lisbet, if she was still alive, or from Karen. He was likely to travel all the way to Norway and get a door slammed in his face. He had dithered about this for too long, and as time ran out he realised he should have done it anyway. It was ridiculous when he was considered to be a war hero, and yet he confessed to Joakim, he had no courage when it came to meeting his own daughter.

Joakim decided he simply had to persuade Lisa to come over to Norway to find Edvard's family. If he had to lend her the money he would. He had no wish to sail back to Bergen. His leg still felt sore and he didn't want to make it worse by attempting a return journey on the yacht. He had made up his mind to fly back from Shetland to Bergen, and he hoped Lisa would come too.

He sent a text to Lars to tell him he would fly home and asked what they had been up to that evening. Lars replied immediately to say they were sitting in someone else's boat at an impromptu party. Joakim was relieved not to be there. He would not have enjoyed a party. He seldom did these days.

He thought back to the time before he had been shot. Life had been so different then. He had loved his job with the Coastguard; loved training for the Olympics and loved his life with Astrid. He shut his eyes and an image of them emerging from an Oslo nightclub, into the flash from paparazzi cameras appeared. Astrid had won two gold medals in the previous Olympics and had been a world champion skier. Her success and her beauty had earned her a secondary career in modelling. She was the Norwegian face of Omega watches and Yves St Laurent cosmetics. Her face had graced the pages of many magazines and newspapers; and there had been a certain amount of interest in Joakim too, especially during the short time between being nominated for the Olympic team and when the news got out about his traumatic injuries.

Life was so different now. Astrid had married someone else; a well-known television presenter. Joakim enjoyed running his own business, but it was nowhere near as exciting as his life with the Coastguard; and as for sport – it simply wasn't part of his life anymore. His social life had diminished overnight, as most of his closest friends had been fellow skiers. His two remaining close friends lived in Bergen, which was a lengthy drive from Larvik.

In effect, his world had shrunk, and it was only now in a rare trip away from home he realised he was not happy with this situation. He normally put his misery down to his injury, but now he realised this was not the main cause for concern. He simply wasn't doing enough to make the most of what he did have going for him. Talking to Edvard, and hearing how much he regretted in his life, despite the fact most people considered him to be a hero, made Joakim anxious not to have regrets of his own.

15

Lisa couldn't sleep either. She felt annoyed and embarrassed in equal measure. She hated the fact her life was such a mess she couldn't simply head off to Norway on a whim. She had friends the same age who were married, had kids, owned their own houses, and had established great careers and all the normal accoutrements, like holidays, cars and gold credit cards. Meanwhile, she was living rent-free with her grandfather and was still struggling. She had more qualifications than most of her friends and yet she worked part-time in the supermarket and she had hardly anything of value to her name. Her car was roadworthy – that was about the most she could say.

She stared up at the ceiling and watched the pale light from the rising sun shimmering above her. Her bedroom window was open to the breeze and white wisps of linen fluttered above the headboard.

When Moffa died, God forbid, she would have to leave her new home. Her mother was already full of ideas about what she wanted to do with the house when it was hers. In some ways she couldn't blame her mother for impatiently wanting a better life. Her marriage had broken down when Lisa was five, when her husband had gone to work offshore and had hardly ever returned. He had been stingy with child support, especially after he had remarried and had two sons who Lisa had never met. Ingrid had never recovered from this heartbreak; and over the years she had gone on to have other equally unsuccessful relationships.

Perhaps her mother was right; she ought to stop studying and get a proper job. She wouldn't be living rent free forever; this was the perfect opportunity to get a decent job and save money to buy her own place one day. Hansi's long term security should be uppermost in her mind, not the relentless pursuit of degrees. If she had a proper job she would be able to afford to go to Norway and track down Moffa's daughter.

She sat up in bed, wide awake now, the sun streaming in through the window despite the fact it was only four in the morning. It was going to be a perfect day. She reached for her laptop, which was always close to hand.

A few minutes later she had scoured the local jobs and decided to apply for a few. Shetland was booming; and jobs were readily available, although not necessarily in the field she was interested in. However, she could suffer an office job for the time being, until something more interesting came along.

Surely sitting in an office all day would beat working in the supermarket.

One of the vacancies was promising – working for Scottish Natural Heritage. It had nothing to do with archaeology, but it was related to the environment she loved so much. It also offered a child friendly workplace, great holidays and a pension.

By five, the application form had been completed online and submitted. Lisa slammed the lid down on the laptop with a flourish, and then sprawled out on the bed exhausted.

An hour later, Lisa took Hansi downstairs for his breakfast. She strapped him into his highchair and made him some porridge with raisins and cinnamon. She attempted to feed him, which he resisted in his usual independent way, so she handed him his spoon and let him get on with it for a moment, while she tiptoed over to the door of the lounge to see if Joakim was still asleep.

She found him sitting outside on the bench, reading a book. He looked up and smiled.

'Lovely day, isn't it?'

'It is; I've been outside for an hour already. I was looking through this book I found, about Shetland archaeology.'

'There are some brilliant sites here, if you are interested in seeing them. I mean, if you want to. I don't want to take up all your time.'

'I would love to visit Jarlshof. An original Viking building would be interesting.'

'Oh, it's even more interesting than just Vikings. There are some Pictish ruins at the same place, and some Bronze Age and medieval stuff.'

'Could we go today? Would it be too much trouble for you?'

'Not at all! Now, let me go and make sure Hansi puts more porridge in his mouth than on the floor and I will make you some breakfast too. What would you like?'

'Porridge sounds good.'

Lisa grinned.

'Hmm, let's see if you like my version of porridge. It isn't very Scottish.'

Lisa went back to the kitchen and grabbed another spoon and finished feeding Hansi. Moffa's bedroom door was still closed. It was unusually late for him to still be in his room, but she heard his radio, and his tuneless humming along to the music.

Lisa made some coffee and knocked on Moffa's door.

'Coffee?'

'*Ja, ja! Kom inn.*' Lisa pushed open the door and set the coffee down on the bedside table. '*God morgen,*' Moffa said. He was sitting on the edge of his bed trying to button up his shirt. His fingers trembled and he was struggling, so Lisa sat down next to him and helped him finish the task.

'You seem happy today, Moffa. Did you sleep well after all that Aquavit?'

'Ja, but I need my coffee now, thank you.' Lisa reached for the mug and handed it to him. 'I'm about to make Joakim some porridge, would you like some too?'

'With cinnamon and raisins?'

'Yes, just how you like it.'

Moffa sipped his coffee.

'Joakim told me about your family in Norway. I'm sorry Moffa; you should have told me. I might have been able to help you get to meet them.'

Edvard was silent for a moment. His eyes clouded over in grief; Lisa leant against him and put her arm around his shoulder.

'It's not too late; I'm going to get a proper job and then I'm going to fly over to Norway and find them for you. Unless of course you feel up to coming too; it would be fun.'

Edvard drained the coffee and put it down clumsily, almost missing the table.

'I'm a useless old man now; I can't walk farther than a hundred feet without getting tired. How can I go home now?' His shoulders sank and he bowed his head; more in defeat than self-pity.

'Well then, I shall have to bring them here to see you.'

Edvard grasped her hand.

'I'm so sorry *kjaere*; you must think I'm a bad man leaving a baby behind.'

'You didn't know though, did you? And after all you had been through; nobody blames you, Moffa. I'm sure your daughter knows enough about what happened to understand.'

'I'm not so sure. But I would like the chance to apologise to her, and her mother too, if she's still alive.'

Lisa stood up, mindful of the fact Hansi was still sitting in his high chair and would no doubt be fighting against the restraint.

'I had better go and sort Hansi out.'

Lisa removed all traces of porridge from Hansi's face and fingers and then carried him into the lounge and put him down on the floor beside his garage, but Hansi was not interested in his collection of toy cars. He made a dash for the open French doors. Lisa followed him outside and laughed as Hansi stopped in surprise when he saw Joakim.

'Hallo Hansi,' Joakim said, putting down his book and smiling at the boy.

Lisa sat down on the bench next to Joakim and held her arms out to Hansi, but her son ignored her. He stood in front of Joakim and frowned. Joakim pulled a face.

Hansi giggled, and then he spotted Joakim's Omega watch. Like a magpie, Hansi was drawn to bright shiny things and he leant against Joakim's leg as he studied the watch. He reached a chubby finger to trace the face of the watch. Joakim held it up to Hansi's ear and laughed when Hansi was surprised at the ticking.

'Careful, he'll get it all sticky.'

'Don't worry; it's waterproof.'

Hansi maintained his interest in the watch for a while and then he attempted to climb up on Joakim's lap. Lisa was about to stop him when Joakim lifted him up. Hansi grinned triumphantly at Lisa.

'*Hei lille mann; snakker du norsk?*'

Hansi reached for a silver chain around Joakim's neck and tugged on it.

Lisa shook her head at Hansi, but he ignored her.

He's a confident little thing isn't he?' Joakim said, as Hansi prodded Joakim's face, curious about the stubble on his chin.

'You don't mind do you?'

'No, it's fine. My sister has children. I'm used to being a human climbing frame. I left my leg by the sofa, so I'm trapped here now. I think he senses my weakness.'

Lisa laughed.

'Shall I get it for you?'

'No it's OK; I'm an expert at hopping around now. It's not dignified; but it is efficient.'

'Well then, I had better make that breakfast I promised you ages ago.'

After breakfast Lisa cleared up the kitchen and when she returned to the lounge Joakim was re-attaching his prosthesis, watched by Hansi and Moffa. Moffa was talking and nobody noticed Lisa standing there. She saw Joakim grimace when he tightened the fastening.

'Does that still hurt?'

'It's a bit sore where the skin has been rubbed. But don't worry, I'll be fine.'

'Let me see; I might be able to find something to make it better.'

Joakim didn't move.

'No, it's OK.'

'Don't be daft; you don't want to ruin your holiday being uncomfortable for no reason.'

Moffa stood up and put the television on, as if he didn't want to get involved in the argument. The news was about to start, and he was unable to resist watching it.

Reluctantly, Joakim gave in to her demand. He unstrapped the prosthetic leg and pulled it off, and then unpeeled the two layers of sock that covered the stump.

Lisa sat down on the sofa next to him and frowned at the painful red welt that had developed around the area where the artificial leg had been secured. Scars from the stitches were still clear, but the stump itself was smooth and rounded in shape.

'I know what will help with this; wait there,' she said, as she hurried out to the bathroom. She returned with a grey plastic jar and sat down on the sofa.

As she applied a generous application of *Sudocreme* to the sore skin, she met Joakim's eyes. He was staring at her. She snapped the lid back on the jar, suddenly aware he might be embarrassed by her action, but possibly too polite to say anything.

'That should help. It's an excellent healing cream.'

Joakim reached for the jar and examined it.

'Yeah, we have this in Norway. It's nappy cream, yes?'

'Well, it is used for lots of things, but yeah, I buy it for Hansi.'

He laughed. 'Well I will give it a go.' He reached for the sock to cover his leg.

'So, do you still want to go out and see some archaeology?'

'Sure, why not?'

Lisa set the baby carrier down on the tarmac next to the car and then lifted Hansi into it. With an experienced flourish she hoisted Hansi onto her shoulders. Joakim meanwhile was standing by the wall of the car park and looking out to sea. Lisa stuffed the car keys into the pocket of her jeans and strode towards Joakim.

'Are you sure you don't want me to carry him. He's heavy.'

'Don't worry; I'm used to it. I have abs of steel now,' she said, tapping her tummy and grinning.

They set off across the grassy path towards the archaeological ruins. The ground was soft underfoot and Joakim felt a moment's anxiety at the idea of walking over the uneven ground, but the ointment Lisa had applied to the sore was already taking effect so he chose to ignore the discomfort and to concentrate on having a good time. He felt relaxed in Lisa's company now. Lisa was marching ahead of him, deliberately jiggling Hansi up and down and making him laugh.

Despite a cool breeze the sunshine was warm on their faces as they explored the ruins. Lisa talked about some of the finds that been uncovered from the site during recent digs; and about the research she had done at University. Joakim listened attentively, fascinated by her passion for history. Although interested in history and culture, he had never felt real passion for anything other than sport before now.

Lisa climbed up a grassy bank that surrounded the foundations of the remains of a wheel-house. She gestured for Joakim to join her on the vantage point. She held her hand out to him as he climbed up. He did not let go when he stood beside her.

'This is a great site. I must take some photos.' He reached into his pocket and withdrew an iPhone and snapped some photos as they peered down into the ancient circular stone dwelling. Then he let go of Lisa's hand and stepped away and snapped some pictures of her and Hansi.

'So, when are you going to come over to Norway to find your grandfather's daughter?'

Lisa stopped smiling and turned away, staring out to sea.

'I can't afford to do it this year. But I have decided I'm not going to do the PhD now. I'm going to get a job instead.'

'Oh!' Joakim said.

Lisa lifted her hands in despair. 'I applied for a good job this morning. If I get it I will be able to afford to visit Norway next summer.'

'Don't wait until then. Come back with me this week. Who knows if your grandfather will still be here next year? Don't put it off.'

'But I can't. I've told you; I don't have any money.'

'I'll buy your ticket.'

Lisa shook her head.

'Pay me back next year.'

Hansi was getting bored and tugged at Lisa's ponytail.

'Ow! Don't do that sweetie.'

Lisa reached up to untangle her hair from Hansi's grip, but some of it had caught on the toggle of his jacket and she couldn't move her head. Joakim walked over and released her hair. He stood beside her, making a face at Hansi who laughed and threw his head back and kicked Lisa in his excitement.

'Whoops, I'm not helping, am I?' Joakim said, grabbing Hansi's foot and shaking his head at the boy.

'So you're flying home?' Lisa said, still deep in thought about his invitation. The comment about Moffa not being around the following year had hurt, but there were no guarantees he would live for many more years.

'Ja, I don't want to risk another rough crossing; at least not until my leg feels better again. I had a look at the Flybe website; there are some spare seats on the Wednesday flight back to Bergen. My car is in Bergen anyway, so it's perfect. Lars and Anders are going to set off on Monday, so they will get back around the same time as me.'

'How much are the flights?'

'I can't remember, but they weren't expensive.'

'For a Norwegian!' Lisa said, laughing.

Joakim grinned and shrugged helplessly.

'So, if I can pay you back next year, you could buy our tickets then?'

'Yeah, of course; I would love to show you around Norway. My parents have been nagging at me for months to take a proper holiday from work. It will be an adventure. I would love to help track down Edvard's family for him.'

'OK then. Let's do it.'

16

That afternoon while Hansi was having a nap, Lisa and Joakim went online and booked their flights. They would fly out on Wednesday and Lisa and Hansi would return the following week. Lisa had taken Moffa aside and told him what she was doing, and immediately he had handed her his bank card and told her to take out some money for the trip. It was then Lisa knew she was doing the right thing. Moffa was desperate for news of his daughter, but had been too afraid to say anything about it before.

On Wednesday afternoon, Lisa, Joakim and Hansi arrived in Bergen. The taxi stopped outside a smart apartment block and while Joakim paid the driver, Lisa put sleepy Hansi into his pushchair and picked up her rucksack.

'We can't go without saying goodbye to Anita and Freya - Lars' wife and daughter.'

Lisa felt a little shy about going to meet someone new but she followed Joakim into the building.

Anita opened the door before they had even had a chance to knock. A little girl in red jeans and a blue tee-shirt appeared behind her and gawped at Hansi.

'Come in, come in. Lars told me all about you coming over to find your family. That's so exciting,' Anita said to Lisa, taking her arm and leading her into the bright sunlit apartment. Hansi woke up immediately and squirmed to get out of his pushchair. 'Hello, what's your name?' Anita added, crouching down to his level.

'His name is Hansi.'

'Hansi? How unusual. Is that a common name in Shetland? It sounds Norwegian.'

'It's an old traditional Shetland name.'

'Well, this is Freya. Darling, come and meet Hansi. Why don't you show him your toys? I expect he would love to have a run around after his journey. Let's go and have a cup of tea while they play.'

Lisa unstrapped Hansi from the pushchair and let him chase after Freya. She leant her rucksack against the wall and followed Anita into the kitchen.

'Now, what would you like to eat? I made some cake earlier, and I'll make some sandwiches, or I could cook something?'

'Sandwiches would be great, Anita. Don't go to any trouble for us.' Joakim said.

'It is no trouble at all. We hardly ever get to see you these days. I'm glad you stopped by to before you left. Lars and Anders don't think they will get back until much later. The wind's against them. It's been a bit rough I think.'

Joakim pulled a face at Lisa and she laughed.

'Bet you're glad you're not on the boat with them again.'

'No way, once was enough.'

'Wasn't it a good trip down? I thought you did well in the race.'

'We did, but it was a bit rough and my prosthesis was a pain. I got a big blister on my leg.'

'Oh dear, is it better now?'

'Yes thanks. Lisa gave me some nappy cream to put on it.'

'*Sudocreme*!' Lisa said to Anita, who laughed and nodded in approval.

Joakim sat down on one of the kitchen chairs, but Lisa hovered near the door, keeping an eye on Hansi.

'They'll be fine. Sit down, make yourself at home,' Anita said to Lisa. 'Now, tell me about who you're looking for.'

Lisa pulled out the chair next to Joakim. Anita was busy pulling jars and packets out of a giant stainless steel fridge. The kettle was on and a freshly iced carrot cake was sitting on the worktop. Lisa relaxed; she felt truly welcome.

'Well, where do I start? I live with my Norwegian grandfather. He is eighty seven and a little bit frail after having a stroke. Anyway, he came over to Shetland not long after the war ended. He had no family left in Norway as they had been executed by the Nazis. It was because of this he had joined the resistance movement – the Shetland Bus, as it became known.'

'Oh yes, I've read about that. They used fishing boats to smuggle people out of Norway.'

'That's right. But my grandfather doesn't like to talk about it much; which is annoying seeing as how I wanted to do a research project on the Shetland Bus, and I have hardly been able to get anything out of him. But Joakim here got chatting to him the other night, and suddenly my grandfather is all talk. He told him about a daughter he has over here. He had a girlfriend who he met during the war, but he left Norway suddenly without saying goodbye and without knowing she was pregnant. I think he felt so bad he couldn't tell anyone before.'

'But with the help of a little Aquavit, I got it all out of him,' Joakim added, grinning at them both.

'You certainly did. Poor Moffa! Ever since he found out about his daughter, which was only a few years ago, he has wanted to come back to find her. So here I am on his behalf. We have no idea what kind of reception we might get. She might well slam the door in our faces. But still, we have to try.'

'My goodness, that's some story. How many children did he have in Shetland? What do they think?'

'Only my mother, and to be honest, she's not impressed with the idea of them meeting up.'

'Would I be able to use your PC for a few minutes, Anita?' Joakim said. 'I need to see the map of where we are going later. We don't know for sure but we think Lisbet was living near Ålesund. I wanted to check the route.'

'That's a hell of a drive. You're not setting off today are you?' Anita stood with her hands on her hips, and frowned at Joakim.

'Well, yes.'

'Nonsense! It will take at least eight or nine hours to get there. What about the little boy, he won't like that? Don't be daft. Stay the night here and set off in the morning. Then at least you will arrive at a time when you can find somewhere to stay.'

'Is it really that far?' Lisa said.

'It's about 300 miles, Lisa. But what a drive; it's beautiful. You'll love it,' Anita replied.

Lisa turned to Joakim. 'It's up to you. You're the driver.'

'OK, we'll stay. But if we got up really early that would be good.'

'That's fine with me; I have my early morning alarm clock playing in the other room.'

'Well that's settled then. You can have the spare room, and I have a travel cot Hansi can use.'

'I'll sleep on the sofa,' Joakim said quickly, looking faintly embarrassed.

Anita laughed. 'Oh sorry, there was me thinking you were a couple.'

'Ah no, we only met last week.' Lisa replied, smiling at Anita.

After they had eaten, Anita suggested they took the children out to a nearby park to have a run around. The sun was bright and warm, much warmer than it had been in Shetland. Lisa felt a stab of envy at the weather in Bergen, which after all was on the same latitude as Lerwick. It didn't seem fair. She was also struck by how many trees grew in the city and in the surrounding landscape. Mature trees in full leaf, and hedges of azaleas and rhododendrons. It was a beautiful place to be on a summer's day.

Lisa and Anita pushed Freya and Hansi on the swings and chatted. Joakim sat down on a nearby bench and leaned back with his eyes shut, soaking up the sun.

'So how did you come to be living in Norway? Do you like it here?'

'I love it. Lars and I met a few years ago in Peru. A holiday romance, but it seems to have lasted.'

'Peru?'

'I know! Mad eh? I went backpacking after university.'

'So what do you do now? Do you work here?'

'I'm an editor, for a publishing company in London, so I don't earn a Norwegian salary, unfortunately. But it's handy being able to work from home with Freya around.

Anita stepped closer to Lisa and lowered her voice.

'So what's the story with you and Joakim?'

'I don't think there is a story. We're just friends. He's lovely though.'

'He is; although he needs a good woman. God knows how he ended up living in Larvik on his own. He gets so lonely. Ever since he split up with Astrid – and now's she's married – he's been a little off-grid. We hardly ever see him. His rehabilitation has been slower than we expected. Don't get me wrong; he gets around brilliantly, and his business is doing well. But he needs to think about meeting someone again. But he never seems to meet the right women; which is funny, as he used to be popular with the girls.'

'I can imagine.' Lisa said, taking a surreptitious glance at Joakim who had fallen asleep on the bench.

'So what about it? Aren't you interested in him?'

Lisa shrugged and looked pointedly down at Hansi.

'I never told him about my son before we met. Not every man wants a ready-made family.'

'I can't imagine Joakim would mind.'

'Hmm; could you imagine him settling down with a poor single mother before he lost his leg? I get the impression his ex-girlfriend was a bit of a celebrity. I'm not the same kind of woman as her, I bet.'

'True, you're not. Astrid was lovely, don't get me wrong. We all loved her, but that's over now, and good luck to her. But you're lovely too. Why would you think you weren't good enough for him?'

'I don't know. But I don't get the feeling there's any chemistry between us. But he is nice to have as a friend. And that's good enough for me.' Lisa pushed the swing again before Hansi complained. 'Did you know Joakim before he lost his leg?'

'Yes; I met him two years before. He was a different person then.'

'In what way?'

'He couldn't sit still. He was always doing something. He was obsessed with sport and went running every day. He hardly ever drank alcohol and was incredibly fussy about what he ate. It was all about the training for the Olympics. Astrid was pretty much the same. They were made for each other back then.'

'And now?'

'And now he is barely recognisable.' Anita gestured to where Joakim sat; his arms were stretched out along the back of the bench, with his face lifted to the sun. 'He would never have sat like that before. He would have been running around, kicking a football, and showing off.'

Lisa frowned.

'Oh I don't mean showing off in a bad way. He wasn't like that. But he would have been fooling around, making people laugh. He wanted to entertain.'

'I haven't seen that side of him at all. It's like you're describing someone else.'

'I know. But I like this quiet side of him too. He is so kind and helpful. And he's still gorgeous, don't you think?'

Lisa grinned.

'Yeah, he is.'

Lisa watched as Joakim sat up straight and reached into his pocket for his phone. He appeared to be reading a text. He stood up and walked over to them, with only a barely discernible limp.

'I've just had a text from Anders. They are not far from Bergen now; maybe another couple of hours.'

'I've got time to make a nice celebratory dinner.' Anita put her arms around Joakim and hugged him. 'See, aren't you glad you haven't set off already.'

Joakim smirked. 'That depends on what you're going to cook for us. I still remember a strange Peruvian chicken stew you made, with condensed milk.' Joakim pulled a face and dodged out of Anita's way when she attempted to slap his arm.

'Well yes, that wasn't my finest hour in the kitchen. But I'm making something much better tonight. A fish stew, and there won't be any condensed milk in it. This is more of a Moroccan style dish, with tomatoes and onions and couscous; a little spicy, but Lars loves it.'

Around seven, after Hansi and Freya had eaten their supper and gone off to bed, Joakim drove down to the harbour to pick up Lars and Anders. Lisa helped Anita lay the dining table and clear away the toys scattered across the floor, mostly by Hansi.

'Thank you for inviting us to stay. It's been lovely meeting you. I'm looking forward to seeing Lars and Anders again too. In fact I have Lars to thank for persuading me not to give up on Joakim straight away. We didn't hit it off at first, although that was partly because his leg was hurting, but I didn't know that. I thought he was a grumpy bastard.'

'Lars is always looking out for other people.' Anita opened a bottle of wine and poured out two glasses. 'No sense in waiting for them. You know what men are like around boats. I bet they won't be in a hurry for their dinner.'

Lisa clinked her glass against Anita's. 'That's true. My grandfather used to drive my gran mad; he almost lived on his boat, especially in the summer. But I used to love going fishing with him when I was little. He taught me a lot.'

'You sail too?'

'I don't know much about yachts, but I can manage alright in a small fishing boat.'

'So there is something of the Shetland Bus in you too.'

'I suppose there is.'

It was nearly nine before they sat down to eat. The doors to the balcony were open, letting in a light breeze. Lisa sat next to Joakim. She felt grown-up suddenly, and realised she missed the company of people her own age. She was usually in the presence of the very young or the ancient.

Lars told them about their journey home again. It hadn't been the best weather and Joakim commented he was relieved he had flown home instead. 'But next year, count me in. I'll be better prepared then.'

Lisa smiled quizzically.

'So, you want to come back to Shetland then?'

'Of course, I like it there. The natives are friendly.'

'And next year, we will win!' Lars said.

Lisa ate her dinner, smiling inwardly at the idea Joakim wanted to come back to Shetland; even if it was just for a yacht race, and a whole year away.

Joakim put his hand over his glass when Lars went to top it up with more wine.

'Early start tomorrow!'

'Ah yes, you're driving up to Ålesund. Do you know the address of where you are going?'

'Not exactly. But we hope we might be able to find someone to help us when we get there.'

'What's her name? I have a good friend in the police force up north. He might be able to help.'

'Edvard's ex-girlfriend's name is Lisbet Olafssen; her maiden name was Bergum. She's about eighty six, if she is still living. And her daughter's name is Karen and she would be around sixty eight,' Lisa said.

'Hmm, not much to go on, but I'll call Peter tomorrow and see what he can come up with. I can text you with anything I find out.'

'That would be great, thanks.' Lisa smiled gratefully at Lars.

'So, what do you think of my fish stew then, Joakim?' Anita said.

'It will do.' Joakim said, pretending to examine it doubtfully.

Anita looked under the table and grinned.

'Which is your real leg; so I can kick you?'

17

They left the apartment before seven. Anita and Lars saw them off and made Lisa promise to keep in touch.

'Find me on Facebook. I want to hear how your search went,' Anita said.

'I will do. And thanks. It's been lovely.'

Joakim hummed to himself as he slung their bags into the spacious boot of his Volvo estate while Lisa strapped Hansi into the car seat she had borrowed from Anita.

Joakim fiddled with a built in sat-nav as Lisa put on her seat belt. The sat-nav said something in Norwegian and Lisa laughed.

'Just as well you're driving, I wouldn't have a clue.'

'I can change it to English, if you like.'

'No, that's fine. I'm going to enjoy the view. I'm sure you can find the way.'

Joakim started the engine and within fifteen minutes they had reached the northern outskirts of Bergen and were on their way. As they left the suburbs Lisa was stunned into silence by the scenery.

She stared up at the jagged mountains, grassy pastures, dark forests, brilliant blue seas and the numerous tiny islands scattered along the coast. They barely spoke for the first hour. Hansi had gone back to sleep and Lisa was deep in thought.

'Are you OK there; you're quiet.'

'Oh sorry; I'm not much company am I? I was thinking about what it must have been like to grow up in Norway and then end up living in Shetland. It is so different here. I came here a few years ago, but we never left the city, so I haven't seen the real Norwegian countryside before. It's lovely.'

Joakim glanced up at the craggy mountains that cast the road into shadow.

'I suppose I take it all for granted, but I couldn't imagine leaving Norway. It was a great place to grow up. Although I don't think it would have been so nice during the war; for Edvard.'

'The bloody war! Honestly, when you are driving through such amazing scenery you can't imagine why anyone would want to start a war and kill people. It's so peaceful here; I can't picture the Nazis invading.'

'Well they did. But all that is in the past. I don't think about it much. I guess I was always one for looking at the future more than historic events.'

Lisa didn't reply for a moment. She remembered what Anita had said about how different Joakim was compared to when she first met him. Was he quieter and less enthusiastic about life because he saw no future? She understood him not wanting to dwell on his own past, but surely he must see a brighter life for himself one day.

'I don't know why I'm so passionate about history. I always have been, since I was a child. We used to live in a house overlooking Clickhimin Broch, the old Iron Age ruin we drove past in Lerwick?' Joakim nodded, so she continued. 'I used to play there when I was little. It was like a castle in my mind and I used to pretend I owned it. I spent so long dreaming about being a little girl living in the Iron Age. I had no idea, at six, that the Iron Age was not a great time to live in. I also had no idea about the reality of Vikings either. I saw the annual Up Helly Aa processions and thought Vikings were like visiting royalty.'

Joakim laughed.

'We were!'

'Very funny!' The conversation paused for a few minutes. Lisa was content to gaze out of the window and daydream.

'Why did you join the Coastguard? That seems a bit random, when you loved skiing so much.'

'I had to do my national service somewhere. And I liked boats too. My father had a boatyard, so I spent a lot of time with him, helping him out.'

'Do you regret it now?'

'No, not at all. I enjoyed my time in the Coastguard. In fact I joined up properly after my national service was over. They were good to me. I was able to take enough time off for my training. They supported my sporting career and I made friends with Lars and Anders when I worked with them. It was great, until ...'

'Are you tempted to take up some other kind of sport, as a Paralympian?'

Joakim shook his head. 'No!'

The vehemence with which he replied surprised Lisa and she regretted saying anything. Seconds later they were plunged into the darkness of another tunnel.

'These roads and tunnels remind me of the Romans,' she said, attempting to change the subject.

'Romans?'

'Well, back when they ruled most of Europe they created this vast network of paved roads. But they tended to be very straight, going from A to B without deviating too much because of hills or rivers. I imagine a modern day Roman Emperor would approve of simply tunnelling through a mountain.'

'I suppose so. Imagine how long the drive would be if we had to drive around these mountains and hills instead of through them. That would take forever.' Joakim grinned, seemingly happy with the change of subject.

'You don't mind driving all this way do you?' Lisa said, suddenly feeling guilty for being the cause of this epic journey; even if it had been his idea.

'These days, driving is what I love doing best. I can't imagine a better place to be than on the road, driving on a sunny day, in – as you said – this lovely scenery and with such great company.'

'Thank you. I appreciate it. I don't know when I would have come over if you hadn't persuaded me. But if you get tired of driving, let me know.'

Joakim squeezed her hand. 'I won't get tired; stop worrying. I am the king of the road!'

Lisa giggled, and was a little disappointed when he let go of her hand and held the steering wheel instead.

They were driving through a small town and they slowed for a junction. The car in front slowed too. Inside the other car was a man and a woman and the heads of two small children were just visible in the back seat.

'What do you see when you look at that car in front?' Joakim said.

Lisa stared at the white Volkswagen *Touran*. It was fairly new. She couldn't see the occupants clearly but she guessed they were in their early to mid-thirties. She shrugged.

'An ordinary married couple with children; why?'

'What do you think we look like to them?'

Lisa looked back at Hansi and then at Joakim.

'Much the same I suppose.'

'Exactly. That's why I'm enjoying this drive so much. I'm an ordinary person when I drive this car. I'm no longer a would-be Olympian; and no longer disabled. I'm not the victim of some stupid smuggling attempt gone wrong.'

'I don't think I would ever describe you as "ordinary." That implies boring; and you're certainly not that.'

'How am I not boring? Compared to what I used to do, my life is very uninteresting.'

'To you maybe; but that's possibly because it is not what you envisaged for yourself. I think other people, well me anyway, see you differently.'

'So how do you see me? Tell me honestly.'

Lisa shifted in her seat and studied him. He was wearing expensive Michael Kors sunglasses, along with his Omega watch. He wore a pale green Ralph Lauren polo shirt and new Levi jeans. The car would have cost a fortune and he seemed at ease with money. He was tanned and good looking; even more so when he smiled. Although when he glowered, as he was doing now under her scrutiny, he was a little fierce. His arms were muscular and his whole physique was lean. In short he was bloody gorgeous, and Lisa suddenly felt self-conscious and inadequate. If it wasn't for the fact he had lost his leg he would now be the Olympian he wanted to be. He would be married to the gold medal winning skier turned supermodel, Astrid, with her perfect hair and perfect face. He would not be driving a scruffy single mother from Shetland up to Ålesund in order to track down her grandfather's daughter.

She felt her good humour evaporate and struggled to find an answer for his question.

'I'm that bad, eh?' Joakim said. He winked at her. 'I should not have been fishing for compliments; that's OK.'

Within a second he had dwarfed in stature; his confidence diminished. The accoutrements of wealth lost their sheen. He was just a young man who had been through hell and back.

'I think you're lovely.'

Lisa turned away quickly. She hadn't meant to say that aloud.

'Really? I've never been called that before.' The road was in shadow as they drove through a forest and Joakim pushed the sunglasses up onto his head. He grinned wickedly at Lisa. 'I'm lovely; and I'm the king of the road!'

18

When they stopped for lunch Joakim read a text from Lars that brought the welcome news that Lisbet lived in a town called Stranda, which was closer than Ålesund. Consequently their journey was a little shorter than anticipated. They left the café and walked back to the car.

'So this is it; next stop Lisbet's house,' he said, as Lisa fastened her seatbelt. He noticed the flicker of anxiety and smiled reassuringly.

'Don't worry. It will be fine. Just enjoy the journey. We'll figure out what to say when we get there.'

'I expect you'll have to do most of the talking.' Lisa replied.

'True. She may not speak any English at all. My grandparents never did. You had better fill me in with all the details. I guess I know most of it. But tell me about your mother. I expect they'll want to hear about Edvard's family.'

Lisa talked about her mother and explained about her failed marriage and the fact Lisa had grown up with only her mam for company. She talked about her grandmother and how close her mother had been to her, although she had not been as close to Edvard.

'It's all starting to make a lot more sense now. I never knew Moffa was keeping such a secret. It must have been hard. Although I know he was happy with my gran.'

'He was. He told me he felt at home in Shetland – safe. He could never get over that sense of being on the run when he was in Norway.'

A road sign indicated Ålesund was 230 kilometres away.   Stranda had not been included on the sign but the sat-nav said they had less than two and a half hours to go until their destination. He was starting to feel excited about finding this old woman. When he had suggested coming to find her with Lisa he imagined it would be harder to track her down. He hoped they weren't going on a wild goose chase. He didn't want to let Edvard down. It was an opportunity to help a real-life war hero and Joakim was only too happy to help bring some happiness back to him.

He wondered how he would manage the situation if they discovered it was the wrong Lisbet, or whether the old woman had passed away after all, or was too ill to see them. She might have Alzheimer's for all they knew. His optimism wavered. This could be a disaster.

He reached for Lisa's hand that was resting on her thigh. He squeezed it reassuringly, although he needed the comfort too.

'Is Stranda a big enough place that there'll be a hotel?' Lisa said.

'Of course and there's always the ski resort at Strandafjellet which will be open for summer visitors. Anyway, worst-case scenario I have a tent in the boot of the car and sleeping bags.'

'Really?' Lisa said doubtfully, hoping it wouldn't come to that.

'Yeah, I keep them in the car all the time; you never know when you might need a sleeping bag, especially during the winter.'

'Of course; you might break down in a snowstorm.'

Joakim thought back to the last time he had been in Strandafjellet. He had come away with gold and a bronze medal from the competition. Not long after he had been offered his first sponsorship from a prestigious sports company. He would only have been about twenty at the time.

'We'll stay at the ski centre. It's about a hundred years old, but lovely. A proper old fashioned skiing hotel.'

'A ski centre in the summer; are you sure it will be open?'

'Yeah, of course. Tourists still visit for the scenery; the mountains, the fjords, the wildlife.'

'Right, well, in that case you have to let me pay. It's my treat this time.'

Joakim narrowed his eyes at her. He had a feeling the price of a hotel room at the ski resort, even if it wasn't peak season, might make Lisa faint. But he had an idea about that.

As they continued their drive north, Joakim felt renewed pride in his homeland, seen through Lisa's eyes. She was blown away by the beauty; the mountains, lush valleys and vibrant blue of the fjords. They had not bothered to put on any music this time and they chatted instead, comparing stories of their childhoods, discussing what films and music they liked and what food they enjoyed.

He was conscious of the fact Lisa had not attempted any kind of flirtation with him. She was friendly, charming and kind, but he had not seen any evidence she fancied him. He thought back to the first night he met her – a week ago – only a week; it felt longer. He remembered how she had held his leg while she had applied the cream to the sore skin. She had done it with the no nonsense approach of a nurse. He had been shocked by her actions. As kind as she had been, it had felt a little invasive – a little too personal, and it underlined the fact she did not see him as a potential boyfriend.

'How about we get some lunch first; then go and find the house. I might make a call to the hotel and get a room too.'

'A room?' Lisa said, raising her eyebrows at him.

'I meant two rooms. It got lost in translation.'

'Yeah, right!' Lisa elbowed him and he laughed.

'I thought Stranda meant beach in Norwegian. It doesn't look like we are close to any water yet.' Lisa said.

'All will be revealed when we get down from this mountain'

In true Norwegian, and as Joakim had observed, Shetland style, the landscape changed dramatically and quickly from grey craggy rocks to a large body of water. The road descended to the town and they passed a caravan park on the edge of the fjord and some apartment blocks. Joakim followed the signs to the centre and found a place to park near the pier. There was a little quay for a ferry which had just left the berth and was steaming across the fjord. They could see passengers on board standing on the deck taking photographs.

'Right, food; I'm starving and I bet Hansi is too. There's a restaurant across the road. Shall we take a look?'

A couple of hours later they parked outside what they believed to be Lisbet's house. It was a large three storey building with balconies to the first and second floor, and overlooking the fjord. It was freshly painted, white with a dove grey trim to the windows and doors.

Lisa stared up at the beautiful timber house. The lawns were immaculate with a colourful display of flowers in the beds and hanging from baskets around the porch. She couldn't imagine an old lady living here on her own. She would have to be fit to keep the lawn in such fine condition.

'Do you really think she lives here? All by herself?'

'Maybe she has a young fit husband. Or perhaps she employs a housekeeper. It's a big house isn't it?'

'She must be wealthy.'

Joakim shrugged. 'It's no bigger than any of the others on the street. We don't know what her husband did, do we?'

Lisa shook her head. She felt shy now and was almost too scared to go and knock on the door. Luckily Joakim was not willing to leave it a moment later.

'Come on, let's go. Bring Hansi; a baby is a great ice-breaker.'

Lisa picked Hansi up and grabbed a toy in case she needed to distract him. Then she faced the house. Joakim locked the car then took Lisa's hand and led her up the path. He squeezed it and let go when they got to the door. Lisa rang the bell.

A moment later a young Asian woman answered the door. Lisa couldn't hide her surprise, and disappointment.

Joakim stepped forward and greeted the woman. Lisa couldn't understand every word but she got the gist of it. He asked the woman if she knew Lisbet Olafssen. When she said yes, Joakim asked if it was possible to see her. The woman was reluctant to let them in. Joakim asked her to tell Lisbet they had an important message from Edvard Christiansen, who had once gone by the name of Peter Andersen. He made her repeat the names back and then they waited on the doorstep.

'She's Lisbet's carer,' Joakim explained as the woman closed the door on them. 'Let's hope that means she's not too frail to see us.'

They heard footsteps and the door opened again and the woman asked them to come inside. They followed her into a formal sitting room.

Almost immediately an elderly woman appeared from another room. She was immaculately dressed in a pale green dress, with a darker green cardigan and a set of pearls around her neck. She had long white hair worn in a tidy French pleat. This woman was in her eighties, yet she seemed so youthful. She held an old framed photo in her hands. Lisa guessed it was Moffa.

'Edvard Christiansen?' The woman said, looking curiously at Joakim.

'Nei, Jeg er Joakim Haaland, og dette er Lisa Balfour; hun er Edvard barnebarn.'

Lisbet snapped her attention to Lisa. She stepped forward and held the photo up to Lisa.

'Han er bestefaren din?'

Lisa looked at Joakim for help. He quickly explained Lisa did not speak much Norwegian, but confirmed the photo was of Lisa's grandfather.

Lisbet slumped onto a sofa in stunned silence. Her carer sat down next to her and whispered something to her. Lisbet shook her head. Her carer glared at them, showing her clear displeasure with the visitors.

Joakim continued to speak, explaining that Edvard lived in Shetland. He spoke calmly and quietly and after a while Lisbet stood up. She waved her hand, dismissing them without another word. The carer followed Lisbet out of the room and then returned quickly. She asked them to leave. Joakim smiled sympathetically at Lisa, and put his arm around her as they left.

Lisa carried Hansi back to the car and strapped him into his seat. She closed the car door and stared back at the house.

She could not believe they had found Lisbet so easily but had failed in their mission to smooth the way for Edvard to contact her. From her reaction, Lisa didn't imagine Lisbet would even welcome a letter from him. She felt heartbroken on his behalf. He wouldn't get to meet his daughter. She hadn't realised she was crying until Joakim pulled her into his arms. Then she wept, her shoulders heaving, tears streaming down her face into his shirt.

'I'm sorry,' he said, stroking her hair. 'I didn't expect that at all.'

'She must hate him,' Lisa said, pulling away from him and rubbing the tears away with her hands. She reached into her handbag for a tissue and blew her nose.

'Why would she keep his photo then?'

'I don't know, maybe she is ripping it up as we speak. What did you tell her about him?'

'I said he was too ill to travel but he only heard a little while ago about their daughter. I said he was now widowed and you lived with him and took care of him. I said he wanted to meet his daughter before it was too late.'

Lisa rubbed her eyes again and then raked through her hair with her fingers. She wanted to leave now and hurried round to the passenger seat got in and slammed the door shut. She waited impatiently for Joakim to get back in the car but he didn't. He was walking back to the front door. Lisa craned her neck to see what he was up to. The front door was open and Lisbet's carer was speaking to Joakim. Lisa wondered whether she ought to get out of the car and join them, but she could add nothing to the situation.

Joakim walked back to the car, with an obvious spring in his stride. He got back into the car and shut the door and then patted Lisa's knee.

'We are to come back tomorrow. Karen will be here in the afternoon. Lisbet was simply overcome with emotion, which is why she disappeared. She has gone for a lie down. Lily said she would be ready to talk more tomorrow.'

'Lily?'

'That's the carer's name. She's from Malaysia. She's been looking after Lisbet for the last five years.'

'Wow; tomorrow? Oh God, I feel so stupid now, crying all over you.'

'That's alright. I was disappointed too. I didn't realise how much I was hoping for a happy ending until the door slammed in our faces.'

'Well let's hope we've not been invited back just so Karen can slam the door in our faces.'

Lisa was relieved to see the back of Lisbet's house for a while. She felt exhausted now. The events of the previous forty eight hours were taking their toll. She shut her eyes and hoped they didn't have far to go until they got to their hotel. It was only four thirty in the afternoon but she hoped Hansi might be persuaded to have an early night.

Fifteen minutes later they pulled up outside the hotel. They walked into the reception and Joakim gave the receptionist his name. She immediately picked up the phone and announced his arrival to someone. A moment later a smartly dressed middle aged man appeared from another office and walked across to greet Joakim; his hand outstretched ready to shake hands.

Lisa held Hansi in her arms and waited until Joakim and the manager had exchanged pleasantries. Ordinarily she might have been impressed by the warm regard the manager held for Joakim, but right now she wanted to sit somewhere quiet to reflect on what had happened at Lisbet's.

She didn't know whether she should ring Moffa and report their findings. She decided not to, in case nothing positive happened tomorrow. She wasn't particularly confident about how the meeting would go.

Eventually the manager slapped Joakim on his shoulder and shook hands with him again. He smiled at Lisa and then snapped an order at the receptionist, who responded by reaching for their key. The receptionist pointed them in the direction of the lift and a few minutes later they were in their room; or rooms. The suite was a two bedroomed apartment with a sitting room and a little kitchen area. Fresh flowers were in a vase on an antique dresser. A bottle of Champagne sat in an ice-bucket.

A moment later there was a tap on the door. Two porters came in carrying a cot and bedding. They placed it in one of the bedrooms and left silently. Hansi stood in front of the giant television and grunted at Joakim to turn it on. A blue talking cow appeared on screen. Hansi sat down in front of the TV and gawped at the cow who was singing a song in Norwegian.

Lisa sat with her head in her hands.

'Champagne?' Joakim proffered the bottle in the manner of a waiter.

'No thanks,' she replied, sighing.

'You're right; this wasn't a good year for Champagne. I will send it back and get some tea for madam instead.'

Lisa stood up.

'I'm sorry. I don't mean to sound ungrateful. I appreciate everything you have done for us, but...'

'I understand. Maybe you need a little time to yourself. There's a spa here. Why don't you go and have a sauna or go for a swim. I can watch cartoons with Hansi. That blue cow and I go way back.'

Lisa shook her head. 'I wish I'd brought a swimsuit with me. That might wake me up.'

'I bet they sell them in the hotel shop.'

Hansi was already starting to lose interest in the television. He had spent far too long sitting in the car and he needed some exercise.

'Hansi loves swimming, maybe I should take him with me. Why don't you come too?'

'Er, no, I don't think so.'

Joakim walked over to the coffee maker. He picked up a coffee pod and inserted into the machine.

'Chicken!' Lisa said, flapping her arms like wings. 'Can't you swim?'

'Of course I can swim.'

'So why won't you come with us?'

The coffee machine gurgled into life. Joakim scowled at her and for a moment she wished she hadn't teased him. Then he smiled.

'OK; I'll come to the pool with you.'

An hour later they had the whole swimming pool to themselves which surprised and delighted Lisa. It was only a small pool, but there was a little children's play area and a Jacuzzi set into a bay window with a stunning view of the mountains. Lisa had bought herself a plain red swimsuit, which was disappointingly school-girlish, rather than *Baywatch*, not that Joakim seemed to have noticed yet.

Joakim emerged from the changing room and walked over to the edge of the pool and then removed his prosthesis while he held on to the edge of the ladder.

Lisa watched him swim a few lengths. He was fast and streamlined in the water. She found some arm bands for Hansi and soon he was bobbing around beside her, enjoying splashing in the warm water.

Joakim swam towards them and Lisa instantly moved away leaving him to supervise Hansi. She felt self-conscious around Joakim, particularly after seeing him swimming up and down in the pool. She had to force herself not to stare at his athletic body. She reached the deep end of the pool and turned to watch

Joakim and Hansi from a safe distance. Joakim had crouched down in the water and was level with Hansi. They were splashing each other. Hansi giggled as he bobbed up and down in the water.

Lisa swam back to them and Joakim sprinted to the end of the pool. She guessed swimming must have been part of his rehabilitation as he clearly had no difficulty in the water and he swam faster than Lisa ever could.

Despite her self-consciousness she was glad they had decided to come down to the pool. Hansi was enjoying himself; she held him as he floated on his back and thought about Lisbet and wondered what would happen when they returned tomorrow.

'I'll look after him, why don't you go and relax in the Jacuzzi?'

Hansi's face lit up when Joakim appeared beside them.

'Brilliant, thanks.'

Lisa left them to it. She needed some time to think. She tried to imagine how she would feel if she was Lisbet or Karen. How would she feel if Neil returned from Australia in seventy years' time to meet Hansi? She would slam the door in his face. Although to be fair, the circumstances were a little different. Moffa hadn't known about Karen, whereas Neil had never been in contact, although he knew perfectly well Hansi had been born. She hated him for that. She couldn't understand why he wasn't even a little bit curious. Then again, her own father had vanished equally effectively when she was a little girl.

She sat down in the Jacuzzi and tried to relax. With her eyes partially closed she watched Joakim playing with Hansi. Joakim had found a large rubber ring which Hansi was now sitting in and Joakim was dragging him around the shallow end of the pool. Hansi's laughter reverberated around the pool.

A moment later, Lisa's peace was disturbed by a middle-aged woman who made a beeline for the Jacuzzi.

Lisa shut her eyes, trying to avoid the need to make any conversation.

'Ooh, that's lovely,' the woman gushed, in an American accent, as she descended into the Jacuzzi and sat down heavily.

Lisa opened her eyes and smiled politely. She hoped the woman would presume Lisa couldn't speak English but unfortunately Joakim chose that moment to bring Hansi to the edge of the pool closest to the Jacuzzi and ask Lisa if she was alright. Lisa sighed; she would have understood that in Norwegian.

'Oh, you're English. Where are you from? I'm from Michigan. Isn't this a lovely place?'

'I'm Scottish. And yes it is lovely.'

'Scottish? Oh wow. I love Scotland. We stopped off there on our way over last week. We went to Edinburgh and then went up to Loch Ness; we didn't see the monster though.' The woman chuckled.

Lisa realised the woman was not going to leave her in peace. 'I studied in Edinburgh, but I live in Shetland.'

'That's where the dinky little ponies come from. We have one on our ranch, he keeps my horse company. Funny little thing he is, very stubborn, but so strong. My grandson loves him.'

'Yeah, that's one of the things Shetland is famous for.'

'So are you over here on holiday too?'

'I suppose I am; I hadn't thought of it as a holiday. I came over to find a relative.'

'Me too! Well, not relatives as such, but my ancestors are from around here. My husband and I decided we would come and see where my father and grandparents came from. Daddy moved to the States during the war when he was a baby. I've never been here before. We're doing a tour of Europe and in a couple of days we are flying down to Stockholm and then on to Paris. But I wish we could spend more time here.'

'That is a pity. But you will have lots of lovely photos to take home, I'm sure.'

'My husband is downloading pictures from the camera right now, and emailing them to our children.'

'That's nice!'

'Is that your little boy? He's a cutie! What's his name?'

'Hansi.'

'What a lovely name. It suits him. I'm Angie, by the way.'

'I'm Lisa, nice to meet you.'

Angie was quiet for a moment as she watched Joakim playing with Hansi.

'Oh, is your husband Norwegian? I thought he looked it, but I just heard him speaking.'

'Er, yes he is...' Lisa was about to say they weren't married, but couldn't be bothered explaining. She would never see Angie again, so what did it matter?'

At that moment Joakim grabbed hold of Hansi and then plunged back into the water kicking his legs into the air.

'Oh, goodness me,' Angie said, 'oh, poor man. What happened to his leg?'

Lisa was surprised at her blunt question and wanted to tell her to mind her own business. She felt defensive on Joakim's behalf.

'I'm sorry dear; I hope you don't think I'm rude. My son-in-law was in Afghanistan and he lost his leg. He's doing fine now, bless him. But it was awful for him at the time, and for my daughter Anne-Lise. He was in the army, but he's retraining to be a social worker now.'

Lisa nodded sympathetically; she realised she wouldn't be able to get away without sharing something.

'Joakim worked for the Coastguard. He was shot.'

'You must be so proud of him dear. What does he do now?'

'He builds boats. He has his own business.'

'That's good. He's lovely looking isn't he? Your son takes after him.'

Lisa didn't know what to say to without digging herself into a deeper hole.

But thankfully Angie decided she had had enough time in the Jacuzzi. She climbed out and said goodbye to Lisa and headed over towards the sauna and steam rooms.

An hour later, Lisa had given Hansi his dinner, a combination of the picnic Anita had given her that morning and some baby food Lisa bought in the shop. Now Hansi was full and had drunk some warm milk he was sleepy. He was good at going to sleep in unfamiliar rooms, but even Lisa was surprised at how fast he dropped off when she laid him down in his cot. He turned over and was asleep in seconds.

She heard a gentle tap at the door.

'Is everything alright? It's gone quiet in there,' Joakim said, when Lisa opened the door to him.

Lisa closed the door behind her as she followed Joakim back to the sitting area.

'I should take him swimming more often; he's zonked.'

'Zonked?' Joakim raised his eyebrows.

'Passed out asleep! Sorry, your English is so good I forget you might not know all the slang.'

'I like that word. I'm ready to zonk too.'

Lisa giggled. 'That's not how you use it; although maybe it should be.' She walked over to the sliding door that opened onto the balcony. Now Hansi was safely tucked up asleep she wanted to go outside without the risk of him trying to launch himself over the railings.

Traces of snow were still visible on the highest peaks of the mountain. There were people dining outside in the hotel restaurant. A glazed canopy stretched out over the tables and chairs. Lisa recognised Angie at a table with her husband and another couple. Angie was talking animatedly, waving her wine glass around as she spoke. Lisa couldn't hear, but she smiled at the thought Angie was clearly enjoying her holiday.

Lisa would love to have gone downstairs to eat, but that would be impossible. She sat down and stared up at the mountains. She tried to imagine Joakim hurling himself down the slopes on skis. She saw something moving through the air in the distance and realised the ski-lift was in operation. She watched its progress up the mountain and saw a red and white chalet near the top. She yearned to be at the top of the mountain.

'Shall we order room service?' Joakim pulled out a chair and sat down. 'Lovely evening; best dining room in the world eh?' Joakim said, tapping the cast iron patio table.

'I was wondering if there is a nice café at the top of the mountain.'

'Most likely; we could take Hansi there, tomorrow. He would love it.'

'Ooh no; we'd have to go up in the cable car. It's so high up.'

'And do you think that boy is scared of heights? He would be perfectly safe.'

Lisa stared back at the mountain. When would she ever get the chance to do something like this again? 'OK, we will; although we may not have time if we are going back to see Lisbet.'

'We'll stay another night or two. What's the rush? You're not flying back until Wednesday. It is only Friday now.'

Joakim handed her the room service menu. It was in Norwegian and her brain was not functioning well enough to attempt to translate it.

'What are you having?'

'Rudolf!' Joakim said, grinning wickedly.

'As in reindeer? That's evil!'

'But it is so nice with the chef's special blend of loganberries and spices.' Joakim rubbed his tummy and licked his lips.

Lisa shook her head in disgust and giggled. She had woken up a little now she was sitting outside. Hansi was safely asleep; perhaps it was time to relax and make the most of the situation.

'Does he come with chips?'

'Mashed potatoes and vegetables; but I'm sure I can get you chips if you want.'

'No; mashed potato sounds good.' Lisa suddenly craved something warm and comforting. She watched Joakim as he went inside and picked up the phone to order the food. He was wearing jeans and a red shirt. His dark blond hair was sticking up untidily where he hadn't combed it after his swim. Lisa ached to reach up and smooth down his hair. He looked adorably boyish. He put the phone down and went over to the fridge and took out the Champagne.

Lisa was conscious this was the first time she had been properly alone with

Joakim. Every other evening she had spent in his company had also been shared with his friends or her grandfather. This suddenly felt a little intimate. She got up and went to her bedroom to check on Hansi. He was still sleeping soundly. The black-out blinds had been drawn in the room and it was in total darkness. Lisa went to the bathroom and locked the door behind her.

Her plaited hair was still damp from swimming. She pulled off the elastic bands that secured the ends and released her hair which fell in kinked waves around her face. Lisa had not brought any make-up with her, other than her lip-gloss which was in the bedroom. She decided it would not be worth the risk of waking Hansi to get it. She had no perfume either and as she sniffed at her bare arm she realised the shower she had taken after swimming had not removed all traces of chlorine from her skin. She picked up a bottle of the hotel's complementary body lotion and rubbed some of it on her arms and neck. It smelled delicious; of roses and geranium oil. It would have to do.

She frowned at her reflection. Her dark blue tee-shirt had seen better days, and her jeans were held together with goodwill. She thought of the photo of Astrid she had seen online before they left Shetland. The image of glossy shiny perfection shamed her and she felt ridiculous.

'Oh for God's sake; it's not like anything is going to happen anyway,' she muttered to herself. But as she left the bathroom she couldn't make up her mind if she was disappointed.

Joakim had poured two glasses of Champagne and was sitting outside. Lisa joined him on the balcony and took a glass from him.

'Here's to a successful mission; cheers!'

'Cheers!' Lisa sipped it cautiously. 'I'm not so sure how successful it's been yet. Maybe we should have saved this until tomorrow.'

'We found her, didn't we? I'm sure she will want to talk to us tomorrow.' Joakim put down his glass and leaned forward and squeezed her hand.

Lisa jumped at his touch and Joakim released her immediately. He picked up his glass and nodded in the direction of the mountain.

'That's the main competition ski-run over there. And in that direction is where they built a big ski-ramp for jumps and tricks; a bit like a skateboard park for skiers.'

Lisa was glad of the change of subject. Joakim reached for his iPhone and a moment later he passed it to her. A video played on the screen. She watched as a series of people propelled themselves off the snow covered ramp and did somersaults in the air before landing expertly on their skis. She gasped at their courage.

'Are you in this?' she said, as the video ended. She handed the phone back to him.

'No, I didn't have time to try that. I wish I had though.' He continued to play with the phone for a moment and passed it back.

'This is me.'

Lisa held the screen up and shaded it from the sun with her hand. She would not have recognised him as his face and hair were covered by helmet and goggles. What she saw of his features were frozen in grim determination. A clock at the side of the picture counted the time and she realised she was watching a race. He raced down the side of the mountain, sometimes lifting into the air and flying, then zig-zagging around the flag poles. As he got closer to the finish line she heard the frantic accompaniment of cowbells clanging and the spectators cheering him on. Safely across the line he came to a stop and there was a close-up of him removing his goggles and smiling. Joakim lifted his arm in triumph and then a moment later he was embraced by team members and one beautiful blonde girl kissed him. Lisa handed the phone back.

'Did you win?'

'Ja!' Joakim put his glass down as if he was not impressed with the taste of it.

'You miss it, don't you?'

Joakim did not reply. She had a glimpse of how impossible it would have been for him to carry on his relationship with Astrid. There would be no way to escape the subject if he had married someone who was still competing.

There was a knock on their door and Joakim got up to open it. A young man pushed a trolley into the room and then set the table out on the balcony. Lisa picked up the two Champagne glasses and stood up to give him some space.

Joakim disappeared into the bathroom and Lisa sat down at the table and waited. The waiter had set out plates, glasses and cutlery. The dishes of food were covered with porcelain lids and sat on food warming trays, heated by nightlights.

'Ow, fuck!'

Joakim stumbled over the wooden door frame as he stepped out onto the balcony. 'Sorry, I didn't mean to swear,' he added, as he sat down. He put his hand down and held his leg and Lisa realised he had jolted his prosthesis.

'At least you didn't stub your toe; now that would hurt.'

Joakim raised his eyebrows in surprise, then burst out laughing when he realised she was joking.

'Rudolf tastes good,' she said, as she finished her reindeer steak. 'I think I might try and buy Moffa some reindeer steaks sometime. I might even make them for his Christmas dinner.'

'Now who's mean?'

Lisa finished her glass of Champagne and Joakim poured her some more. She realised she had drunk far more of it than he had. Joakim seemed to prefer water, although he had gone to the fridge and taken out a bottle of beer. She felt her worries drifting away. The sun had set behind the mountain and the sky was tinged with pink. The trees around the hotel whispered in the light breeze and as Lisa listened she heard birds singing; competing with the burble of laughter and conversation drifting up from the restaurant.

'It's a lovely hotel. Did you stay in the suite the last time you were here?' Lisa said.

'No, I was sharing a room with three other team members. It was more like a youth hostel than this. But then I was too young to have appreciated it. I didn't care where I slept in those days. It was all about the snow.'

'I think you should try again.'

'Oh Lisa; if you only knew how many times I have heard someone tell me that. Don't you think I would if I could?'

'I think maybe you tried too soon; before you were ready.'

'Hmm, I didn't even make a good sailor last week so I hardly see how I can take to the slopes again. It's not as easy as you think.'

'I know it wouldn't be easy. Then again, I don't think I'd be any good at skiing in the first place.'

There was a knock on their door. Joakim got up to answer it. Lisa expected it to be the waiter coming to clear away the table. However, it was the receptionist.

'Lisbet's daughter is downstairs. She wants to see us,' Joakim said, when he returned to the balcony.

'Oh!' Lisa's hands flew to her face in surprise. She stood up quickly almost knocking her glass over. 'What's she doing here?'

'I told Lily where we would be staying so I guess she told Karen. Anyway, the receptionist is going to send her up here. I didn't think you would want to go down to reception.'

Lisa sat down again, her shoulders slumping in misery.

'I expect she's come to tell us not to bother her mother again. Oh dear!'

'Don't worry. I'm here. It will be fine, whatever happens.'

19

There was a quiet, almost hesitant knock on their door. Lisa hurried to open it. The woman who stood in the corridor appeared younger than someone in their late sixties. She was taller than Lisa and she stood almost to attention, and was more confident in the flesh, for someone with such a timid knock. Karen did not smile at Lisa but scrutinised her as if she was trying to recognise her. Lisa stared back, struck by the similarities to Ingrid.

'I'm Lisa Balfour. Edvard Christiansen is my grandfather.'

'And he is my father,' Karen replied coldly, as if there was some weird kind of one-upmanship at play.

'Hello, I'm Joakim Haaland. I'm a friend of Lisa and her grandfather. I'm here to help her find his family. Pleased to meet you!' Joakim stuck his hand out and shook hands with Karen. Lisa held hers out too, and then stood back as Karen stepped into the room warily, without shaking her hand.

'Come and sit outside; we've just finished our dinner. Lisa's son is sleeping and we wouldn't want to wake him. Shall I order some coffee or would you like a drink.'

'Nothing, thanks.' Karen followed Joakim outside and sat down with her arms folded tightly. She wore a grey wool coat buttoned to the neck, although it didn't appear to cold enough to warrant it.

Lisa hurried out after them and pushed their plates away to the end of the table.

'Why are you here?' Karen said, as Lisa sat down next to Joakim. Lisa desperately wanted to grab hold of his hand but he was fiddling with the label on a bottle of beer instead.

'My grandfather is getting old; he has already had two strokes and couldn't travel here himself. I only found out about you last week and I came over to find you and your mother. I wanted to meet you and I also hoped you might want to meet my grandfather. He didn't know about you when he left Norway. He's sorry.'

'Oh he's sorry! Well too bad. He's had plenty of time to get to know me and he chooses now, when he's on his deathbed. Does he hope God will forgive him now?'

Lisa bristled at Karen's righteous anger.

'He doesn't believe in God. And he is not quite on his deathbed, thank you.'

Karen shrugged as if those details were immaterial to her.

'He told me he only heard about you about five years ago. He was too ill to travel then as he had not long had his first stroke. I'm sorry if you feel angry about that. Perhaps we have wasted your time,' Joakim said, calmly peeling the label off the bottle and depositing it on a plate.

'That's a lie. I found out where he was living twenty years ago and came over to Shetland to meet him. His wife and daughter said he didn't want to meet me. I left him a letter, to which he never replied.'

Lisa turned to Joakim and frowned, expecting him to know more. He shrugged and shook his head.

'But he has never spoken about this. I'm sure he would have told us. We spent all day Sunday talking about you and Lisbet. Are you sure he knew you were in Shetland?'

Karen narrowed her eyes as she stared back at Lisa. She did not reply.

'He can't have known. Was he in the house when you called?'

'No, he was out fishing. But your mother said she would give him the letter and tell him which hotel I was staying in. I waited for four days but he never showed up.'

'You gave the letter to my mother?' Lisa sighed, and rubbed her face with her hands. Her bloody mother! Lisa suspected she had thrown the letter away. Twenty years ago her grandmother had been ill.

'When exactly did you visit? What month?'

'It was the 20th June; my birthday,' Karen replied, folding her arms and standing up. She leaned against the balcony rail with her back to them.

'My grandmother died on the 22nd June.'

Karen snapped her attention back to Lisa.

'What?'

'She died two days after you came to the house. She had a heart attack. She had been ill for about a year, but she died suddenly; unexpectedly. My grandfather was away at sea at the time. They had to call his boat back.' Lisa stood up and hurried to the bathroom without excusing herself. She heard Joakim's voice, talking soothingly to Karen in her own language.

Lisa splashed cold water on her face. She sat down on a stool and held a towel over her face. What Karen had told her explained everything. Ingrid had changed so much after her mother's death. At the time Lisa had thought it was grief, but as time moved on her mother seemed so hostile towards Moffa; as if she had blamed him. Well it was now clear she did blame him. It also explained why she had removed so many of her mother's belongings from the house. She must have thought someday Karen would come looking for him again and make a claim on his estate.

Lisa returned to the balcony. Joakim had poured Karen a glass of red wine and he had got another beer for himself. Karen looked as if she had been crying.

'I'm sorry about your grandmother; I had no idea she was so ill. I only saw her briefly. Your mother did all the talking.'

'That's alright; you weren't to know. But now can you see Edvard didn't know about you until much later. My mother clearly didn't tell him. He found out when a friend of his died, another Shetland Bus man, and someone from the Norwegian government came over to his funeral. This man knew

Lisbet and told Edvard about you. Really, I'm certain that's when he found out. Believe me, Moffa doesn't tell lies.'

'Moffa?'

'That's what I called him when I was little. I couldn't pronounce Morfar and then the name kind of stuck.'

'That's what my daughter Cecilie called her grandfather – my stepfather.'

Lisa smiled at Karen.

'Does your mother know about what happened in Shetland?'

'No; I didn't tell her anything. She would have been too upset. It was a year after her husband died. She was still grieving. So was I; I think that's why I wanted to find Edvard. I hadn't felt able to search for him while Olaf was still alive. It seemed disrespectful to the man who became my father. He was a great man; a wonderful father.'

'So, does that mean when we came to visit this afternoon, it was a complete shock to her?' Joakim said.

'Definitely! But I think in some ways she has always been waiting for him to come back. She really loved him. He helped save her life.'

'I know.' Lisa held her head in her hands and stared down at her feet. There didn't seem to be any point in going over history. She looked at her watch. It was nearly ten but it was an hour earlier in Shetland. Moffa would still be awake.

'Can I borrow your phone?' Lisa said to Joakim. He handed it to her with a smile.

Lisa dialled Moffa's number, praying he would answer it.

'Don't tell him about your visit to Shetland,' she said to Karen, while she waited for Moffa to answer. Karen looked startled as if she wasn't ready to talk to her father.

'Hello Moffa. I'm in Stranda; that's where Lisbet and Karen live. I have someone who wants to talk to you; your daughter.'

Lisa thrust the phone into Karen's hand and hurried inside to give her some privacy. Joakim got up and followed her, closing the balcony door behind him.

'Sorry, I should have said that was a long distance call I was going to make.'

Joakim waved his hand, dismissing her apology. He grabbed hold of her as she was about to go and check on Hansi.

'Come here,' he said, pulling her into his arms and hugging her. Lisa leaned into him, feeling drained but buzzing all at the same time. Her head was a mess, she wanted to cry. She wrapped her arms around him and closed her eyes, breathing in his warmth and the scent of *Davidoff Cool Water.*

'Well, what a surprise.' Joakim stroked her hair and then pushed her away so he could see her face; his hands still gripping her shoulders.

'I wasn't expecting that. What a mess. What an absolute bloody mess. No wonder my mother has been so weird all these years.'

'Do you blame her? It must have been a shock to meet her half-sister. I'm a little surprised Karen would turn up like that. I think I would have tried to get Edvard on his own first. I'm sure your mother must blame her for your grandmother's death.'

'I'm certain of it; and in all honesty it probably didn't do her any good to find out this news. But she was ill; I doubt she would have lasted many more weeks. My mother was always nagging at Moffa not to go away on the boat. It was like he was in denial. I thought that was the reason she was mad with him; for not being there. Now I know it was something completely different.'

'Well I'm glad I managed to persuade you to come over to Norway. I think this was the only way to have patched things up with Karen. Edvard might not have had a chance to speak to her; she would have refused to see him.'

Lisa hugged Joakim tighter. 'I can never thank you enough; seriously, you're so lovely to do this for us.'

Joakim rested his chin on Lisa's head but said nothing.

20

The door to the balcony opened and Karen smiled uncertainly at Lisa. She handed the phone to Joakim, and held her arms out to Lisa.

'I guess I'm your auntie,' she said. Lisa rushed towards her and hugged her. 'Thank you for coming to find us. I'm sorry I was so angry earlier.'

'That's OK; I understand. Is Moffa OK? How did he take it, speaking to you after all this time?' Lisa said, brushing away tears with the back of her hand.

'Oh, he cried. I cried. It was a mess!' Karen grinned, and sat down on the sofa and leaned back with her eyes shut. She opened them again and sat up sharply. 'He wants to see me. He wants me to fly over to Shetland. I need to go home and speak to Michael, my husband, and sort something out. Oh wow, I never imagined this would happen today.'

'I'm flying home next Wednesday; come back with me,' Lisa said, sitting down next to Karen.

'Oh, I don't know dear. I need to sort a few things out and I need to speak to my mother. Come over tomorrow for lunch and we will talk about it some more.'

The phone was still hot from where Karen had been holding it. Joakim thought about Edvard and wondered how he was feeling. He wouldn't have had time to prepare for the surprise Lisa had thrown at him. He stepped out on to the balcony and closed the door behind him and pressed redial.

'*Hallo Edvard, er det Joakim her; er du OK?*'

Edvard was still emotional, but happy. He didn't expect to sleep much that night. He asked how Lisa was getting on with Karen and Joakim reassured him that Lisa was sitting in the lounge holding hands with her new aunt. He promised Lisa would ring again tomorrow after they had been to see Lisbet.

Edvard was silent when Joakim said her name. He sighed heavily and asked Joakim to tell her he was sorry.

When he finished the call Joakim picked up his bottle of beer from the table. He went back inside to join them.

'I spoke to Edvard again, to make sure he was alright. He was very cheerful,' Joakim said, smiling at Lisa. 'I said you would ring him again tomorrow.'

Karen stood up. 'It's getting late. I had better go home and let you get some rest. I'll see you tomorrow.'

Lisa hugged her aunt goodbye and when she had closed the door she leant against it.

'Wow. That's all I have to say on that matter. Wow.'

'I think we should go to bed now. You look exhausted.'

Lisa froze for a moment and Joakim realised she wasn't entirely sure what he meant. He laughed. He wasn't sure what he meant himself. He watched her reach up and run her fingers through her hair. It was in a stressed-out anxious kind of way, rather than trying to draw attention to her hair.

Joakim liked Lisa's wild hair. It reminded him of Astrid when he first met her, back in the days when she had been relaxed about her appearance and thought more of her sport than what people thought of her; before she was offered sponsorships and modelling opportunities. From that point on her hair was always immaculate, even after winning the gold at the 2014 Olympics in Sochi; he had seen her on the news, still picture-perfect. It was barely the same woman he had fallen in love with. Astrid was one of the most beautiful women he knew, but he still preferred the less polished version than the one she was today.

Lisa was still leaning against the door as if she felt the need to stay close to the exit. Joakim walked over to the balcony door and locked it and then he headed towards his bedroom. He paused at the door.

'I hope you sleep well. Goodnight.'

'Goodnight!'

Joakim sat down on the edge of the bed and took off his jeans and then unfastened his prosthesis. He stared down at the ugly scars as he peeled off the protective sock and examined the skin that was still a little irritated. His right leg, although still intact was not perfect either. A bullet had pierced his calf and torn through the muscle, leaving a hideous scar.

He glanced out of the window at the twilight. It was strange being back in Stranda. When he had first set the address into the sat-nav all those hours ago he had almost forgotten he had ever been here before. He had pulled the plug on those memories; but they were good memories and he was starting to wonder whether he had done the right thing by trying to forget his earlier career.

He loved it up here in the mountains. The ski resort at Stranda was one of the best in the whole world; and he should know, having competed at so many in Europe and Canada. The views from the top of the ski-slopes were eye-wateringly beautiful. He had recognised that even at the age of nineteen when he had won his first gold medal. He thought about what Lisa had said about trying to find a way back into skiing. Maybe he was wrong to dismiss it so quickly.

He left the blinds open. He loved this time of year with its almost permanent daylight. He got into bed and stared at the sky. There was only one star visible in the clear sky, twinkling against the violet night. He heard Lisa brushing her teeth in the bathroom and then heard her bedroom door close. Silence.

So much had happened today and a lot more would happen tomorrow. In some ways he was obsolete now. Lisa didn't need an interpreter as her Aunt spoke perfect English. In fact she had been an English literature teacher at the university at Ålesund. He wondered what would happen once Lisa returned to Shetland. He imagined they would simply carry on their friendship online and at some time in the future it would fizzle out. They would be reduced to making the odd comment on Facebook.

He couldn't see a future for them as much as he liked her. He could never live in Shetland. It was a lovely place, what he had seen of it, but he would miss the mountains and the snow; especially the snow. He would miss the warmth of the sun in the summer, and the language. He couldn't imagine having to speak English all day long. It was like watching television with the sound too low. He had to concentrate in order to understand, and sometimes he missed the subtleties and nuances of words.

Joakim couldn't see Lisa leaving Shetland either. She had a life there and he doubted she would want to move to a country where she couldn't speak the language.

He heard her bedroom door open and a moment later a quiet tap on his door.

'Come in,' he said, sitting up.

'I can't sleep,' she said. She leaned against the door frame, wearing track suit trousers and a tee-shirt. For a moment he thought she was about to go out running and then he realised she was wearing them as pyjamas.

'Neither can I.'

Lisa grinned and walked over to the window.

'I had to close the blinds in my room because of Hansi, so I haven't got a nice view to look at. I could look at this for hours. I still cannot get over how Moffa left this behind in favour of Shetland.'

'Shetland is beautiful too.'

'Oh I know, but this is like Shetland on steroids. Everything is so much bigger here; you have mountains where we have hills. You have giant fjords where we have little voes. You have forests; we have a few tree plantations. You get proper snow in the winter, whereas we get wind, rain and more wind. And when the sun shines here, it is hot sun, not lukewarm – keep a cardi with you at all times in case it disappears.'

Joakim shuffled over to the edge of the bed and looked out the window.

'This has been the best, worst, scariest and most fun week of my life. It's been so up and down and crazy. I can't believe I only met you a week ago, you know properly, in person. And here we are in this amazing place. I should be back at home contemplating my next shift in the supermarket, not sitting here in this luxury suite. And tomorrow we are going to have lunch with my new aunt and her mother. It's too much. It's really too much.'

Lisa sat down on the bed, accidentally sitting on his leg. She jumped up again. 'Sorry!'

'It's alright. I'll move over, sit down.'

Joakim moved back to the middle of the bed. Lisa sat down again.

'Now you have family here, do you think you will come back again?'

'Oh yes, and not just for them. You promised me a skiing lesson didn't you?'

'I did. And I keep my promises.'

'So when I go home, I'm going to get a proper job and start saving up so I can come back and visit. If the airline keeps doing those direct flights to Bergen – please God – then I can come over every year.'

'Can't you fly to Oslo from somewhere in Scotland? It's nearer to where I live.'

'Yeah, I can do that too.'

'Right, so if I sail over next year for the race then I will get to see you maybe three times a year.'

'Yeah; could you cope with that?'

'I suppose so; it might get a bit boring though.'

'Bloody cheek!' Lisa put her hands on her hips and although he couldn't see her smiling he heard it in her voice.

'For you, not me. It would be great to see you; and Hansi. I think I could make an Olympian out of that boy, given a chance. I bet he would take to skiing, he has great balance. I've watched him walking around. He's got great co-ordination.'

Lisa was silent and he wondered whether he had made her uncomfortable talking about her son.

Joakim reached for his phone from the bedside table. It was nearly midnight.

'I'm sorry, you must be tired. I'll let you go back to sleep,' Lisa said.

'I wasn't asleep. You don't have to go.'

Lisa didn't move.

He wondered if she was thinking what he was thinking. She turned her head towards the window and saw her face in the moonlight.

She was fiddling with the hem of her tee-shirt, a shadow of a smile on her face. Part of him wanted to reach over and pull her into bed with him. But the last time he had slept with a woman had not gone well. It had been awkward and uncomfortable. He couldn't even remember her name; just someone he had met in a bar. Thankfully the alcohol had taken the edge off the memory, but he could still see the repulsion on her face when he took his prosthesis off. He shuddered at the memory and pulled the bedcover up.

'Are you cold?'

'No – just shy!' He pulled the cover up even further, exaggerating his modesty.

'Very funny; I doubt that.'

'It would have been true a few years ago.'

'Have you had any girlfriends since?'

Joakim coughed and sat up straighter. He picked up a cushion and set it against the headboard before leaning back again.

'Yeah, but no.'

'Yeah, but no?'

'Well, I was with Astrid for a year or so after. Then there was nobody else apart from a couple of one night stands. Nothing good; nothing to write home about. What about you? Have you been out with anyone since Hansi was born?'

'Are you kidding me? Who wants to go out with a single mother like me? I'm too tired, too busy, too shabby and too poor to be of any interest to anyone. I barely go out with my girlfriends, let alone any man.'

'You won't always be too tired or too busy. And I don't get it about being too poor?'

'I'm still too shabby.'

'True!'

Lisa gasped out loud. 'Bastard!'

Joakim sunk down into the bed and pulled the sheet over his face. Lisa pulled it away. He pulled it back, effectively pulling her towards him. Her face was inches away from his. He could kiss her if he wanted to.

He wanted to.

But he didn't. He stared into her face, but he was still at a disadvantage to her. She was in shadow and her hair fell forward shielding her eyes from the residual light. He had no idea what she was thinking.

He was a coward. He had waited for her to make the first move, but she had already made the first move. She had come to his bedroom in the middle of the night hadn't she? Did that mean anything? He couldn't be sure, but just as he was about to test it out he heard the sound of a disgruntled wail from the other room. Hansi had woken up.

Lisa scrambled off the bed and hurried next door. He heard her soothing the boy. Then the light clicked on in the kitchen. Lisa had taken him to get some milk. He sounded wide awake now; Joakim sighed. He wondered whether he should join them in the kitchen, but he would have to put his prosthetic leg back on. He shut his eyes. Perhaps it was for the best. He wondered if Hansi had sensed an intruder into his mother's life – a competitor for her affections. It had been such perfect timing on his part.

He listened as Lisa kept up a quiet running commentary while she prepared the milk in the microwave. He heard the ping and then there was silence. He guessed Hansi had the bottle in his hands now. He leaned over and peeked through the gap in the door which Lisa had left ajar. She was sitting on the sofa stroking her son's head as he sat on her lap, nestled in her arms. Joakim felt a stab of envy and then felt stupid. How could he be jealous of a little boy?

Hansi didn't take long to drink his milk. Lisa carried him back to his bedroom after switching the kitchen light off. She was still talking quietly, it sounded like she was trying to negotiate with him. He realised she was changing Hansi's nappy. It sounded like a struggle. He pictured the boy trying to wriggle free and he smiled to himself. He heard Lisa laugh, and then scold Hansi in a happy good humoured way. Hansi giggled and then almost instantly protested. Lisa appeared to be ignoring his protests. He heard taps running, then the toilet flushing and then the taps running again. All the while Hansi called out to Lisa, presumably from his cot.

Too tired, too busy, too shabby, too poor; that's what she thought of herself. He could kind of see where she was coming from. It explained her lack of confidence, despite her pretty face, her naturally blonde hair and slim figure, not to mention her obvious intelligence and good humour. She had been worn out by the demands of a small boy; unable to take any time for herself at all. He couldn't imagine being solely responsible for a baby. It was a job for two people; in fact two people with a nanny, if he was perfectly honest.

There was silence from the other room. He guessed Hansi had gone to sleep again. Joakim picked up his phone and saw it was nearly one o'clock. Lisa didn't return and he wondered whether she had gone to sleep.

He needed the bathroom now so he put on his prosthesis. Afterwards he hovered at her door, pushing it open a few inches.

'Hansi won't go back to his cot. He has gone to sleep in my bed so I can't move,' she whispered.

'Well, it's late now. I'll see you in the morning. Goodnight.'

21

The next morning Hansi woke up bright and early and demanded Lisa did likewise. Lisa stumbled into the kitchen to warm up some milk and as she waited for the microwave to ping she thought about the previous night and wondered whether she had dreamed she had nearly kissed Joakim.

She felt a huge sense of relief she hadn't; it would have destroyed their friendship, and to what end? Then in direct contradiction of her first thought she started to regret that she hadn't kissed him. She wondered whether she would get another opportunity.

She carried the bottle of milk back to Hansi and let him snuggle up next to her while he drank it. After he had drained every last drop he dozed off again in Lisa's bed. She shut her eyes and thought about the lunch. She was looking forward to seeing Karen and Lisbet again.

A few hours later they returned to Lisbet's house and this time the welcome was far warmer. Lisa sat on the sofa and tried to follow the conversation. Lisbet did not speak English so Joakim had to do most of the talking on her behalf. He explained how they decided to come over to find Lisbet and Karen a few days after Edvard had confessed to having an earlier family.

Lisbet showed them some photographs of Edvard, including some taken during the war. Lisa would not have recognised him. He was tall and good looking with dark hair, but seemed much older than his years. He didn't smile in any of the photos. There was one photo of Edvard and Lisbet, taken together with her parents and younger brother. Edvard did not look comfortable in the family group.

Lisa held on to the photographs studying them for clues to Moffa's state of mind. He had not been happy. She knew him as someone who was quick to smile. All the photos she had of her grandfather were of someone who misbehaved in front of the camera. He pulled faces; he laughed and he always animated, even as a frozen image in time.

She wanted to show Lisbet a recent photo of Moffa but she didn't have one on her. However, Joakim had taken a couple of photos of him on his phone and he showed them to Lisbet and Karen. Lisbet put on her reading glasses and peered at the screen for a long time, trying to recognise the old man.

'Han er fornoyd,' she said, smiling at Lisa. He is happy.

'Ja,' Lisa nodded. 'Very happy.'

Over lunch Lisbet talked about the war and the mission Edvard took part in that effectively saved the lives of her family. Her father had worked for the Norwegian Royal Family and had helped them to leave Norway after Germany had invaded. He had taken his own family out of Oslo and escaped up to Stranda where his parents had a house. However, that had not been a safe place to stay for long, and he discovered the Nazis were still searching for him. The family had moved further north, trying to find a way out, either across the border to Sweden or to the UK.

They were finally smuggled out of Norway during one of the Shetland Bus missions. Edvard had brokered the arrangement, risking his life by coming to find them and then guiding them under cover of darkness to the boat that would transport them. They had almost given up being able to escape. It had become so hard to know who to trust. The German destruction of the town of Televag and the arrest, execution or internment of all of its men, women and children had scared many people from helping the resistance.

The sheer numbers of German soldiers in all of the main towns and cities was overwhelming. Added to which there were Norwegians who supported the Nazis; and whether this was genuine or coerced it didn't matter, fear was endemic.

Lisa heard snippets of this conversation as either Joakim or Karen translated what Lisbet was saying. Hansi soon grew bored and wanted to run off and play. Lisa excused herself from the table and carried him outside. She found an old wooden swing in the garden. Hansi sat in it for a little while, but grew bored of that too, so Lisa took him on a tour of the garden, looking at the flowers and butterflies.

It was warm in the garden and Lisa found a bench and sat down and admired the fragrant roses and lavender in the immaculate flower beds. Lisbet's house was perched high above the fjord and Lisa watched a pleasure boat steaming along in the sunshine. It seemed like a little piece of heaven, and a million miles away from what Lisbet had been describing over lunch. Lisa simply couldn't reconcile the Norway she saw around her, with the frightening, devastating experiences people had suffered during the war.

She heard footsteps and saw Joakim walking towards her. He sat down beside her and put his arm around her shoulders and hugged her.

'Lisbet is talking to Edvard. You don't mind do you? I spoke to him first to make sure he was alright.'

'Why should I mind?'

'Well, I suppose it might be upsetting for him. Lisbet was a bit emotional when she heard his voice.'

'Hardly surprising. Although it's a little strange isn't it, talking to someone you haven't spoken to in seventy years. I wonder if I would even remember someone after that long.'

'They did share something unique though.' Joakim withdrew his arm from Lisa's shoulders. 'I found out something interesting just now; I think I understand why Edvard left Norway and hasn't wanted to return.'

'Oh?' Lisa allowed Hansi to get down from her lap. He sat down on the lawn and plucked a daisy and scrutinised it before attempting to eat it. Lisa didn't even need to tell him not to. He shook his head in disgust and spat it out and glared at the remains of the flower.

'After the war, Lisbet's family moved back to Oslo and Edvard went to stay with them. I get the feeling Lisbet's parents were not keen on having him there. They might well have been grateful for his help during the war, but when life started getting back to normal they felt he ought to move on, but he had nowhere to go and Lisbet wanted him to stay. Edvard had no qualifications and no training for a proper job, he tried being an apprentice mechanic but he didn't get along with his employer and left. He wanted to start his own haulage business but didn't have any money, so he all he could do was a bit of fishing. Then one day Lisbet's father asked him what had happened to his parent's house in Haugesund.

'So he went with Lisbet to find out. The house had been boarded up so they went to the law office where Edvard's father used to work. There they had good news and some very bad news.'

Hansi stood up and waddled over to Lisa, oblivious to the fact Lisa was desperate to hear the rest of the story. Joakim stopped speaking as Lisa picked Hansi up and looked for something to distract him for a few minutes. However, the garden had nothing of interest for a toddler.

Karen stepped out onto the patio and then walked across the lawn. She held out Joakim's phone to him.

'Thanks. My mother has gone to have a rest in her room for a while. It's all a little overwhelming for her.'

'Is she alright?' Lisa said, feeling a little guilty at the stress they had brought to the household.

'Oh she's fine, thanks. She often has a nap in the afternoons; but she was a little tearful after speaking to Edvard. You might want to see if he is alright. He asked us to go and visit him. I guess we should think about it sometime.'

Lisa felt her head being pulled towards Hansi and she untangled her hair from his grasp and set him down on the ground again.

'Well, you shouldn't leave it too long.'

Karen nodded thoughtfully as she stared down at Hansi who was tottering towards a beautiful hedge of Camellias. Lisa hurried after him before he could de-head the crimson blooms.

'Which is the best way to get to Shetland? It would involve a lot of flights I imagine. I don't think my mother would be able to cope with too long a journey.'

'You can fly direct from Bergen to Shetland a couple of days a week. That's how we got here.' Lisa remembered they had talked about this the night before but clearly Karen had forgotten in all the excitement.

'So if we fly down to Bergen from Ålesund airport we would be in Shetland an hour or so later? Are there any nice hotels near your grandfather's house?'

'Why would you need a hotel; he has room for you to stay?'

'But that might be too much for him.'

'I doubt it. Anyway Hansi and I live with him. It would be me who does all the cooking and cleaning and I would love it if you came over. You can't imagine how much it would mean to him.'

'Lisa and Hansi are flying back on Wednesday.' Joakim said. 'Why don't you go back with them?'

'Oh, I don't know. I would need to sort so much out before I go. I will speak to my mother. Otherwise maybe we could do this in a few weeks.'

Lisa nodded, and then yelped when Hansi prodded her in the face, just missing her eye. 'You little beast,' she scolded. Hansi simply giggled.

'Let me,' Joakim said, taking Hansi from her and swinging him up onto his shoulders.

Lisa watched them walk away; trying not to worry about the way Joakim limped under the weight of Hansi, who was squealing with laughter.

'How do you two know each other?' Karen asked.

'It's a bizarre story. I found a message in a bottle from someone with the same name as him, Joakim Haaland, and I found him on Facebook and wrote to him. It was the wrong man, but we got chatting anyway, and then he happened to come over to Lerwick last week for the yacht race and he met Moffa and well, here we are.'

'Joakim Haaland; that name rings a bell.'

'He was a champion skier who used to date Astrid Bergstrom.'

Karen swivelled round to see Joakim who had wandered over to a little fountain and was splashing water at Hansi.

'Oh, the one who was shot and lost his leg; I thought he was familiar.'

'That's the one. I guess if I had googled him first I wouldn't have contacted him. I didn't realise he was kind of a celebrity.'

'He seems nice. He is good with your little boy and I'm glad he brought you to meet us.'

'He was the one who got the truth out of Moffa too. I don't think he would have told me otherwise. Joakim plied him with Aquavit and got him talking.'

Karen laughed.

'So, you're staying in Stranda for a couple more days?'

'I suppose so. We're going to go up to the top of the mountain later on.'

'It's beautiful up there. I much prefer to go up the mountains in the middle of the summer than the winter. I wasn't any good at skiing although my daughter Cecilie loves it. I will have to tell her I met Joakim, she'll know who he is. And you can't really come all the way to Stranda without going out on the fjord. Geirangerfjord is famous for its beauty. It would be like going to Paris and not visiting the Eiffel Tower.

22

Joakim drove Lisa and Hansi back to the hotel. Hansi was almost asleep when they got to their room and he seemed relieved to be put in his cot for a nap. Lisa closed the door on him and then went out to the balcony to find Joakim. He handed Lisa a cup of coffee as she sat down.

'I could do with something stronger,' she said.

Joakim was about to stand up, when she waved him down again.

'I was joking; coffee's good thanks. It's too early to hit the wine. Hansi will be awake again before too long.'

'Maybe we can take him swimming again later. He seemed to like that.'

'Good idea; but I want to go up there too,' Lisa said, pointing to the top of the mountain.

'We can do both. Anyway, now I can finish the story about Edvard and Lisbet.'

'Oh God, yes; please carry on.'

'Where was I? Oh yes, they went to see Edvard's father's law firm in Haugesund.'

'Good and bad news,' Lisa said, picking up her coffee and taking a sip.

'That's right. Well the good news was the house would become Edvard's, although not straight away. They needed to get a court to approve that his family could be considered dead. Obviously he didn't have death certificates for them, so there would have been some formalities to go through which would take time.'

'So what was the bad news?'

'They found out it was one of his father's colleagues who had reported the family to the Germans. Edvard's father had been helping people to leave Norway, and two Jewish families in particular. He was managing their property so they could leave the country in the expectation he would send them the money once their homes had been sold. He loaned them money against their properties to help them escape.'

'Jesus! What harm was he doing by helping people escape?'

Joakim shook his head and shrugged.

'Anyway, his colleague was arrested and charged with treason after the war. He went to prison for what he did.'

'Good! What a bastard.'

'But it was a bit of a shock for Edvard; this man had been a friend of the family, or so he thought. Lisbet said it really shook Edvard up to find this out. He was devastated.'

'Poor Moffa, no wonder he never likes talking about what happened.'

'Lisbet said the lawyer gave him two letters. They were from his mother and one of them was for his brother, Jan. His mother had been worried something might happen to her and their father and had put some money away with the letters. They had been in the safe at the law office for a few years. The letters both contained some money, enough to leave Norway and instructions on how to contact a relative in America. In Jan's letter she had enclosed her engagement ring and asked him to look after his brother if anything happened to her and their father.'

Lisa put down her cup and put her hands over her face and sighed.

'This gets worse and worse.'

'It does. Lisbet took Edvard back to Oslo. He was completely broken. He barely spoke for nearly two weeks. She tried to cheer him up; she persuaded him to get engaged and he gave her his mother's ring, which she still has. Then one day she went to see him – he lived in a little apartment above her parent's garage – and he had gone. No letter, no explanation; nothing.'

'Goodness, she must have been heartbroken.'

'She was. She kept expecting him to come home. She thought he might have gone to Haugesund to his parents' house. She tried to find him but nobody had seen him. Then she discovered she was pregnant. Her father was furious and sent her to live with his parents up here in Stranda. She never went back to Oslo.'

'Never?'

'Well not until after her father died. She never spoke to him again.'

'Poor Lisbet. What a horrible thing to happen. God, I'm surprised she even wanted to speak to Moffa again.'

'Well, I think she realised he was in a bad way and she didn't blame him. With hindsight I suppose it was obvious he was suffering from post-traumatic stress. Anyway, she married Olaf a couple of years later and she stopped looking for Edvard. She assumed he had gone to America to stay with the relative his mother had written about. She didn't think for a minute he would go back to Shetland, since she associated that with the war and thought he would avoid everything that brought back memories. She had no idea if he might have written to her in Oslo even. She simply had to give up.'

'But clearly she didn't stop loving him.' Lisa said, sadly.

'No, she didn't, and I don't think she ever stopped hoping to see him again. That's why we must get them back together. I think they need closure.'

'Absolutely.'

'So, who wants to go up in the cable car?' Joakim said.

Hansi had woken from his afternoon nap. He pulled his bottle out of his mouth and grinned, although clearly he didn't understand the question. He merely seemed delighted to have Joakim's attention.

'Shall we? Is it safe with him?'

'Of course; we Norwegians love our children too.'

Lisa smiled, but felt embarrassed.

'Sorry, of course it's safe. I'm just a little bit scared of heights.'

'So I've noticed.'

'Will it be cold up there?'

'Colder than here I expect. Probably a little windier; but you have a jacket don't you?'

Lisa waited until Hansi had finished his milk and eaten his banana and then she packed his jacket and hat into her bag and they set off for the cable car.

There was a little wooden cabin next to the cable lift. Joakim bought tickets for the ride and then they stood and waited for the next run. A few minutes later the cable car descended and some passengers got out. Joakim stepped in, and then reached out to take Hansi from Lisa. Once inside with the door firmly shut the car started to ascend the mountain. At first it didn't seem so high off the ground and Lisa looked down without fear, then as the mountain gained height so did the cable car and soon Lisa started to feel giddy. She wanted to enjoy the view but the whine and clatter as the cable car progressed upwards made her feel uneasy.

'Come here; it's perfectly safe. Look how Hansi is enjoying it.'

Joakim was still holding Hansi who was leaning against the glass and gawping in wonder at the scenery.

'Sorry! Shall I take him?' Lisa said, raising her arms to claim her son back.

'No, he's alright; relax and enjoy the ride.'

Lisa stood next to Hansi and tried to look down. She spotted a group of people walking below them. It exaggerated the height. She felt Joakim put his arm around her shoulders and she leaned against him gratefully. She giggled nervously.

'This is silly. I shouldn't be afraid.'

The journey ended a minute later and Lisa stepped down onto the platform with a sense of relief. They walked over to the building where the café was and found a children's play area. Hansi was happy to wander off in the safe confines of the soft play park. Lisa and Joakim sat down and watched Hansi as he stood at the side of the padded ball pit and watched another child playing. A moment later Hansi had climbed in and was throwing balls around and laughing.

'I want to come back here in winter,' Lisa said, turning in her seat for a better view. 'I can't imagine it all covered in snow. It feels like it must always be green and lush.'

'I can safely vouch for the fact it gets snowy up here. Although there is a snow-maker here too in case the weather is too mild for the ski season.'

'A snow-maker? Wow, what a fun job that would be. I would love to see snow being made.'

Joakim laughed. 'It's done by a giant machine, not a person.'

'Well obviously – I'm not stupid; but I would love to operate the machine and make it all snowy outside.'

Lisa glanced at Hansi and then at Joakim. He was leaning back in the seat with his arm along the backrest, although he was not touching her. She stared at his profile. His face was smooth shaven and tanned. He had crinkles around his eyes from many years of squinting in the sun. His hair was cropped short at the back and sides but was longer on top, like a film star from the 1940s. The vintage style suited him. There was something old fashioned about him; solid, trustworthy, dependable.

Joakim frowned as if he was uncomfortable with her scrutiny. When he didn't smile he was so serious, almost frightening. His eyes turned icy in seconds.

Lisa leaned towards him and felt a huge sense of relief when he dropped his arm around her shoulders and held her for a moment. She revelled in the warmth, although she had not been cold before. She wanted to snuggle up even closer. She wondered what might happen later when Hansi was asleep again. Would she allow him to kiss her? Would he even try?

'*Hei*!' Joakim stood up and had pulled Hansi out of the ball pit before Lisa had seen what had happened. An older boy had thrown a toy at Hansi and hit his face. Hansi was screwing his face up as if he was about to wail. A woman hurried over to retrieve her son and apologised to Joakim; at least that's what Lisa thought she was saying. '*Jeg beklager*!'

Joakim acknowledged her with barely a smile as he carried Hansi back to Lisa. There was a tiny graze on the side of his face, but Hansi was less bothered by that than being taken out of the ball pit. He put his arms out to Lisa and sobbed.

'Is he alright?' Joakim said.

'Yeah, but he thinks you were telling him off and not the other boy.'

'Oh, dear! Sorry Hansi. It wasn't your fault.'

Hansi hid his face from Joakim.

'Shall we go and get some hot chocolate or something? Maybe that will cheer him up?'

'Or make him high as a kite and unable to sleep tonight.' Lisa stood up. 'I would like a hot chocolate though; he can have a little taste. I expect he will love the marshmallows.'

They found a table by the window. Hansi was soon strapped securely into a high chair, drinking juice and snacking on an unorthodox combination of tiny shortbread cookies, marshmallows and cubes of cheese and ham. Lisa tried not to think about how unhealthy this was as a meal. However, he had eaten some vegetables at lunch time.

'Do you think you will have children one day?' Lisa said, instantly regretting the question when Joakim looked up in surprise.

He shrugged. 'I would have to get married first,' he replied, as if it was some impossible obstacle to overcome.

Lisa considered his response in silence. It seemed a little old-fashioned.

'You still have time,' she said.

'Time, yes; I have plenty of time.'

Lisa didn't know what to say. She finished her hot chocolate and thought about Moffa instead.

'Do you think I should ring my grandfather? Just to make sure he's OK.'

Joakim handed her his phone. Lisa walked over to a quieter part of the café to speak. Moffa seemed tired but happy. Margaret had just come round to see him and they were sitting in the garden. Seagulls were squalling in the background, and she heard the distant sound of a lawnmower. For a moment she wanted to be home in Shetland giving Moffa a hug. But there would be time enough next week.

'I had better go now. Hansi will start misbehaving soon. Take care, Moffa.'

'Farvel, kjære!'

Lisa didn't hurry back. She held the phone up to her ear as if she was still talking. The late afternoon sun had dipped behind the mountain and cast shadows over the valley. Only the top of their hotel was still in sunshine. It would soon be time to go back to their hotel and Lisa was a little nervous now. She was becoming more and more attracted to Joakim, but had no idea what he thought of her. She didn't want to make a fool of herself with him.

She walked back to the table and gave Joakim his phone.

'So what would you like to do this evening?'

'We could have dinner in the hotel restaurant tonight if you like. They might even have a baby-listening service if you want to put Hansi to bed first.'

Lisa shook her head; she wouldn't relax if Hansi was left alone in the room.

'OK then; room service again.'

Lisa sat down next to him and reached for his hand and held it in hers.

'Sorry; I would love to go and have dinner with you without a small grubby little monster throwing stuff at us; but I wouldn't relax if we left him.'

'I would miss the food throwing.' Joakim grinned.

Hansi stared at them for a moment and then picked up his beaker of juice and dropped it deliberately, splashing juice on Lisa's jeans as it landed.

Lisa bent down to pick it up, letting go of Joakim's hand.

'Beastly boy!'

'I think we should take him swimming again; that might buy an extra hour's sleep tonight eh?'

'I like your thinking!' Lisa said, as she picked up a napkin to wipe the gooey marshmallow stickiness from Hansi's mouth.

They went for a little walk around the top of the mountain but it was significantly cooler than it had been down in the valley. Lisa shivered as they made their way back to the cable car. There was a queue of people waiting to go back down the mountain and when they got in the car they were squashed up together. Joakim held Hansi as Lisa was pressed against the window, forced to look down into the valley as they descended. This time she managed to enjoy the view. The jolly chatter of the other occupants took her mind off the height.

When they walked through the hotel reception they saw some men bringing in musical instruments and setting up equipment in the bar.

'Live music tonight!' Joakim said, as they walked over to the lift.

'That would be nice,' Lisa said. She watched a young woman walk past, carrying a guitar case. She was tall with ebony skin and long hair in elaborate cornrows. She was breathtakingly beautiful, dressed in a short red floaty dress, over the top of tight jeans and high heeled boots.

Joakim watched the female musician. 'I would love to hear what *she* sounds like?'

'Really?' Lisa tried not to sound sarcastic, but failed.

'Don't you?'

'Actually, I would love. I bet she brings in the crowds.'

The lift pinged open and they went up to their suite. A little while later they took Hansi down to the swimming pool and did their best to tire him out. Two hours later they had succeeded. Hansi was fast asleep in his cot; it was only seven and the evening stretched out ahead of them.

Joakim picked up the telephone and rang down to reception. Lisa presumed he was talking about getting room service but since she hadn't even looked at the menu she was a little confused. He didn't appear to be speaking about food either.

'The hotel has a babysitting service. Someone could sit here while we go downstairs if you wanted. It would be an experienced nanny.'

Lisa couldn't imagine how much that would cost. She wanted to protest, but it was that or spending the whole evening in the suite. This was awkward.

'OK then, if you're sure. I don't suppose he will wake up for a while now.'

Joakim picked up the phone again and arranged for the babysitter to come.

'Half an hour; she'll be here. She speaks English too.'

'I don't suppose Hansi would mind if she didn't to be honest. He seems to be fine with people speaking Norwegian.'

'That's true. It's time you learned too.'

'Ja!'

Lisa tiptoed into her room to get a different top to put on. There was nothing she could do about her jeans. She had only brought two pairs with her and they were both equally shabby. She put on a black silk shirt with long chiffon sleeves she had bought from Oxfam. Once again she resorted to plundering the body lotion from the bathroom instead of perfume, although she did find her lip-gloss. She undid her hair from the ponytail she had worn earlier and fluffed it around her face. It fell in shiny waves and for once she felt a little more confident.

When she returned to the lounge she found Joakim had also changed his shirt and was now wearing a formal long-sleeved shirt and a waistcoat, but thankfully no tie.

'Very rock-chick. They will think you are one of the band members.'

'Ha ha.

'I wasn't trying to be funny.' Joakim was confused and Lisa realised he had genuinely meant to compliment her.

There was a knock at the door and when Lisa opened it there was a young woman carrying a bag crammed with text books. Lisa was relieved at the studiousness of the babysitter.

Lisa explained where everything was in case Hansi woke up and the girl reassured her she would call down to the restaurant if there was a problem.

'Go, have a nice time. I've seen that band before; they're great. Don't worry.'

Lisa was about to pick up her handbag but decided she would have no need of it since they weren't leaving the hotel. They left the room and waited for the lift to come back up to the top floor.

'Thank you!' Lisa said, as they got into the lift and Joakim pressed the button for the ground floor.

'My pleasure.'

Lisa leaned against the wall of the lift and realised they were now officially on a date. Joakim seemed to be daydreaming. She wondered if he considered this a "date". He smiled at her as the doors opened, and then stuck his arm out for her to take hold of it.

Joakim greeted the restaurant receptionist and pointed to a table by the window. Lisa was little in awe of the swanky surroundings. Pristine linen tablecloths, puritan-plain but clearly expensive crystal wine glasses, stylish cutlery, and a perfect arrangement of pink gerberas. Lisa was underdressed and outclassed.

Joakim was apparently born to dine in such surroundings. The wine waiter came over and Joakim ordered something without even referring to the menu. Lisa felt even smaller.

She saw Angie sitting at a table with her husband. Lisa was relieved to see a friendly face. Joakim turned to see who she was smiling at and raised a hand in greeting to the American couple.

Lisa opened the menu and closed it again almost immediately.

'What would you like?'

'I don't know. I don't understand it.'

'Did you even try?' Joakim said, lowering the menu with a mocking smile on his face.

Lisa opened the menu again and tried to translate it.

She recognised lamb, beef, salmon and lobster. 'What's *kylling*?'

'Chicken.'

'I think I understand the rest.'

'See, it's easy.'

'I wouldn't go that far.'

The waiter brought the wine over and proceeded to uncork it. He poured out two glasses after Joakim had approved it.

Joakim raised his glass to hers.

'Skål!'

'Skål!'

At first she thought the red wine was a little heavy for her taste. Then again she barely ever spent more than a fiver on a bottle of wine. It warmed her blood almost immediately. She grinned at Joakim.

'This is nice.'

'It's my favourite.'

Now they were alone together Lisa was tongue tied. As Joakim spoke to the waiter and gave him their order she looked up at the mountains. They were even more majestic in the pale sky. She followed the line of spruce trees running alongside the edge of the ski runs. The trees were menacingly dark and shadowy, by contrast to the bare green slopes. She remembered the famous story of the Norwegian resistance man who had fled across Norway pursued by the Nazis in the middle of winter. He lived to tell the tale, only just, and had lost most of his toes due to frostbite. Lisa had read his biography by David Howarth, *We Die Alone*, and had found it difficult to imagine the frozen landscape and the vast scale of the mountains and forests. Now she had a better idea. She also had a better idea of what her grandfather had gone through and she wondered how he could be such a warm and loving man. It would have been so easy to become diseased with hatred and bitterness.

'Are you OK, Lisa?'

'Perfect, thanks; I wish I could bring Moffa over here; he would love it.'

'Maybe you can persuade him when you go home.'

Lisa was reminded she only had a few more days until she would be home again. Frankly, it would all feel a little mundane after this adventure.

'Good evening; I hope you are enjoying your stay here.' The manager had appeared beside their table. Lisa smiled.

'It's lovely, thank you.'

'Joakim; I was wondering if you could spare me a few minutes of your time before you leave. I wanted your professional opinion on something.'

'Of course; why don't you join us for coffee after dinner?'

Lisa watched the manager walk over to another table, pausing to say hello before leaving the restaurant. It struck her there wasn't a hotel in the world where anyone would go out of their way to ask her opinion on any subject.

'Well, I guess there is no such thing as a free upgrade,' Joakim said, grinning at her. 'I didn't like to tell him my professional opinion on anything other than boat varnishes isn't worth much these days.'

'He obviously still thinks you're someone special.'

'Well I suppose I should be grateful someone does.' Joakim winked at her, and then turned to look around at the other diners.

'Are you fishing?'

'Fishing?' Joakim shook his head and frowned.

Lisa mimed casting a fishing line into the sea and reeling it in again. She laughed when he still did not understand. 'You were clearly fishing for compliments,' she said.

'Ah, yes; maybe I was. But I didn't get any did I?'

Before Lisa could reply their first course arrived. Lisa admired the stack of tiger prawns artfully arranged on a bed of baby spinach and wild flowers.

'This is too pretty to eat,' she said, tilting her head to the side as she studied the nasturtiums and lavender, wishing she had her camera with her.

Joakim nodded. He had ordered the same thing. He glanced around the restaurant quickly then used his phone to take a picture of Lisa and the food. 'One for Facebook,' he said, as he put the phone back in his pocket.

Lisa gingerly picked up one of the prawns, wondering how she was going to eat it in a ladylike fashion. Then again you could hardly pull the head off a creature and devour it and worry about the way you looked.

Lisa was relieved that while she may not have eaten in many upmarket restaurants she had at least spent most of her life eating seafood in all its guises. She could crack open a lobster or a crab like a professional. A prawn was simple by comparison.

The prawns had been cooked with lemon and garlic and they were delicious. Lisa wiped her fingers on the napkin. She could get used to this kind of life; although as soon as she thought that, she reminded herself she didn't normally live in the kind of world where dining out in glamorous hotels was the norm.

'What's wrong?'

'Oh nothing; that was lovely! Too lovely in fact; all future prawns will be dull by comparison.'

'You must have some nice restaurants in Shetland.' Joakim said, surprising Lisa by how tuned in to her thoughts he seemed to be.

'We do, but I don't tend to go out much; especially not with Hansi.'

'Of course; but he won't always be so little.'

Lisa realised he didn't get her after all; it wasn't because Hansi was so little she didn't go out.

They spent the rest of the meal talking about Joakim's childhood in Norway. Lisa steered the conversation back to him whenever he tried to get her to open up about her life.

She was fascinated by his life which seemed charmed by comparison to hers. His parents were still happily married. His mother was a retired paediatrician and his father owned a large boatyard which he still worked in from time to time. His sister, Hanne, was married with two little girls. She was a radiographer married to a surgeon. They lived outside Oslo.

Their childhood had been full of travel, adventure and love. Joakim admitted he had taken life and happiness for granted right up until he lost his leg.

Lisa couldn't help but think he still had a good life compared to hers. His family were close and supportive, and he was clearly wealthy despite the disability. Lisa was sure if a similar thing had happened to her she would be destitute. She was feeling sorry for herself and was glad he couldn't read her mind.

After they finished their meal Joakim suggested they went to find the manager so they would still have time to go and see the band play for a little while.

'You go and find him. I'll see how Hansi is getting on.'

'OK, come and find us in the lobby.'

Lisa hurried up to their room and knocked quietly on the door before letting herself in. She found the babysitter at the table poring over text books and writing notes in a jotter.

'He hasn't woken up at all.'

'Oh good. He doesn't usually, once he's fallen asleep. What are you studying?'

'I'm doing a degree in archaeology,' she said, almost apologetically, 'my final exam is on Monday.'

'That's what I did too. I've just finished my Masters.'

'Where did you study?'

'Edinburgh and Shetland.'

'I would love to go to Shetland. I was thinking of going to another country to get a post-grad in museum studies. Where would be a good place to go?'

'St Andrew's University in Scotland does a Masters course in Museum Studies. It's about an hour away from Edinburgh.'

'St Andrew's; isn't that where Prince William met Kate?'

Lisa grinned and nodded.

'Sounds perfect; I could get my degree and meet a prince.'

'I should have gone there myself,' Lisa said.

'Oh, but your husband is gorgeous.'

'We're just friends.'

'Really?'

Lisa shrugged. 'Well I had better go and find him again. The band will be playing soon.'

'OK, I will ring down if your little boy wakes up. Have fun!'

Lisa found Joakim in the lobby sitting with the manager. A tray of coffee was on a low table between them. The manager instantly poured Lisa a cup and handed it to her as she sat down next to Joakim.

'*Tak*!'

The men resumed their conversation in Norwegian, and Lisa quickly lost track of what they were talking about, although it seemed to be about skiing. Joakim seemed happy though, so Lisa relaxed and drank her coffee, happy at the thought she had been wrong about nobody wanting her opinion. She had helpfully recommended a university course to a fellow student.

After a few minutes of serious discussion the manager leaned forward and shook hands with Joakim and said good night to them both.

'Shall we go and see the band then?' Joakim said.

'Sure!'

They went to the lounge bar which was packed with people. There was nowhere to sit so they stood to one side of the stage in time to see the musicians climb up on the stage and start tweaking and tuning their instruments.

'Are you alright standing?' Lisa said, as they waited.

'Ja!' Joakim snapped.

Lisa wondered why Joakim seemed a little tense now. The musicians all seemed to be ready and a moment later the young black woman they had seen earlier climbed up on the stage. She had changed out of her folksy outfit and was now wearing a skin-tight black Lycra outfit with red platform shoes. Her elaborate hairstyle was now tied back with a red bandana. Lisa could not imagine what kind of music the band would play. The band's name was etched on the bass drum – *Red Fish Blue Fish*.

The room was silent for a second, and then without any introduction or musical accompaniment the woman burst into song … "Well, you know you make me want to shout…"

Lisa was surprised to hear this energetic rendition of Lulu's famous song from the 1960s. The band joined in a moment later creating a raucous cacophony of sound bringing more people into the lounge. The area around the stage became crowded. Joakim pulled Lisa in front of him and held her shoulders, only letting go to applaud when the song ended.

The set included an inspired mix of songs from all eras and styles. The singer, Alberta, had an incredible vocal range, and confidently tackled smoky jazz classics and upbeat soul-diva songs and a little bit of rock, singing mostly in English but also in Norwegian, and curiously, another song *Ne Me Quitte Pas* in French. Lisa was glad they were standing for the performance and she couldn't resist jigging about in time to the music and she was glad Joakim seemed to be enjoying it, even though he stood perfectly still throughout.

'That was brilliant,' Lisa said, as they headed for the lift after the encore had finished. It was almost midnight now, although it was still light enough outside to see fairly clearly. Lisa had contemplated asking Joakim to go outside for some fresh air, but remembered they needed to let the babysitter go home.

The babysitter reassured them Hansi was still fast asleep. 'I looked at St Andrew's; I think I might apply,' the girl said, as she stowed her books into her bag.

'I hope you find your prince then,' Lisa said, laughing.

Joakim reached for his wallet.

'It goes on the room bill, don't worry,' the babysitter said to Joakim.

'*Ja; jeg vet.*' Joakim handed over some folded notes which the girl stuffed into the pocket of her jeans.

'*Tak! God natt!*'

'What a great night, thank you.' Lisa said, leaning against the door.

'Shall we sit out on the balcony for a while? I'm not ready for bed yet, my ears are still noisy.'

'In English we would say "my ears are still ringing", which mine are too. It was loud!'

'Ringing – noisy; it's the same thing, ja?'

Lisa followed him out onto the balcony and leaned over the railings. A couple walked along a pathway through the landscaped gardens in front of the hotel. They were holding hands and stopped to kiss. Lisa was jealous. She sat down where she couldn't see the couple.

'What did the manager want?'

'To talk about skiing? Do you want a drink? I might get a beer from the fridge.'

'I'll get it.'

Joakim seemed a little subdued and Lisa couldn't understand why. The meal had been excellent and the band had been entertaining. His mood could only be attributed to one of two things; either she had upset him or the manager had. She wasn't sure which it would be, but she hazarded a guess it was the manager. Joakim had changed the subject quickly when she had asked him earlier. She wasn't sure whether she should pursue it.

'What exactly about skiing did he want to discuss? It seems like a strange thing to talk about, considering you don't ski anymore.'

Lisa wanted to slap herself for being so blunt, but it was too late now. She stared at Joakim, waiting for his reaction but he simply put his beer down and sighed.

'His brother has a ski-lodge near Bergen. He wants to start a winter-sports school for disabled people and needs to recruit another coach. He wanted to see if I had ever thought about doing that.'

'And have you?'

'No!'

'It was nice of him to ask though. I expect people would love to be taught by someone like you who was won so many competitions. I think it sounds like a great idea teaching people to do sports.'

'I have taught before. I qualified as a coach years ago.'

'I know, so why don't you see if you can do it again?'

'Because I would need to be able to ski again.'

'But if other disabled people can ski, why can't you? You said yourself you were thinking of trying it again.'

Joakim did not reply. He went indoors and Lisa was left outside, shivering in the cool air. She hugged her arms around her body, regretting her tactlessness. It was blindingly obvious Joakim had issues with his disability and yet she could not seem to stop prodding him into discussing it.

She got up slowly and went inside, locking the balcony door behind her. She sat down on the sofa and finished her beer. She rubbed her face with her hands. She heard the toilet flush and the taps running in the bathroom. A moment later she heard Joakim brushing his teeth.

'I'm sorry,' she said, as Joakim emerged from the bathroom and switched off the light.

'Sorry?'

'For pestering you about skiing; it's none of my business – I'm sorry.'

Joakim shrugged and disappeared into his bedroom without replying.

Lisa slumped in despair, but a moment later got up and went to the bathroom to get ready for bed. She brushed her teeth, washed her face and then stared at her pale miserable reflection in the mirror. Such amazing things had happened this week and yet she would give anything to be home in her own bed, far away from Joakim.

She turned off the bathroom light and shut the door behind her, intending to go to her own room.

'Lisa?'

Lisa stood in the doorway of Joakim's room. He was sitting on the edge of the bed, wearing a tee-shirt and boxer shorts. He had removed his prosthesis. Lisa stared down at the stump. It didn't repel her in any way, although she was fascinated by it. She was curious to know what it felt like to lose a limb, but she had done enough damage already. This time she stayed silent.

'I would like to try to ski again. I just don't think I could. That's why I get upset when people talk about it. I'm sorry. It's not your fault I'm in a bad mood.'

'It's been a long day,' she replied, turning to go.

'Don't go.'

Lisa put her hand on the door frame, silently questioning him.

'I'm going to check on Hansi,' she said.

Lisa peered around the door of her room. Hansi was undoubtedly asleep, judging by the gentle snoring coming from the cot. She listened for a while, her eyes adjusting to the darkened room. He was lying on his tummy with his head to one side, the blankets kicked off. He was always hot when he slept so she didn't bother to cover him again. He would not appreciate it.

She tiptoed back to Joakim's room and stood by the door not sure what he wanted from her.

'Come in.'

He patted the bed beside him. He was already under the covers.

Lisa sat down on the edge of the bed and folded her arms across her body.

'Is he asleep?'

Lisa nodded.

'I bet if I tried to kiss you again he would wake up.' Joakim said, with a warm smile in his voice.

'I'm sure he would.'

'I'd better not try then.'

'Oh...' Lisa let her disappointment slip out, and hoped Joakim wouldn't notice.

'It's not that I don't want to; of course I do. But where would it lead?'

'Where does a kiss usually lead? Is it so different in Norway?'

'No, of course not; but...'

'But?'

'But you live in Shetland and I live here, and...'

'And,' Lisa said, with a sense of finality. 'You're right; it couldn't work.'

Lisa stood up.

'I never said it couldn't work,' Joakim said, reaching over and tugging her hand, pulling her towards him. 'I don't think I can offer you much. I'm a wreck of a man.'

'You're not as much of a wreck as you seem to think; but I don't think I would be able to persuade you otherwise. So, yes, perhaps I wouldn't be right for you. Maybe one day you'll realise what you're still capable of.'

Joakim let go of her hand as if he had been stung.

'This is our sticking point.' Lisa said. 'It's late; I'm going to bed now.'

Lisa got as far as the bedroom door and then strode back to Joakim who was still lounging against the headboard. She put one knee on the bed and bent towards him. With one hand resting on his shoulder she kissed him; softly, then as he pulled her closer she relaxed and kissed him with intent. Then just as quickly, she pulled away and stood up.

'God natt!'

'What? Are you serious?' Joakim sat up straight, and reached for her hand.

'Absolutely!' Lisa stepped out of his reach.

'But why?'

'Because we're not sure and I don't have space in my life for a short term fling; do you?'

Lisa closed Joakim's bedroom door behind her before she changed her mind. She hurried into her room as quietly as possible, put on her pyjamas and slipped under the sheets and pulled them up to her neck. Her eyes were still open but all the light from outside was shielded by the black-out blinds. It was uncomfortably dark and she would have raised the blinds had it not been for Hansi.

A few minutes later when she knew sleep would evade her, she got out of bed and went out to the balcony and stood outside, watching the sky get lighter as the sun rose.

She relived the kiss. Her lips still tingled and she got butterflies when she remembered how he had held her. It was so tempting to go back and see what would happen. But she wasn't sure; that was the truth. Would a few hours of pleasure be worth the heartache of saying goodbye to someone she might never see again after their trip ended? There were no guarantees either of them would ever cross the North Sea in either direction again. The whole reason they had ever met was by sheer chance and misdirection. He was the wrong Joakim Haaland. Somewhere in Norway was another young man who had thrown a message in a bottle into the sea. If Lisa had looked the name up on Google instead of Facebook she would have found Joakim's name immediately and all the details of his career. She would never have contacted him. He would have seemed unapproachable with his almost celebrity status.

And yet, because she had reached out to him in a moment of alcohol-induced bravado she had discovered things about her family that would have stayed secret forever. She had met new members of her family; she had an aunt, and cousins. Moffa had cried with happiness at being reunited with his daughter on the phone. How much happier would he be when Karen came over to Shetland?

Lisa owed a great deal to fate and to Joakim. She would be forever grateful and whatever happened over the next few days, weeks or years, she would remember him with fondness forever.

Her heart fluttered again; yes, she was growing fond of him. She put her fingers to her lips, remembering the softness of his mouth against hers. The urge to kiss him again was too strong to resist. She turned away from the sunrise and went inside. She would find out what it was like to kiss him again. She was a grown up, she could handle the outcome, whatever it was.

She was almost at his bedroom door when she heard the unmistakeable sound of Hansi waking up. He was grumbling in his half-asleep way, and in a moment the noise would escalate if she did not get to him quickly.

It was unnerving how Hansi's radar seemed to have picked up her intentions. She went to her room and closed the door and picked up her son and held him close, stroking his hair as she soothed him back to sleep. He would only stay settled now if she stayed next to him so she carried him to bed and lay down next to him. Hansi nestled in the crook of her arm, his fingers gripping her pyjama top.

23

Joakim woke early after a restless night. In between lustful thoughts of Lisa he had spent some time thinking about what the hotel manager had discussed with him earlier. At the time he had immediately dismissed the idea of becoming a professional ski coach, but in the early hours of the morning when sleep was impossible he had thought about the possibility of it. In doing so, he had awoken memories of the best times of his life, and he knew he still had ambitions that would never be realised in his new career. Perhaps it was time to revisit the idea of returning to sport.

As he put on his prosthesis he knew it was time to accept his situation and to make the best of it. Hiding in a boat yard for the rest of his life was not an option. That was his father's dream job; not his. He resolved to contact his physiotherapist and rehabilitation advisor with a view to getting a new prosthetic leg suitable for attempting skiing again.

With a renewed sense of optimism he sat out on the balcony with a cup of coffee and stared up at the mountain with hope and expectation.

'You're up early,' Lisa said, stepping out onto the balcony with Hansi and making Joakim jump.

'I didn't sleep well, so I thought I may as well get up. It's a beautiful day isn't it?' He lifted his arms to take Hansi from Lisa seeing as the little boy was trying to escape from her. 'Get yourself some coffee and come and enjoy the view. We can go down for breakfast in a little while. I was thinking of going for a swim this morning. Are you up for that, little man?' He ruffled Hansi's hair.

Lisa fetched some milk for Hansi and a cup of coffee and sat down. She passed Hansi the beaker of milk which he accepted although he was too distracted to drink.

'I wonder when we will hear from Karen today. I hope she comes over to Shetland soon. The more I think about it the more I realise Moffa needs to make his peace with his family. I always thought of him as being a happy person, but now I know, deep down, he's been carrying a hell of a lot of sadness too. It's time to let it all go and try and enjoy his last years.'

'I think she will. Who would let that opportunity pass?'

'It's only Saturday; my fourth day in Norway and so much has happened, I can't get over it.'

Joakim reached for his coffee. He held the cup away from Hansi who was leaning against him.

Joakim thought about the last time he had been home. It was nearly two weeks. He had only planned to be away for a maximum

225

of ten days. He realised he ought to ring his colleague who was managing the boat yard in his absence. He would also need to discuss his new plans with him too.

'I'm sorry about last night,' Lisa said.

'Don't mention it. You're right; I have no idea what I'm doing at the moment.'

'Me neither, but it was tempting; I nearly came back to you after I had gone to bed, but Hansi woke up.'

'I told you he had remarkable powers. He wants to keep you all to himself. And I can't say I blame him.'

'Shall we get some breakfast then?'

Lisa took Hansi from him and went inside to fetch her bag. Joakim watched her take a tissue from her pocket and wipe her son's mouth. Hansi beamed when she smiled at him. They were a happy little family, and for a moment he wanted to be a part of that. He shut the balcony door and picked up the room key and followed them out to the lift.

As the lift door shut he reached for Lisa's hand. She seemed surprised, but her fingers closed around his.

Despite the early hour the restaurant was busy. The musicians from the band were sitting at the table next to theirs. They ate their breakfast in silence as if they were too tired to speak. Alberta waggled her fingers at Hansi as he twisted in his seat to stare at her. He giggled and hid behind the back of the chair and then peered over to see if she was still there.

'He has an eye for the ladies already,' Joakim said.

'He's a terrible flirt, although he seems to prefer hanging out with men. It makes me sad sometimes that the only man he spends time with is Moffa.'

'His father is a fool. If I had a little boy like Hansi I would be very happy. I couldn't imagine being thousands of miles away from him.'

Joakim watched Lisa squirm in discomfort in her chair. After the waiter took their order he noticed Peter, the manager, standing at the entrance surveying the restaurant. Joakim raised his hand and beckoned him over.

'Have you got time for coffee with us?' Joakim said.

'Of course.' Peter sat down and signalled to the waiter.

'I was thinking about what you said yesterday. Maybe I should reconsider.'

Peter nodded, and then smiled apologetically at Lisa.

'Do you mind if we talk in Norwegian, my English is not good enough for business?'

Lisa nodded and turned her attention back to Hansi who was becoming impatient for his breakfast.

Joakim explained he had been thinking about Peter's proposition about taking up a position as a professional ski instructor at his brother's resort. He explained he would need to sort out his current business in Larvik, and sort out his own personal fitness before the ski season started in the winter. He wasn't sure whether it would be possible, but he was willing to give it a go.

Peter was overjoyed and when the waiter appeared with their breakfast he said he would leave them in peace and go and ring his brother.

'What was all that about?' Lisa said, as she cut up a hardboiled egg and some ham for Hansi.

'My new career,' Joakim said, grinning with pride. 'I've decided to give skiing another chance.'

Lisa shrieked and jumped up out of her seat and hugged him.

'That's brilliant. I can't believe it. But you should, you really should.'

'I have you to thank.'

'Me? How on earth?'

'I couldn't sleep after you kissed me and ran away. So I started thinking about what Peter said last night. I realised I should give it another chance. I haven't been on the snow since I lost my leg. The one time I tried was a disaster; but I think with some help from my physio and the prosthetic clinic I might become more confident on skis. I might be good enough to teach, although competing at any kind of level is beyond me now.'

Lisa had abandoned all attempts at eating her breakfast. She sat in stunned silence, staring at Joakim. She reached for his hand and linked her fingers through his.

'That's fabulous. Have you told anyone else yet? What will your parents think?'

'I think my mother will be pleased, but my dad might be disappointed as my business will have to be sold, or managed by someone else. But I think he'll understand my heart was never in it.'

Lisa tore an apple-filled pastry apart, and gave a piece to Hansi. 'Where will you live now? Will you have to move?'

'Yes I think so. The resort is just outside Bergen so I will need to move there. But that means I will be closer to Lars and Anders too; another bonus.'

'And it means if I come over to Bergen again then you won't be so far away.'

'I guess I'm going to be busy for the next few months getting back into shape, but yes, you will have to come over again.'

'You seem in pretty good shape to me.'

Joakim grinned, recognising that Lisa was flirting with him.

Peter caught them as they were leaving the restaurant after breakfast. He handed Joakim a piece of paper with an address and contact details on it.

'Henrik wondered whether you might be able to drop in and see him as you are passing. You mentioned you had driven from Bergen; will you be driving back that way?'

'Yes, I have to take Lisa and her son to the airport. But we would have time to stop off. I will give him a call when we have decided when we are leaving.'

While Lisa took Hansi to their room to clean him up after breakfast, Joakim stepped out onto the balcony and gazed out at the view. He had missed the mountains. As much as he loved the sea, he knew it was the mountains and fjords he felt at home in. This would be his again, if he was lucky. But was he lucky? He shifted his weight onto his prosthesis. It would take some serious work on his part to get back to his previous levels of fitness and agility. It would be harder and more painful than when he was younger and whole.

'Have you called him yet?' Lisa said, making him jump.

'Just about to! Would you like to come with me? Perhaps we could stay the night there; get a feel for the place. Then we could carry on to Bergen and spend our last night with Anita and Lars.'

'This week is going too quickly,' Lisa said, sitting down suddenly. Hansi toddled out onto the balcony and Lisa reached for him and pulled him onto her lap and rested her cheek against his head.

'We've achieved a lot this week. A new family for you - a new career for me.'

'I know. I guess we should go and see Lisbet again before we go, and see what they have decided about coming over to Shetland.'

When they arrived at Lisbet's house Karen had just arrived with her husband, Michael. Karen and Lisbet had just booked their flights and would be coming to Shetland on the same flight as Lisa. They discussed their arrangements over coffee.

'Now that's all sorted, maybe you should relax and see something of Geirangerfjord. Michael keeps a boat in the marina if you'd like to go out on it,' Karen said.

'Wow, that would be lovely,' Lisa replied. 'But I'm not sure it would be a good idea with Hansi. He would be a bit of a handful on a boat.'

'There are lifejackets on board. It's just a little motor cruiser, but it has a cabin, and a little galley kitchen.'

Lisa turned to Joakim.

'What do you think? Would you be able to manage going out on a boat?'

'Yeah, it wouldn't be rough out on the fjord.'

'Karen told me you used to be in the Coastguard,' Michael said. 'So you don't need me to come with you, do you? Why don't you leave the little boy with us? We could look after him if you want to go off on your own.'

Karen nodded and put down her coffee. She patted Lisa arm.

'What a great idea! After all you've done for us it's the least we could do. You deserve a little treat. And don't worry, Michael and I are used to babysitting.'

'Really? Do you think you could manage Hansi? He can be a bit of a handful sometimes.'

'No problem at all. There is a room full of toys upstairs that my mother has kept for decades. My children and grandchildren have had hours of entertainment in this house.'

An hour later Joakim was steering the boat out of the marina. Lisa stood beside him at the wheel and waved goodbye to Michael who stood on the edge of the quay. She had been nervous about leaving Hansi behind with

Karen, but he hadn't seemed to mind. He had been diverted by the huge cache of toys that Karen had found for him. As the boat moved into the vast open water of the fjord she started to relax. The scenery was stunning.

It was cloudy and a little cold compared with the previous days, but this did not detract from the awesome sight of mountains towering over them from both sides of the fjord. They motored at a steady pace away from the town and soon they were passing waterfalls, cascading into the fjord.

'Melted snow from the mountains,' Joakim said, as Lisa marvelled at the volume of water rushing over the rocks.

'I've seen so many photographs of the fjords, and even seen them as we drove here, but it's so different viewed from a boat. I know people who have come over here on cruises, and I could never see the appeal before. But this is spectacular.'

'There's a cruise ship up ahead of us.'

Lisa picked up some binoculars and trained them on the ship.

'The Marco Polo. That comes to Lerwick sometimes.'

'This is one of the most popular places in Norway for cruise ships. We had better get out of its way.'

Joakim steered the boat out of the path of the ship, towards the shore, where Lisa could get a better view of the waterfalls. A few minutes later the Marco Polo passed them and their boat started to sway in the wake. Lisa put her arm on Joakim's shoulder as the boat rocked.

Joakim took his hand off the throttle and let the boat slow to a drift. He checked to see how far they were from land and other vessels then he turned to face Lisa.

'I have you all to myself now. No small child to interrupt us.'

Lisa put down the binoculars and stepped backwards. She glanced over at the shore and then turned back to Joakim. She recognised that she now had the perfect opportunity to kiss him again; to see where a kiss might lead. But now she felt nervous, exposed, with no child to hide behind.

Joakim didn't give her time to fret. He stepped forward, towering over her. She hadn't appreciated how tall he was until he tilted her chin and bent his head to kiss her.

All thoughts of Hansi vanished as Lisa kissed him back. She pushed him back against the door frame of the cabin. The boat lurched under the weight of the sudden movement, but Lisa ignored it. She was too intent on kissing him to notice the swaying.

She slipped her hand under his shirt and even though her eyes were closed, she squeezed them tighter with delight when she ran her fingers over his taut abdomen. His skin in contrast to the rigidity of his stomach was smooth and warm to the touch. She inhaled the scent of aftershave, mixed with the salty freshness of the fjord. The boat rocked unexpectedly. Joakim pulled away from Lisa and looked to see what had caused the disturbance. He laughed.

'It's the Coastguard.'

Lisa turned to see a large grey military vessel pass slowly. A uniformed man appeared to be watching them through binoculars. Joakim lifted his hand in greeting. Lisa giggled.

'Do you think they saw what we were doing?'

'Probably. But there's no law against it.'

'No, but maybe this isn't the best place. We might drift into another boat, or those rocks over there if we're not careful.'

'That would be a little embarrassing.'

Lisa peered into the well-equipped cabin. She wanted to drag Joakim inside, but as she looked out of the window she could see another boat coming towards them. 'It's kind of busy here, isn't it?'

'Yeah, maybe we will have to concentrate on where we are going.'

'Sadly, I think I might have to agree with you.'

Joakim held Lisa's hand and started the engine again. 'Let's see if we can find somewhere a little more secluded.'

24

Lisa collected her boarding cards from the check-in desk, picked up her carry-on bag and followed Joakim and Hansi to the coffee shop, her heart increasingly heavy at the prospect of saying goodbye.

Joakim picked up a bag of cheesy snacks and held it up for Hansi's approval. Hansi reached for them despite the fact it had not been long since he had eaten his lunch at Anita's apartment.

'Would you like some coffee?' Joakim said, as Lisa joined them near the counter.

'Um, yeah, sure,' Lisa said, turning her face away almost immediately. Tears pricked her eyes. She found a free table and sat down and then realised she had left Joakim to carry both the tray and Hansi. She hurried back and reclaimed her son and found a highchair for him. She watched Joakim walk across the café floor, his head held high, and a big grin on his face. He had not stopped smiling since their visit to Henrik's ski centre. Joakim handed her coffee to her.

'Edvard is going to be so happy this afternoon. I wish I could be there to witness it.'

She stirred her coffee and set the spoon down in the saucer. Hansi had lost interest in his snacks already and was dropping them over the side of the high chair. She snatched the almost full packet away from him and put it in her bag for later.

'I want to see you again,' Joakim said, reaching his hand out to her.

'I know! It won't be easy though, will it?'

Joakim shrugged. 'No, I suppose not. But I will have most of the summer off next year, so I can come over and visit. And maybe you could come here too.'

Lisa smiled, but didn't feel so confident about her ability to visit Norway again. She already owed Joakim lots of money for her flights and accommodation. He had refused to discuss it, but Lisa knew she wouldn't want to come over again until she had repaid him. It wouldn't feel right.

'I'm going to miss this little man.' Joakim said, ruffling Hansi's hair, then picking a soggy cheesy puff from the front of the little boy's tee-shirt and depositing it safely on the table. 'You will call me and tell me how the reunion went, won't you? I'll be home this evening, kind of late, but call me anyway.'

'I might be able to make a quick call; it's expensive to ring Norway, but I can send you a message on Facebook, or an email.'

Joakim shook his head.

'Not good enough.' He stood up. 'Don't go anywhere.'

Lisa drank her coffee as she waited for Joakim. She gave Hansi his beaker of juice and then checked her watch again. She would have to go soon. She shut her eyes and replayed the way Joakim had kissed her the previous evening. A swarm of butterflies erupted inside her and she wished she had been braver. Their passionate kissing had not been followed up by anything much more satisfying. Hansi had put paid to any chance of more intimacy. Lisa had told herself perhaps this was for the best. It wasn't as if their relationship could progress from such a distance.

'A present for you, so you can talk to me for free, anytime you like.'

Lisa looked up in surprise at Joakim's voice. She took the bag he held out, peeped inside and gasped.

'Oh my God, an iPad. For me?'

'Of course it's for you. I did think about getting you an iPhone, but then I thought Hansi would like watching videos on the iPad. My nieces love it. I bought them one for Christmas last year. They're already experts on it.'

Lisa stood up and threw her arms around Joakim and buried her face in his chest.

'That's so generous, thank you. I can't believe you did that. I already owe you so much. This week has cost you a fortune.'

'No it hasn't. I have regained my enthusiasm for life which you can't put a price on. If it wasn't for you I would not be going back to skiing. It's you I owe a lot to. I think we should call it quits, ja?'

Lisa put the iPad in her bag.

'I should go soon.'

Joakim nodded. He stood up and lifted Hansi out of his highchair and swung him up in the air, grinning as Hansi giggled. 'I'm going to miss you both,' Joakim said, as Lisa stood up and took Hansi from him.

At the departure gate a teenage girl was saying goodbye to her parents, presumably for a long time judging by the tears. Lisa felt her own eyes prickle with empathy. She had yet to say goodbye to Joakim, and she had no idea when, or if, she would ever see him again. In the last week she had grown closer to him than any other adult, but she couldn't exactly claim to be in a relationship with him. She had no idea how to classify the situation; a brief holiday romance, a new friendship or the start of something permanent?

She felt a tug on her bag. Joakim swung it on to his shoulder. He took her hand and nodded toward the gate. With Hansi balanced on her hip, his arms clinging around her neck she followed Joakim. They stopped near the barrier and Joakim put Lisa's bag down on the ground then wrapped his arms around her.

Lisa leaned into him and sighed involuntarily, shutting her eyes. She opened them quickly in response to Hansi pulling her hair. Lisa pulled away from Joakim and shook her head at Hansi. She put him down on the ground next to the bag. 'Don't move!' Hansi stood still as Joakim pulled Lisa back into his arms.

'That's better, maybe now I can kiss you without someone punching me in the face.'

'Who says I won't?' Lisa replied.' Joakim grinned, as he pushed back a strand of her hair and then disentangled a sticky half eaten jelly sweet from it. He stepped away and dropped it into a bin and rubbed his hand on his jeans pulling a face at Hansi as he did.

'Oh God, that child; talk about killing the moment,' Lisa said, checking her hair for other misplaced sweets.

Joakim laughed. He hugged her for a moment and then loosened his grip as he bent his head to kiss her. Lisa closed her eyes and for a few seconds forgot all about Hansi who was clinging to her legs. Lisa had her hands on Joakim's shoulders and she reached around his neck and pulled him tighter, wishing she didn't have to let go so soon.

The tannoy announced her flight and they pulled apart.

'Try out your iPad tonight and call me. I want to hear how Edvard got on with Lisbet and Karen. I wish I could come back with you now, but I guess I have a lot of things to sort out now. Hopefully I will get over to Lerwick again this summer.'

Lisa slung the bag over her shoulder and then reached into the side pocket for the tickets and passports. Then she picked Hansi up.

'We'd better go. It's been lovely. I can't thank you enough.'

'Stop trying. We're quits remember. Call me!'

Lisa battled her way through security with an uncooperative Hansi who did not want to stand still while she put her bag on the conveyor belt after taking out her new iPad, nor while she was trying to put it back again after they had gone through the metal detector, and her belt buckle had set off the alarm. Hansi had wandered off while the female security officer was patting her down, and Lisa had been forced to chase after him and nearly forgot to pick her new iPad.

Lisa was still feeling bereft after saying goodbye to Joakim when she spotted Lisbet and Karen walking towards her. Her spirits lifted a little when she saw the smiles on their faces.

'You're here. We wondered if you were still getting this flight,' Karen said, as she hugged Lisa.

'I was saying goodbye to Joakim, and then this little monkey was causing a nuisance going through security.'

Karen smiled sympathetically. She lowered her voice, even though Lisbet could not speak English. 'My mother's handbag was stuffed full of things she couldn't take through security. Nail scissors, perfume, a giant tube of hand-cream, honestly! She made such a fuss when they confiscated it all. I had to buy her more perfume in the duty free store, and no doubt she will have it in her handbag on the way home again. She won't listen to me.'

Lisa glanced at Lisbet who was picking imaginary pieces of fluff from her sleeve.

'Is she looking forward to seeing my grandfather again?'

'Oh, yes. She has been up since five this morning and has been fussing about what to wear as if she was a teenager going on her first date.'

Lisa grinned and hoped Lisbet wouldn't be disappointed when she saw Moffa.

Lisbet was wearing a smart navy blue skirt suit with a cerise blouse. The bright colour suited her, and it was obvious Lisbet had been stunningly beautiful in her youth. Her hair was snow white and once again she was wearing it up in a French pleat. Her bright pink lipstick added a pop of colour to her pale face. Lisbet had style.

Lisa had rung Moffa to warn him she was bringing Lisbet and Karen home with her. She had rung her mother too, who had not been pleased, after which she had rung Moffa's neighbour, Margaret, who volunteered to take Moffa shopping for groceries.

Lisa knew the house would be ready and welcoming for them and she pictured Moffa standing at the kitchen window when they arrived in her car.

She was surprised, therefore, when Moffa was waiting at Sumburgh Airport for them. He was dressed in a dark suit with a pale blue shirt and a tie, an unusual outfit for him unless he was going to a funeral, although in that case he would have worn a black tie, and not the scarlet one he had on today. He carried two bouquets of red roses too. Lisa was leading the way from the plane to the terminal and she spotted her grandfather before anyone else did. She grinned at Karen and Lisbet.

'He's here!'

'*Han er her,*' Karen repeated to her mother. Lisbet let go of Karen's arm, her hands fluttering to her face to tidy her hair, as she strained to see through the window into the arrivals lounge.

Lisa hurried to greet Moffa, giving him a quick kiss on the cheek and then standing back so he could see who was following her.

'Look what I brought you back from Norway,' Lisa said, although Moffa was far too distracted to reply, or even notice Hansi who was attempting to extricate himself from Lisa in order to greet his Pop Pop.

Lisa stepped back to watch the reunion of Lisbet and Edvard. Lisbet stopped a few feet away from him with her hands covering her mouth, utter disbelief on her face.

'Edvard?'

'Ja!'

Edvard dropped the roses onto a nearby table and rushed towards Lisbet, who collapsed against him, audibly sobbing. They held each other, Edvard bending his head towards hers and whispering to her.

Lisa saw Edvard brush away tears from his face with one hand, while he held tight to Lisbet. Lisa walked over to Karen and put her arm around her shoulders, almost embarrassed that Edvard seemed to be ignoring his daughter.

'It's OK; I knew this would happen. They've been storing up so much emotion for so many years,' Karen said, smiling at Lisa. 'Let them have their moment.'

Almost as if he had heard, Edvard lifted his head and held out his hand to Karen.

The luggage carousel started up behind Lisa and she slipped away to retrieve her bag and Hansi's pushchair, then waited. The emotional reunion caught the attention of other travellers who stopped to look at the three people who hugged and cried and laughed. Lisa spotted a friend of hers who had just got off the flight from Aberdeen.

'Hi Lisa, have you been away?' Jenna said, crouching down to say hello to Hansi who was now strapped into his pushchair and looking fed up.

'Yeah, I went to Norway and met my grandfather's ex-girlfriend and his daughter. I brought them back with me – it's the first time he has met his daughter.' Lisa indicated in the direction of her grandfather and grinned.

'Wow! They've got a lot of catching up to do.'

'I'm starting to wonder if I'll be able to get them home.'

'Good luck with that. We must catch up sometime. Call me; I'm home all summer now.'

'I'll do that,' Lisa replied, thinking it would be so good to catch up with her friend, and the opportunity to talk about Joakim would be entirely welcome. She already missed him. She looked at her watch as Jenna walked away. It was less than two hours since she had seen him and her heart ached.

Karen broke away from Edvard and her mother and retrieved their luggage. Lisa fetched a luggage trolley and helped Karen pile the bags onto it.

'You OK?'

'Ja, it feels strange to meet him at last. But he feels like my father. Does that make sense?'

Lisa grinned and nodded. 'In many ways he is more like a father to me than a grandfather; he cares more about me than my dad ever did.'

'I want to hear all about you and your family over the next few days,' Karen said, smiling sympathetically at Lisa. Edvard and Lisbet were finally ready to go. Hansi strained to get out of the pushchair, so she let him get out and he immediately ran towards Moffa who reached down and picked him up, the years melting away as he held him high and kissed him.

'Crumbs!' Lisa said. She hadn't seen Moffa do anything so energetic in a long time.

Lisa drove them all home, all crushed together in her small car. Karen sat in the front passenger seat, as her parents had resisted being parted so soon. They shared the cramped back seat with Hansi; Lisa glanced at her rear view mirror and smiled when she saw Moffa and Lisbet leaning against each other whispering like teenagers, ignoring Hansi who was whimpering for attention.

When they arrived back at Moffa's house Lisbet declared she needed to have a lie down. Lisa was about to show her to the spare room but before she had a chance Moffa led Lisbet into his room and the door closed.

Karen burst out laughing and hugged Lisa.

'Well, that was a little unexpected, but what could they be getting up to at their age?'

Lisa shrugged, thinking it might be a little bit more than she had managed to achieve with Joakim. With that in mind she dragged Hansi away from Moffa's door and carried him into the lounge and dumped him unceremoniously into his playpen.

She made Karen some coffee and some sandwiches which they took out into the garden. Freed from his playpen and already forgetting about Moffa, Hansi played happily in the garden, chasing a cabbage white butterfly and the neighbour's kitten that had escaped into their garden.

The week passed in a blur of sightseeing and scenic drives, long drawn out meals around the kitchen table, sitting up late drinking wine with Karen, or listening to the sound of Moffa and Lisbet giggling over a cup of tea in the garden. It was all over too soon and Lisa was back at the airport hugging her aunt goodbye, wiping tears from her eyes as she watched Moffa say goodbye to Lisbet, and then to Karen.

Lisa had taken Hansi to nursery before they set off to the airport so she stood alone and watched the last group hug before Karen led her mother off to the departure lounge. She took Moffa's arm and they walked out to her car. He seemed elderly again, almost shuffling along the pavement.

'Why isn't it foggy today?' Moffa said, tilting his face beseechingly to the sky, as if he hoped for a sea mist to roll in so tight the flights would be cancelled.

'They'll come back again. You'll see. And you can talk to them on my iPad. Karen is going to teach her mother how to use the Wi-Fi connection at her house, so you can talk anytime you want, and it won't cost a fortune.'

Moffa shrugged.

'It's not the same as them being here.'

'I could take you over to Norway if you like. Shall we look at flights when we get home?'

'My passport has expired. I need to renew it first.'

'We'll do that too,' Lisa said, as she opened the passenger door for her grandfather and helped him into the car. She got in and started the engine but didn't move for a moment; Moffa was muttering to himself and she recognised a Norwegian profanity. She raised an eyebrow.

'Why was I so stupid? Why didn't I contact her when I first found out?' Why did I wait until I was half dead?' Moffa slapped the dashboard and then bent forward, his shoulders shaking with anger and grief. Lisa put her hand on his arm and stroked it.

'We all do stupid things Moffa. But you've found each other now. It's going to be alright. You're friends again; it could have gone differently, couldn't it?'

Moffa sat up straight and nodded.

'Yes, you're right. She might not have wanted to speak to me before. Karen is lovely

246

isn't she? I wish your mother had met her. Why didn't she want to meet her sister?'

'You know what mam's like.' Lisa said, putting the car into gear and reversing out of the car-park.

Moffa sighed and shut his eyes.

'Thank you, Lisa. You will never know how much you have done for me. You are one beautiful little granddaughter. I love you so much.'

Since Moffa wasn't someone who normally discussed his feelings openly, Lisa was surprised.

'Love you too, Moffa. You're my favourite man in the whole world.'

'I thought your favourite man was a much younger Norwegian. You haven't told me what is going on with you two, but I can see you're in love.'

'To be honest, I don't know what is happening with Joakim and me. I haven't spoken to him much since I got back. He's been busy trying to sort out his business so he can start training for his new career. He was visiting his family in Oslo the last time we spoke.'

As Lisa drove along the road that hugged the perimeter of the airport she glanced across and saw the plane Karen and Lisbet were about to board. She pulled into a small parking area by the beach and stopped the car where they could still see part of the runway. She turned the engine off and pushed her seat back.

A helicopter was parked outside one of the hangars and a maintenance crew were milling around preparing it for flight. Moffa watched them for a moment before turning his attention back to Lisa.

'When are you going to see him again?'

'I don't know. I can't afford to keep flying over there, and he is going to be too busy to come over here often. And anyway, nothing much happened between us.'

'Nothing; not even a kiss?'

'Moffa!' Lisa giggled. The idea of confiding in her grandfather about her love life was a little novel, but in some ways he was the only person who would understand what was going on. 'OK, then. We kissed, and maybe, just maybe, it might have led to something else. But what can I say, other than Hansi!'

'Ah, that boy. An excellent contraceptive, I'm sure.'

Lisa choked with embarrassed laughter, and nodded.

Lisa told Moffa about Joakim's plan to become a ski instructor at a resort outside Bergen. Moffa nodded enthusiastically.

'I couldn't see him as a boat builder. His heart wasn't in it.'

'Exactly, it was his father's dream job, not his. But he now has to get fitter, get a new prosthetic leg, do lots of physio and training, sell up his business, move house. He has a lot on his mind.'

Lisa had only had two emails from Joakim and a couple of phone calls since she had seen him a week ago. They had been disappointingly short and lacking in any affection. Essentially, he had simply brought

Lisa up to date on his plans. Had she had imagined the bond between them?

The flight to Bergen took off a few minutes later and they watched it lift up into the sky above them, initially flying in the wrong direction and then turning in a large circle behind them before disappearing behind the cliffs at Sumburgh Head.

'OK, then, let's go home. I have some things I need to sort out.' Moffa said. He looked wistfully in the direction of Norway, as if he hoped to see a last glimpse of the plane, but the sky was empty apart from wisps of white cloud and a flurry of wings from a trio of oystercatchers flying overhead, screeching at each other.

They drove home in silence and Moffa went straight to his room and shut the door, refusing an offer of tea and a slice of cake.

Lisa tidied up the kitchen, putting the breakfast dishes into the dishwasher and cleaning the table as she waited for the kettle to boil. It had been nice having a houseful of people. For a whole week it had been non-stop talking, laughter, some tears and lots of hugs. Hansi had picked up new words and almost seemed to respond more to Norwegian than he did to English.

She picked up her iPad and checked for emails, but apart from the usual junk mail there wasn't anything. She was crushed. She had spent well over a week with Joakim, getting pretty much as close as it was possible to another person and now it was as if that week had not happened.

She logged onto Facebook. Joakim didn't appear to have been online recently, which was a little comforting. Maybe he genuinely was too busy to catch up. He still hadn't emailed her the photos he had taken on his phone. She wished he would hurry up as perhaps it would make it feel more real. It was nearly five in Norway; she imagined he would surely be finishing work right now. She decided to call him. She clicked on the FaceTime icon beside his name and listened as it bleeped for a minute. Joakim didn't answer and she set the tablet aside and sighed. Despite having owned this lovely piece of technology for a whole week she had not once had a proper conversation with him. He never seemed to be available.

Lisa couldn't explain why she thought the connection between them had been broken. It simply felt odd. She thought back to their last night together. They had sat on the sofa holding hands as they talked. Hansi had been asleep. They had talked into the early hours until it was fully light again and exhaustion had forced them to bed.

They had discussed past loves, their childhood, their families, their thoughts and dreams, music and books. There hadn't been a single gap in the conversation; it had been a tight-knit jumble of sentences and laughter. They had talked over each other, interrupted each other, stopped, apologised and done it again, in their rush to interrogate and find out new things about each other. He had teased her about her fears of not being good enough for anyone; so much so, she had almost fallen off the sofa laughing at the silliness of it. By the end of the night, or the beginning of the morning, she had felt good enough for anyone.

But now?

25

Joakim pulled out his phone and saw Lisa was trying to call him. He switched the phone to silent and shoved it back in his pocket. Astrid would be here in a few minutes and he didn't want to have to explain to Lisa who he was with; or to Astrid for that matter.

He took out his phone again, but before he finished composing a text he saw Astrid sashaying across the room towards him; all eyes from the other clientele in the bar were on her.

She was even more polished and perfect than normal, in a green silk shirt, skinny white jeans and gold high-heeled sandals. Joakim stared at her feet in surprise. Astrid hardly ever wore high heels, as she was always too anxious about twisting her ankle; her legs were worth too much to take the risk. Still, it was mid-summer and it was a long time until the ski season.

He was about to stand up to greet her, but she gestured for him to stay where he was. She bent down to kiss his cheek and trailed a hand through his hair; the familiar gesture of affection caught him off guard.

'You look beautiful,' he said, by way of greeting.

Astrid shrugged, and swivelled in her seat to catch the eye of the barman, who wasted no time in rushing to her side.

She ordered a glass of white wine and another beer for Joakim and after the barman had gone she leaned in towards Joakim and put her hand on his thigh.

'So my darling boy, I hear you're going back to skiing. I knew you couldn't stay away forever. Good for you; fuck your bad leg. You'll still be the fastest thing on the slopes.'

Joakim grinned at her forthrightness. She hadn't changed a bit since he had seen her. Other than the fact she wore a diamond studded wedding band she was the same Astrid he had fallen in love with all those years ago.

'I read about your wedding in the paper. My mother showed me the photos in a magazine.'

'You should have come; you were invited.'

'That would have been strange. I'm not sure I could watch you get married.'

Astrid cocked her head to one side.

'Why, do you still have feelings for me? That would have livened up the service a little if you had declared them; a bit more drama for the newspapers.' Astrid looked around the room as if she was checking to see who was watching them. The barman arrived with their drinks and Astrid sipped her wine and waited until they were alone again. 'Why now? Why have you come alive again now, and not when we were together? I did everything possible to support you, but you rejected me. Now I hear some woman has caught your eye and suddenly you're a new man, getting your shit together. It's not fair, Joakim; really not fair.'

'I'm sorry. It took me a lot longer to come to terms with what happened than I imagined it would. I didn't want you to waste your life sticking around with me, waiting for my recovery.'

'Bullshit. That was for me to decide, not you.'

'You're right. But my head wasn't in a good place.' Joakim picked up his beer and sipped it, his eyes meeting Astrid's. She looked lost for a moment. 'But you're married now. Aren't you happy?'

Astrid shrugged and fiddled with her wedding ring, her red manicured finger tips trembling a little.

'Yes, I'm happy. He's a great man; but. But he's not you. Damn you, Joakim. I would have waited for you.'

'I'm sorry, Astrid.' He held his hand out to her, squeezing it briefly, before letting go. She sat up straight, trying to regroup.

'So tell me about her. Anders told me you met her in Shetland. She's pretty, and a bit younger than you. That's all I know.'

'She's pretty yes. She reminds me of you when you were twenty.'

'Ouch! I'm not that ancient and over the hill.'

'I didn't mean it like that. I meant she still has that girl next door thing going on, she doesn't wear much make-up and doesn't wear designer clothes.'

'Right, well, you know that isn't exactly my choice. But I needed the sponsorship. I wasn't born wealthy, like you.'

'I wasn't criticising you. You're beautiful. Every man watched you walk in here; every woman too. You turn heads. I don't think Lisa would.'

'Lisa, that's her name? I can tell how much you like her by the way you say it.'

Joakim shrugged and picked at the label on the beer bottle.

'It's complicated.'

'I bet it is. Have you and her...?'

'No; not exactly.'

'Why not? For God's sake, you're not still hung up over your leg are you? Jesus, I can tell you now, with or without your injury, you were still the best lover I ever had.'

'Don't say stuff like that, Astrid. You're married now.'

'I'm telling you the truth; what's wrong with that?'

'Anyway, she has a little boy. We never had the opportunity.'

'She's not a gold-digger is she?'

'Not at all! She had no idea who I was when we met.'

'So are you going to see her again?'

'I hope so. But Shetland is hard to get to.'

'What does she do?'

'She's about to do a PhD; she's just finished a Masters in archaeology. She's researching the Shetland Bus, as her grandfather was involved in it. He's Norwegian.'

Astrid nodded. 'An intellectual girl, that's new for you? Would that work long term?'

Joakim bristled at the veiled insult, but chose to ignore it. What did it matter what Astrid thought of the situation? Astrid sighed, put down her glass and put her hand on his arm. 'I'm sorry, that was mean of me. Ignore me; I'm jealous. She's going to end up with what I wanted. I hope she appreciates you.'

'Astrid, could we change the subject? I asked to meet you because I wanted to talk about getting back into training, not to talk about my feelings for you, or anyone else.'

Astrid raised her hands in defeat.

'I'm excited by this news. I met a young woman at the Paralympics in Vancouver – we stayed on to support them - and she has real potential. She came in sixth place. But you know what, with some proper coaching she could go for gold. She was only sixteen at the time, so lots of time ahead of her to progress. She's from Bergen and I would love to help her get some coaching with you.'

'What's her disability?'

'She's blind in one eye and almost profoundly deaf; she was involved in an accident. But she's a natural born athlete and is learning to compensate for her eyesight problems.'

Joakim leaned back and smiled.

'It feels more real when you talk about the people I might work with. Until now it has been kind of abstract. I've been thinking about myself too much, what it would be like to get back on the slopes, without thinking about helping people.'

'You'll be so good at this. You always supported others. Remember the training camp we managed, at Holmenkollen? Those kids adored you. You had them doing things they never thought possible. You inspire confidence, Joakim. Remember that; you are perfect for this job.'

They spent another hour or so in the bar talking about skiing and the friends they still had in common.

'I have to go; I'm meeting Bendt for dinner soon. It was good to see you Joakim.'

'It was good to see you too. Let me walk you out. I'm going to see some friends later. It's not often I get to Oslo these days. It's nice to catch up with my old life.'

'Your new life again; welcome back.'

They left the bar and once again, Astrid drew attention. They walked arm in arm to the end of the road and then stopped.

Astrid slipped her arms around his waist and pulled him close. She tilted her head back waiting for him to kiss her. Joakim hesitated, it didn't seem appropriate, and yet it was such a familiar gesture. How many times had they kissed before? Would one more time hurt?

Her lips parted as he kissed her. He felt a rush of adrenaline. It had been a long time since he had kissed her like this. The last time he had been a lost soul, lacking all of his previous body-confidence; now that had returned a little, just as she had described earlier. He was alive again. It felt good, and so did the kiss. He opened his eyes at the sound of a motorbike passing them. He thought he saw a flash of light but when he turned there was nothing there; just the setting sun flashing on a wing mirror of a car.

'Take care and let me know how you get on. We'll always be friends OK. We've been through so much,' Astrid said, before she hurried away.

As Joakim strolled back to the taxi rank he thought about his meeting with Astrid. He wondered whether it would have worked with her after all. She clearly cared about him, and she still had the ability to get under his skin. He brushed the back of his hand across his lips and noticed her lipstick had left its mark on him. He reached into his pocket and found a tissue and removed the rest of the evidence.

As he climbed into the taxi to go and meet his friends he remembered Lisa and rummaged in his pocket for his phone. There were no messages from her, and without Wi-Fi he couldn't call her on FaceTime. He decided he would call her later, or maybe tomorrow. It might be too late tonight.

Lisa sat on the sofa, half watching the news with Moffa, who was decidedly more morose now Lisbet and Karen had gone home. He didn't pass his normal commentary on the state of the world and seemed deep in thought instead.

Lisa picked up her iPad and checked for emails or messages from Joakim. Still nothing. She was bored and restless. Hansi was in bed and she had nothing to entertain her this evening. She logged into Google and typed in Joakim's name, curious to know what else had been written about him. She hadn't had the chance to read much about him before now.

She regretted it immediately. There were countless images of him with Astrid Bergstrom, or pictures of him winning medals. There were stories of him and the incident that had cost him his leg. It was clear he had been considered some kind of national hero. She scrutinised the photos of Astrid then googled her instead, fascinated by the woman who had won his heart.

Impossibly glossy platinum hair dominated every photo. Astrid was stunning and was a natural in front of the camera, whether it was at a sporting event, a charity dinner, or in one photo, doing voluntary work in Africa. Even in combat trousers and a vest top Astrid looked like a supermodel.

The photos of Astrid's wedding gave Lisa some comfort. Astrid was clearly happy with her husband, Bendt. He was also a handsome man, although Lisa didn't think he had the same appeal as Joakim.

She was about to abandon her internet stalking when she saw a photo and headline appear in the newsfeed of the Norwegian newspaper she was looking at; Joakim and Astrid kissing on a pavement with the headline *Sammen Igjen*? Together Again? Lisa clicked on the link and read the articles with the help of Google Translate. The picture had been taken earlier that evening and the story implied they had shared a passionate lover's kiss after an evening spent in a bar in Oslo.

Lisa stared at the photograph, quickly enlarging it on the screen, her heart pounding.

There was no mistaking the fact Joakim and Astrid were in love. They didn't seem to be aware of anything going on around them in the street. Their arms were around each other as if neither of them wanted to let go. No wonder he had hardly been in contact since she left Norway.

Lisa switched off her iPad and flung it on the seat beside her. Moffa was staring at the TV but not watching it. She knew where his head was; back in Norway with his first love. Lisa left the room without saying goodnight. She couldn't speak, and she doubted Moffa would notice.

Lisa was nobody's first love. Nobody was beating a path to her door to get back together, to acknowledge how important she had been to them. Neil had walked away without a backwards glance. She was mortified she had allowed herself to fall a little bit in love with Joakim. He was not the man she thought he was at all. Thank God she hadn't slept with him.

The next day, Lisa woke exhausted. She had barely slept; endlessly replaying the way Joakim had kissed her and measuring it up against the image in the news of him kissing Astrid. If the paparazzi had been remotely interested in taking a picture of her with Joakim, she would have looked like his twelve year old niece in most of them. She felt disgusted with herself.

She got up when Hansi demanded attention and when she returned from the nursery she checked her emails. She was pleasantly surprised to find she had been invited for interview for the job at Scottish Natural Heritage. She had forgotten all about the application she had submitted.

'Hey, Moffa, I've got an interview for a proper grown up job,' she said, as he shuffled into the kitchen for a late breakfast.

'That's good, kjaere. But what happened to the idea of doing your PhD?'

'What's the point? Where will it take me?'

'Wherever you wanted it too, surely? Don't you want to travel, to broaden your horizons? You don't have to stay in Shetland, do you? You could get a job in a university anywhere in the world with a PhD.'

'Why would I want to leave Shetland?' Lisa said, scowling, conscious she had betrayed bitterness in her voice.

Moffa was sitting down at the kitchen table about to eat his scrambled eggs on toast. 'What's happened? Something's not right with you.'

Lisa shrugged. 'Nothing's happened, to me at least. But I think Joakim is having some kind of affair with his ex-girlfriend. There was a picture of them online, taken last night.'

'Oh, I see.' Moffa frowned and pushed his breakfast away untouched. 'I didn't think he was like that, I'm sorry.'

'Me neither, but it's not as if anything happened between us. He doesn't owe me anything. And you know how hard it is to let go of your first sweetheart.'

Moffa shook his head. 'Different circumstances; Lisbet and I would never have met up if either of our partners were still living.'

'Well anyway. He helped me find Lisbet and Karen so it doesn't matter does it? I'm going to concentrate on getting this job and getting my life back on track. And I still want to write a book about you. So now I know all about your disgraceful past and you have no more secrets to hide, perhaps we can sit down and you can tell me all about it.' Lisa grinned at her grandfather, who laughed in agreement.

'My disgraceful past, indeed! Yes Lisa, we will sit down and record this story. Karen wants to hear about it too, so she can tell her children about me. Let's do this.'

Later that morning while Lisa was recording an interview with Moffa, Joakim tried to call her. She ignored it and returned to the story of Moffa's initial encounter with the Shetland Bus. She was gripped by the tale now, and didn't feel any remorse about Joakim at the time.

Lisa was leaving the house to pick up Hansi from the nursery when Moffa's solicitor arrived. Lisa showed him into the house and then drove off. She stopped off at the supermarket to buy groceries and then picked up Hansi. She met a friend outside the nursery who was picking up her daughter. They agreed to meet up for coffee the following afternoon to catch up properly. Lisa drove home feeling a little more cheerful. It had been a productive day so far.

When she got home she found Moffa still deep in conversation with Mr Jamieson, his solicitor.

'This is my granddaughter Lisa; she's writing a book about me,' Moffa said proudly, as the man got up to leave.

'Nice to meet you Lisa, your grandfather is one of my favourite clients. I don't normally do house calls, but it's always interesting talking to him.'

As Lisa put away the groceries, with a little help from Hansi who decided to tear holes in the bag of potatoes and roll them around the floor, Moffa sat and watched her.

'I have rewritten my will. That's what Mr Jamieson was here for.'

'I guessed that, Moffa. But please hang around for as long as you can. I'm kind of fond of you.'

'Don't worry; I've no intention of going anywhere, other than Norway. Mr Jamieson countersigned my passport application. I got some photos taken last week when Lisbet was with me. She wants me to come home soon.'

'Just for a holiday, right?'

'Of course. I would like to stay for a little while though. You don't mind do you? It's just that I think it will be my last big trip and I may as well make the most of it. I have more grandchildren to meet and I'm ready to go home now. I never thought I would say that.'

Lisa hugged him and kissed the top of his head as he sat with a big smile on his face.

'I'm happy for you Moffa, but have you spoken to Mam about this? I think you need to. I know it was upsetting when she didn't come to see Karen, but you know why that was, don't you?'

Moffa shook his head.

'Oh, I thought Karen might have told you by now.' Lisa sighed, and pulled out a chair and sat down. 'Karen came over to find you twenty years ago when Grandma was still alive. Grandma was upset to meet Karen, and Mam was annoyed with you for not telling us about them. It was two days before Grandma died. Karen left a letter for you. I think that is why Mam has been so off with you. She thinks that's why Grandma died so suddenly.'

Moffa sighed and shook his head. He stood up without saying anything else and went to the lounge and picked up the phone.

Lisa stayed in the kitchen with Hansi while she cooked dinner. She heard a raised voice from time to time. She heard the phone slam down on its cradle so she hurried in to see if he was alright.

'Why didn't you tell me before?'

'I only found out when I met Karen. She came to our hotel and told us to stay away from her mother. She was pretty upset, but we managed to persuade her you had never known about her visit to Shetland. I forgot about it until now, sorry. How is Mam?'

'She's not speaking to me. She thinks I betrayed your grandmother.'

'How could you have betrayed her, you had no idea about Lisbet and the baby when you met Gran; did you?'

'Not a clue; I would have gone straight back to Norway. You have no idea how lucky your generation is having such easy access to keeping in touch with people. This wouldn't have happened if we had had Facebook or email.'

'I don't know Moffa, Facebook hasn't stopped Neil staying away in Australia. I never hear from him do I?'

Moffa didn't reply. He leaned back in the arm chair and shut his eyes.

Lisa parked her car outside the Scottish Natural Heritage office and then checked her hair in the mirror. She got out of the car smoothing down her borrowed suit. The navy blue skirt was a size too big and the jacket a fraction too small so she hadn't buttoned it over her white shirt. Lisa was ill at ease in the formal outfit. She had tied her hair into a ponytail but as she caught sight of her reflection in the window of the office she looked like a school girl in a badly fitting uniform.

The office was curiously dark, relying on the natural light from the windows, rather than the overhead fluorescent lights. As Lisa adjusted to the gloom she noticed the view of the harbour and the sea. It was a view she could get used to working with on a daily basis. Her spirits lifted as she was shown into a meeting room.

Less than an hour later Lisa drove home feeling certain she hadn't got the job, and not feeling sure whether to be disappointed or not. Despite the pleasant location, the interesting and worthwhile work and the nice colleagues she might work with, she realised she wasn't cut out for an office job. Everything about it was alien.

She took off the jacket before she had reached her room and slung it on the bed in disgust. She never wanted the kind of job where she needed to dress like that for an interview. It wasn't her at all. She wanted to do something creative, or adventurous, or a combination of both. She thought about her earliest ambition to become a field archaeologist; that wasn't on the cards anymore, not with a small child to care for. Most archaeologists had to travel extensively for their work; the money was appalling, and now she had tried it out as part of her degree course she knew it was also backbreaking.

She changed back into her jeans and hung up the suit ready to take it back to her friend. Then she checked her emails. There was nothing from Joakim this time. He had finally given up on her. A month had passed since she had seen the paparazzi photos of him online. She had read more speculation about Joakim and Astrid, although they did not appear to have been seen together since. Joakim, naturally, had denied anything had happened between them.

'It didn't mean anything', he had said.

'How do you translate "cliché" in Norwegian?' Lisa had replied.

'How do you translate "trust" between friends? In any language?' Joakim replied by text, after Lisa had hung up on him.

He had tried to call a few times, but Lisa had refused to speak to him. She wasn't going to fall for that *we're just good friends* malarkey. There was far too much at stake to get involved with a man who was still hung up on his ex. It would have been hard enough simply to contemplate a relationship with someone who lived on the other side of the North Sea.

But when the emails and texts dried up she did not feel relieved; just lost.

26

Joakim had started his training sessions in the gym with a heavier heart than he had expected when he signed up for his new career. However, within a couple of weeks his energy and stamina had improved, along with his mood. New prosthetics were on order and he was confident a few more weeks in the gym and a season on the slopes would see him back to good form again. He was surprised at how excited he was to be returning to skiing, and not at all surprised at how easy it was to give up his business. His father had agreed it would be a good idea to sell the business to Joakim's colleague, who in all honesty had been much better at the job.

Joakim's new job came with a fully furnished ski-lodge so he decided to sell his apartment in Larvik along with the boatyard. He took a long weekend off from training to drive over to his new home and then drove into Bergen to stay with Anita and Lars.

He sat in the park with Anita while Freya played with one of her friends in the playground.

'Can you blame her? I saw the photos too, and I thought you'd got back together.

There's an expression – the camera never lies – and really, you two looked like you were still in love,' Anita said, as she passed Joakim a sandwich.

'But that's just it; we were in love, past tense. I still care about Astrid, and I know she cares about me. But we're not together anymore and never will be. I don't understand why Lisa won't listen to me.'

'OK, but maybe if Lisa was your sister and the new man she had fallen for had been seen in a similar photo with another woman, what would you say to her?'

Joakim shook his head. 'I don't know, but I expect I would want to hear a full explanation from him. And so far I haven't been able to give my side of the story.'

'Do you care for her that much? I mean, you only spent about a few days together.'

'She's different. I never expected to fall for her; and in some ways I wonder if it's because she reminds me of Astrid when we were much younger. She's pretty, but she doesn't know it. She's clever but she doesn't show off, and she is genuinely caring about people, but without being patronising. She literally doesn't care about my amputation. She didn't pull a face when she saw my leg, she doesn't fuss around me or treat me like I'm about to fall apart. When she looks at me, she sees *me*. As I am now, not who I was in the past, or who she hopes I might be in the future. Does that make sense?'

'Yes it does, and you'd be a fool to give up on her. Maybe she needs a little time. Have you tried writing to her?'

'Email, text, Facebook messenger; I've tried everything.'

'How about a handwritten letter straight from the heart? There's something cold about new technology.'

Joakim nodded. He reached for a bottle of water, and remembered the catalyst for his first meeting with Lisa; a handwritten message in a bottle.

'I'll give it a try. I want to see her again; I need to know whether it's the real thing or not. Perhaps it wasn't meant to be; maybe I am the wrong Joakim Haaland.'

He laughed when Anita wrinkled her forehead and then told her the story about how Lisa had found the message in the bottle from someone else called Joakim Haaland.

'No, you are the right Joakim. By the way, I heard from Lisa this morning. She is busy writing a book about her grandfather. She wanted my advice on finding an agent for it. I've agreed to look at the manuscript when it's finished and see if I can help. I think there would be a market for the story, don't you?'

'You heard from her? What else did she say?'

'Nothing about you I'm afraid. But she did mention her grandfather was coming over to Norway in a few weeks to visit Lisbet and Karen. I wonder if she will come with him, she didn't say though. Shall I ask?'

'Yes please. I could meet them.'

'I would like to see Lisa again, and meet her grandfather. They could always come and stay here for the night if they wanted to break up the journey. I'll invite them, shall I?'

Joakim drove home the next day, composing a letter to Lisa in his head, but he couldn't find the right words to describe either what had happened between him and Astrid, or how he felt about Lisa. When he got home he rang Astrid.

'Hey, what's up? How's the training going?' Astrid trilled, in a way that indicated she was not alone. He heard music in the background which faded as Astrid appeared to leave the room and go somewhere quieter.

'How's Bendt now? Is he still angry with you?'

'No, don't be silly. He knows it was nothing. Anyway, I have some news. I haven't told anyone else yet, other than Bendt, but I'm pregnant, about eight weeks.'

'That's great news. Congratulations. But, wait; you'll miss the Nationals!'

'Of course, but I already have enough gold medals; a baby would be a much better achievement don't you think?'

'Yes it would. Well done Astrid, I'm delighted for you. You'll be the perfect mother.'

'Thank you. And I'm sorry about kissing you. I was feeling nostalgic and it was confusing seeing you again when you seemed like your old self. I couldn't resist it, but it was crazy, and I should never have done that, to you or to Bendt.'

'I'm sorry too. You remember I told you about Lisa? Well she saw the picture online and thinks we are having an affair. She won't speak to me now.'

'Oh, Joakim, I'm so sorry. Do you want me to speak to her?'

'That's not a good idea.'

'Why not? Do you think she won't believe it when I say I'm not in love with you anymore? Are you so vain?'

Joakim laughed.

27

Lisa had finished typing up her notes from the day's interview with Moffa. They had spent every day for more than three weeks talking about his war experience. At first he had taken his time over it, censoring himself as he spoke, reluctant to share all the details, but over time he had relaxed and divulged much more personal stuff. Lisa was becoming more and more excited by the story that was unfolding. For all she had read about the Shetland Bus and seen the exhibits in the museum, it was nothing compared to hearing the story from Moffa. The moments of fear, devastation, and exhaustion were mixed with elation and triumph, when a mission had gone to plan.

Moffa was excited about his forthcoming trip to Norway. His flights were booked; he had been to his GP and come back with a remarkably clean bill of health, and a supply of medication to keep him healthy during his holiday. Moffa seemed to be getting younger by the minute. It was as if by telling his story he was letting go of a heavy burden. He said that he had started dreaming in Norwegian again, after decades of thinking and speaking English.

Lisa closed the document and logged onto Facebook with the intention of contacting Jenna to arrange to meet for lunch on Saturday. She noticed there was a new message waiting for her and clicked on the icon.

The message was from Astrid Bergstrom. Lisa blinked in surprise at the name and immediately opened the message.

Dear Lisa, I found your name via Joakim's Facebook, I hope you don't mind me contacting you. He rang me today to say you were not speaking to him any more as a result of the photo you saw in the news. I'm sorry to hear that. He told me all about you the evening that photo was taken and I was pleased to see how happy he was. He was the happiest I had seen him since before he was injured, and it wasn't just because he had decided to go back to skiing.

Lisa, let me tell you, that kiss didn't mean anything to Joakim. And I could tell; I was the one kissing him. It was my fault. I saw him that evening as a friend, and I was a little bit jealous to hear he had met someone else. He was glowing with happiness, and I felt sad for what might have been; but only for about five minutes, and certainly not after I kissed him goodbye and realised the chemistry was gone. If we had meant to be together then nothing would have kept us apart, but that wasn't how it happened. But the truth is I'm very happy with my husband, so everything worked out as it should have. In fact, I'm now pregnant (but please keep that a secret as it's early days).

I wish you would give Joakim a chance to explain. I know what it looked like. My husband was cross with me too, but not for long, as he knows he is my true love.

Joakim is one of the good guys. Trust me – and more importantly, trust him.

Call him.

Kind regards, Astrid x

PS. Joakim doesn't know I sent this, so it is up to you whether you tell him, but my advice is not to. Let him think it was your idea.

Lisa read the message again, before replying.

Dear Astrid

Thank you for writing to me. I didn't know what to think when I saw the photos of you together. Joakim did try to explain, but I didn't listen to him. I guess my experience with men has made me expect things like that to happen, but I should know better than to treat everyone the same. Joakim spoke about you with such obvious fondness; it was hard not to think he wasn't still in love with you.

Thank you for your honesty. I will contact him again, although as he is so far away, I'm not sure whether we stand a chance of having a proper relationship, but I would hate to lose him as a friend.

Lisa x

PS. Good luck with the baby. Motherhood is brilliant – hard work, but so much fun too.

Lisa went downstairs to make herself a cup of tea while she thought about how to respond to this development. She contemplated ringing Joakim, but felt stupid. He might not be as pleased to hear from her as Astrid believed. It had been weeks since they had spoken now; so long in fact she even wondered if she had imagined how close they had been.

'Are you making tea? I would love some too,' Moffa said, making Lisa jump.

He sat down at the kitchen table, and reached for the biscuit jar and took out a chocolate wafer biscuit, humming while he unwrapped it.

'You seem happy,' Lisa said, as she stirred the teabag in the pot.

'This time in two weeks I will be in Norway. I will see the sun shining down on the fjords, I will gaze up at the mountains of my homeland, and I will be with my family again. Change your mind, why don't you? Come with me.'

'I just might. Do you think that would be OK?'

Lisa smiled as she passed Moffa a mug and then helped herself to a biscuit.

'Has something happened? You're grinning like a mad thing; have you heard from Joakim?'

'No, but I heard from the woman he used to be engaged to. She is happily married and having a baby. She kissed him goodbye, that's all. She said I should trust him.'

'I knew he was a good man. Are you going to call him?'

'Yes I will. I might do it tomorrow though, since it is a bit late in Norway now.'

'Nonsense, it will only be a little after ten. I just spoke to Lisbet and she told me it's a lovely evening over there. She was sitting in the garden as she spoke to me. I could hear the birds.'

'OK, let me finish my tea and I'll ring him.'

'Good girl, then you can book your flights to come back with me. I think it was a good thing you didn't get that job. Now you have time to come on holiday with me; time enough to worry about a job later.'

Lisa pulled a face. It still stung a little that she hadn't got the job, even though she hadn't wanted it.

Lisa sat on the end of her bed and brushed her hair and put on some lip-gloss, before sending Joakim a text.

Can you talk? I'm sorry I was so mad at you before. I miss you. Call me anytime x

Lisa sat up in bed reading for a couple of hours, her iPad and mobile phone close to hand in case Joakim called, but eventually she gave up and switched off the light, wondering if she had been too late with her apology.

Joakim heard his phone bleep while he was driving back home to Larvik from Bergen. He still had some packing to do and had decided to drive back to his old apartment to pick up more of his possessions. The phone was in his bag on the back seat of the car so he left it where it was and carried on. He got home long after midnight and went straight to bed, without remembering to look at his phone.

The next morning Joakim saw the message. It was too early to call Lisa and the phone was nearly out of power so he plugged it in to charge while he made breakfast. He went outside and sat on the deck. He would miss this view. In a few weeks he would be moving out for good. He had a warm sense of optimism about his new life, and now Lisa had tried to contact him he felt better still.

His phone rang from the kitchen and he hurried inside to answer it, hoping it might be Lisa. It was Henrik, his new manager, inviting him to come and meet a potential investor; a wealthy philanthropist who was keen to meet the new superstar coach.

Joakim agreed to leave straight away, although he didn't feel up to a long drive. He hadn't expected to drive back to Bergen for another few days. He decided to fly instead and managed to sort out a flight leaving in three hours. He had enough just time to pack and get to the airport. He would ring Lisa later.

28

On Saturday morning Lisa got Hansi dressed and ready to go and meet Jenna. She was disappointed Joakim hadn't called her back, but confident it was because he was busy. She left her iPad at home, but took her mobile with her and decided not to let herself get too paranoid about Joakim's lack of immediate response.

'I'll be home in time to make you dinner later, but there's some soup left over from yesterday if you want to heat it up for lunch,' Lisa said to Moffa. 'I'm going to see Jenna. So if Joakim rings...'

'OK, I'll tell him you'll be home later. I'm going to call Lisbet soon, and I think I can manage to make my own lunch. I'm a war hero you know, not some feeble old man.'

Lisa laughed and hugged Moffa.

'Say hello to Lisbet for me. See you later.'

A few hours later Lisa returned home with Hansi, after having a lovely time sitting in Jenna's back garden, catching up with her news, while Hansi was entertained by Jenna's little brother and a new puppy.

Lisa unstrapped Hansi from his seat and then reached into the car for a bag of groceries. She carried the bag as she led Hansi up the steps to the house. Hansi ran in search of Moffa while Lisa took the shopping into the kitchen.

Lisa noticed Moffa had left his soup bowl on the table, which was unlike him as he normally tidied up after a meal. She smiled; he was clearly distracted by his forthcoming holiday. Lisa put the bowl in the sink and ran the tap to wash it. While the sink filled she put the groceries away and thought about what to cook for dinner.

As she turned off the tap she realised she couldn't hear Hansi or Moffa. She wondered whether Moffa had gone next door so she hurried to find Hansi, in case he was getting up to mischief.

There was nobody in the lounge and the stair-gate to the upstairs was still securely fastened. Lisa pushed open the bathroom door and found it empty which only left Moffa's bedroom. She tapped on the door but there was no reply. She heard a muffled whimper from Hansi so she put her head around the door and then shoved it opened, slamming it against the wall when she saw Moffa crumpled in a heap on the floor. Hansi was on his knees leaning against Moffa, patting his face, trying to get his attention. Moffa's eyes were open but there was no life behind them. Lisa fell to her knees beside her grandfather feeling his neck for a pulse but not finding one. His skin was icy cold and she knew it was far too late for any first aid treatment. She called for an ambulance, not sure if that was the right thing to do or not. However, the reassuring voice at the emergency call centre said an ambulance would arrive shortly.

Lisa picked up Hansi and carried him into the kitchen and strapped him into his highchair out of the way. She gave him a beaker of milk which he flung on the floor. He wasn't crying, so Lisa left him to go to her grandfather again.

'Moffa, Moffa, what happened to you?' Lisa said, sitting on the floor beside him, stroking his hair. She was conscious of the fact the shock had not hit her yet and realised she had some phone calls to make while she could still speak.

She rang her mother, who took the news silently at first, and then with a barely audible voice said she would meet them at the hospital. Then Lisa rang Karen.

'Hello Karen, it's Lisa.'

'Lisa? How are you? I hear you are coming to see us now. I'm so happy.'

'Um, Karen, I have some bad news. My grandfather has just died. I'm sitting here with him waiting for the ambulance, but I'm pretty sure it's too late to save him. I'm so sorry.'

'He's dead? *Oh min himmelen, hva skjedde?*'

'I don't know yet. He was lying on the bedroom floor when I got home. I think it happened quickly.'

'Are you OK? Is someone with you?'

'Just Hansi, but my mother is going to meet me at the hospital. It's such a shock. He's been so energetic and happy for the last few weeks. Honestly, it's like he had found his youth again.'

'The same for my mother! Oh dear, this is going to break her heart. I had better drive over and tell her. I will ring you later. You take care now.'

Lisa wondered whether to call Joakim, but he hadn't replied to her text message yet. She was desperate to hear his voice but then she heard the sound of a vehicle pulling up outside the house and went out to meet the paramedics.

'He's through here,' Lisa said, as they entered the house. She led them into the bedroom and went to get Hansi who had started to howl in the kitchen. She cuddled him as she watched the paramedics, shielding Hansi's eyes from Moffa. They had already concluded there wasn't anything that could be done, but they still went through their procedure of checking for viable signs of life.'

'Are you alright, love?'

'Yeah, I'll be fine, thanks. I've been out all afternoon and only got home a few minutes ago. I wish I had stayed home now. But you know, the last few weeks he has been so well. He was supposed to go on holiday to Norway soon.'

'We'll take him to hospital where a doctor will have to examine him. You're welcome to come with us, although you might want to think about leaving your little boy with someone.'

'I'll take my car; my mother is going to meet us at the hospital.'

'Are you sure? Are you alright to drive?'

Her resolve waivered. 'Um, I'm not sure. Let me see if my neighbour is home.'

Lisa carried Hansi outside and looked across to Margaret's house. She saw Margaret hovering at the kitchen window, already alerted by the presence of an ambulance that something had happened. Before Lisa reached the front door her neighbour had opened it.

'Is Edvard OK?'

Lisa shook her head, unable to speak.

'Oh, you poor lamb. Here, let me take Hansi. You go with your grandfather. I'll keep Hansi here with us until you get back.'

Margaret took Hansi from Lisa, and then put her hand on her shoulder.

'Chin up darling, you can do this. Your grandfather was proud of you; you know that, don't you?'

Lisa nodded and turned on her heels, too distraught to even say goodbye to her son.

The ambulance men had transferred Moffa onto a collapsible trolley and were preparing to move him to the ambulance. Lisa looked around Moffa's room. The bed had been made and the room was tidy, with no sign that anything tragic had occurred in the room. It was so unreal. She watched as one of the men pulled a cover over Moffa's face. Her legs buckled and she stumbled into the wall. One of the paramedics put his arm around her and caught her before she fell.

'It's a nasty shock isn't it?'

Lisa nodded, shivering violently.

'It might be a good idea to put a jacket on.'

Lisa picked up her Fair Isle cardigan from the back of the kitchen chair, and put it on as she followed them to the ambulance.

She climbed into the back and sat down while the men secured the trolley in place. The driver slammed the door and they set off at a steady pace.

'He had just fallen in love again. He was so happy.'

'In love? Well good for him. That's the way to go eh?'

Lisa looked at the paramedic and smiled.

'Yes, I think you're right.'

When they arrived at the hospital, Ingrid was waiting in her car. She got out and walked across the car-park towards them. Ingrid's face was set in a determined grimace, as if she was trying to hold back a furious rage rather than grief.

Moffa was wheeled into a private room and a nurse bustled out of the reception area to meet them. She folded back the sheet to take a quick look at Moffa.

'A doctor will be along shortly; have a seat,' she said, as she left them alone.

Ingrid went over to her father's body. She tentatively touched his shoulder, but retreated immediately. She sat down heavily on one of the plastic chairs and leaned her head back and stared up at the ceiling.

'Where were you? Why weren't you with him?'

'I went to see Jenna. He was perfectly fine this morning.'

'What do you mean he was perfectly fine, he clearly wasn't fine was he?'

'He only saw his GP last week who said he was fine enough to travel to Norway in a couple of weeks. Nobody could have predicted this.'

'Go to Norway? Why was he going over there? Oh, I get it! How stupid of me? He was going to see his bit of stuff. They got their claws into him pretty damn quick didn't they?'

Lisa was well aware her mother's anger had been stirred up more by distress than anything else, but she didn't want to engage with her about Lisbet and Karen.

'When did you speak to him last?' Lisa asked, trying to change the subject.

'Two weeks ago, and that was only because he rang me to say he was changing his will. So thanks, Lisa, I will have to sell the house to give Karen half, and you'll be homeless. I bet you didn't think of that when you were trying to track down his relatives.'

'I would have been homeless even if he had left the house to you. You made that perfectly clear.'

Lisa arrived home three hours later, having accepted a lift from Jenna who came into the house with her. Margaret was sitting in the lounge with Hansi on her lap.

'I had to bring him over here. He wouldn't settle in my house. He keeps asking for his Pop Pop; poor little lamb.'

'Thanks, Margaret. He's too young to understand what is going on isn't he?'

'He had a little bit of tattie soup for his tea and some bannocks, but he didn't eat much.'

Lisa picked up Hansi who nestled into her neck and wrapped his arms around her.

He didn't cry but it was obvious he was still distressed.

'How's your mother?'

Lisa pulled a face. 'She's pretty upset, but kind of hard to talk to at the moment. She told me I should organise the funeral as she didn't want to speak to anyone for a few days.'

'It hits people hard sometimes. Losing a parent is awful. Be patient with her.'

Margaret left them after explaining she had left a pot of soup on the hob for Lisa and a tray of scones for them.

'Are you really going to organise the funeral yourself?' Jenna asked.

Lisa shrugged. 'I suppose I'd better. I'm pretty sure Moffa would have left some instructions about it though. I'll ring his lawyer tomorrow. There's no way I have enough money to pay for it. But I'm sure he would have sorted something out. I always changed the subject when he tried talking about stuff like that. Now I wish I had listened; but I never expected to have to deal with it. And not so soon.'

'You'll manage. Shame you'll have to move again though. This house is lovely. I can remember coming round here when we were little, and your gran used to let us make cakes; what a mess we used to get into.'

'Oh yeah; this has been one very happy house. I shall miss it. Hopefully I'll be able to get another housing association place again. I hate to say it, but maybe my mother was right; maybe I shouldn't have been in such a hurry to give up my little house to come here.'

'Don't be daft. You've had such a great time with your grandfather. You wouldn't have missed this for the world. I was feeling jealous this afternoon when you were telling me about the book you're writing about him.'

'It won't be the same writing it now though.' Lisa groaned. Hansi opened his eyes from where he had been dozing on the sofa. He glared accusingly at Jenna who was sitting in Moffa's chair and then he turned his back on them both and shut his eyes.

'I should put him to bed.'

'I bet he won't go to sleep on his own. Why don't you let him be for a while? Shall I go and heat up the soup?'

'Sure, why not.'

While Jenna was in the kitchen, Lisa checked her phone in the hope there might have been a text or a phone call from Joakim, but nobody had called her. She was still pondering the lack of response from him when the house phone rang. She picked it up quickly, before it disturbed Hansi.

'Lisa, how are you? Any news about what happened to Edvard?'

'I've just got back from the hospital, Karen; the doctor's initial feeling is he had another stroke. I'll get the death certificate tomorrow and then I can start to organise his funeral. Will you be coming over?'

'Of course, although I don't think my mother will be coming with me. She didn't take the news well, and who can blame her. It's so sad we have only just got to know him and he is taken away from us. I feel like screaming, don't you?'

'Yes, but if it's any consolation, I have never seen him as happy as he was in the last few weeks. It made me realise what he must have been like when he was younger. He has been talking about her so much over the last few days, telling me how they met.'

'Have you spoken to Joakim? Edvard told me you have fallen out. That's such a shame; he was a lovely young man. We owe him such a lot. I was thinking that today. If he hadn't come along when he did we might not have met Edvard at all.'

'I have tried to contact him but he hasn't replied.'

'Oh dear. Anyway, I was ringing to see if there was anything we could do to help with the funeral. Do you want me to contact someone in the Shetland Bus veterans' organisation over here, or the Norwegian press? They will want to know. I expect our government will want to send someone to the funeral. I believe Queen Sonja went to the last funeral of a Shetland Bus man.'

'Oh crumbs. I was going to call his lawyer tomorrow to see if he had written anything down about his wishes. Shall I call you back afterwards?'

'Yes, please do. I was going to bring my daughter Cecilie with me, would you mind if we came to stay with you? She wanted to meet you. I know it's not a great time to meet someone but...'

'Of course, you can both stay here. I will try and organise it for Friday that might make it easier to plan flights.'

'Bless you. Speak to you tomorrow.'

Lisa put the phone down as Jenna came back with two bowls of soup and a plate of ham sandwiches.

'That was my aunt. She's coming over for the funeral with my cousin Cecilie.'

'How old is your cousin?'

'I think she's in her late thirties, not sure. She's a journalist in Oslo. My aunt thinks some Norwegian dignitaries might want to come to the funeral, maybe even Queen Sonja.'

'She's right. The Queen comes over fairly often. She was in the Scalloway Museum the other day, checking out the Shetland Bus exhibition. She arrived unannounced and paid her entrance fee and wandered around with a group of pensioners who had no idea they were in the company of royalty.'

'Maybe I should write a press release for the papers. He was a bit of a war hero; I guess people will be interested in him.'

'You should write a proper obituary with a photo of him; it's not as if you don't have enough material now. You have spent the last month writing down his life story. You owe it to him to tell the story yourself and not some random journalist from the paper who never even met him.'

'You're right. I'll do that tomorrow.'

'Has Joakim called you back yet?'

'No. I don't think he will now, do you? It's been twenty four hours since I sent the text.'

'His loss,' Jenna said, blowing on her soup before tasting it.

29

Joakim opened the door to his new home and put down his bag. It had been a long day. He had flown to Bergen, met the businessman, who had been a bit of an idiot, but had money to invest so Joakim had bitten his tongue and said all the right things. Now he was exhausted and he would not be flying back home again until Monday. The lodge was unbearably stuffy in the August heat and Joakim opened all the windows to let in some fresh air. Then he stepped outside. The evening air hummed with insects and birds.

Joakim had only realised when he went through airport security that he had left his phone charging in the kitchen. Now, when he finally had the time to speak to Lisa he couldn't, as he didn't know her number. However, he might possibly be able to contact her via Facebook if he could use a computer.

He walked over to the hotel building and asked if he could use a computer. The receptionist pointed to an empty office.

Joakim tried to log on to Facebook but a message popped up saying the site was blocked. The receptionist explained the manager had blocked access to social networking sites in the offices so staff couldn't use them while working.

Joakim went back to his lodge and lay down on the bed feeling defeated. He hoped Lisa would still want to hear from him on Monday when he returned home.

Lisa sat in bed typing on her laptop. It was three in the morning and she was wide awake. Hansi was curled up fast asleep next to her and thankfully undisturbed by the backlight of the screen. Lisa blinked back hot tears as she wrote her grandfather's obituary. She wanted to email it to the newspaper first thing in the morning. She was well aware this was an exercise in distraction, both from the shock of losing Moffa and from the disappointment in not hearing from Joakim. Of all her friends Joakim would be the most understanding of her absolute frustration and despair that Moffa would not be returning *home* to Norway.

She finished the article, read over it again and removed some of the overly maudlin sentiment Moffa would have hated and then emailed it to the editor. She sent a copy to Karen as well, in case she wanted to use any of it for the Norwegian press, along with some photos of Moffa from the war, later as a fisherman in Shetland and a recent one of him reunited with Lisbet.

She logged on to Facebook and was again disappointed Joakim had not contacted her. In a fit of pique she deleted him as a friend, although five minutes later she regretted it. How childish she would look. Then she wondered whether he would even notice.

On Monday morning, bone weary with lack of sleep, Lisa got up with Hansi and got ready to face the day. She rang Mr Jamieson, her grandfather's solicitor.

'Oh dear, that is sad news indeed. Edvard was such a character; I was looking forward to hearing how he got on in Norway.'

'I was ringing to see if you had any information on any funeral requests for him. He never got around to telling me what he wanted, and my mother wants me to organise it all.'

'Ah well, that I can help with. He left me with a detailed list of his wishes, in addition to his will, which he only updated a short while ago. If you want to come along to my office, I can let you have all the information you need. He had a funeral plan all paid up, so you don't need to worry about anything.'

'That's a relief. I've never organised a funeral before, but I know they can be expensive.'

'Indeed they are, but in this case, everything has been taken care of. Your grandfather didn't want to be a burden to anyone.'

Lisa gulped back the emotion that threatened to erupt.

'He was never a burden; did he think he was?'

'I'm sure he didn't, but he was a fiercely independent man to the end. B

But I do know he was very happy when you and your little boy moved in. He believed he was taking care of you. And don't you think he would have preferred it that way, whatever the truth of it was?'

After Lisa met with the funeral director she called Karen to confirm the date of the funeral. Karen told her Moffa's death had been on the Norwegian news that afternoon. She had forwarded the obituary to Cecilie who had passed it on to the news-desk for the broadcasting network.

'How's Lisbet today?' Lisa asked, feeling a little overwhelmed by how far her story had circulated.

'She stayed in bed today. She has not felt up to getting up all weekend. She has a little bit of a cold too, which hasn't helped. Poor thing, but Lily is looking after her and I've been in to see her this afternoon. She'll be fine; she's a tough lady.'

'That's good. Well I had better go and find Hansi, he's feeling neglected. It's been a busy day.'

Lisa made Hansi a sandwich for his supper and then let him have a long play in the bath. He had been curiously silent for most of the day. If she left him to play he would wander off to Moffa's room and stand in the doorway, but he wouldn't enter the room. Lisa had no words to explain what had happened.

They both went to bed early and once again Lisa was forced to allow Hansi to sleep in her bed as he refused to stay in his cot on his own. For once Lisa didn't mind, as she was glad of the cosy warmth of his body beside her.

On Tuesday her mother surprised her with a visit. She had been to the solicitor to ask him about the will, which didn't surprise Lisa in the least, although it was far too soon to be concerned with such things.

'He wouldn't tell me anything; he said you were handling the funeral,' Ingrid said, as she slumped onto the sofa.

'Well, you asked me to, remember?'

'Does this mean you know who is getting the house?'

'No, I don't know anything about the will, other than the fact Moffa changed it two weeks ago. I don't care about the will anyway. It's not like I'm going to inherit anything, is it; it will be split between you and Karen.'

Ingrid looked around the room as if she was summing up the contents.

'Well she's not getting any of my mother's things. I'm going to take them before she gets her hands on them.'

'At this stage they're not your mother's things. They were Moffa's remember, and he could distribute them as he sees fit. You do realise it's against the law to take things that don't belong to you.'

Ingrid glared at Lisa.

'You're loving this, aren't you?'

'Don't be ridiculous; how in God's name do you think I could "love" any minute of this?'

To Lisa's surprise Ingrid burst into tears. Lisa stood up and fetched a box of tissues and sat down next to her mother. She put her arm around her mother's shoulders and held her as she cried.

'There's no way Moffa did any of this to hurt you. He was upset when he found out you had turned Karen away all those years ago, but he understood why. Honestly, he had no idea about Karen until a few years ago, and he didn't do anything about it as he was too embarrassed. Yes it is my fault that I tracked Karen and Lisbet down, but don't you think he deserved to find closure. He had a few weeks of happiness knowing his daughter and grandchildren were happy and healthy and had grown up in a lovely family. He had been looking forward to meeting his other grandchildren in a couple of weeks. But that doesn't mean he loved you or me any less, does it?'

'What's Karen like?'

'She's lovely. She looks a bit like you, but older obviously. She used to be an English teacher. And Lisbet was sweet too, although I couldn't talk to her much as she doesn't speak English. I feel sorry for her. Moffa was her first love, and she couldn't believe it when they met again after all this time. You should have seen them together; it was magical. It didn't mean he didn't love Grandma though. I know he did. He has pictures of them both in his room, and you and me, and Hansi too. He was proud of all of us.'

'Are they coming over for the funeral?'

'Karen is, and her daughter Cecilie, but Lisbet isn't. It would be too traumatic for her.'

'What are the arrangements then?' Ingrid grabbed a handful of tissues and blew her nose.

'The service is going to be in Lunna Kirk and he will be buried there as well. Afterwards there will be tea and sandwiches at Fjara. It's all been paid for already. Moffa sorted everything out ages ago. He even picked out his own coffin. He didn't want us to get stressed out about stuff like that.'

'That's typical of Dad to think of others.'

Lisa nodded and smiled at her mother, squeezing her shoulders before walking over to the fireplace and picking up a photo of her grandmother and dusting the glass frame with her sleeve.

'Karen thinks someone from the Norwegian government might come over and I had a phone call from the Convener of the Council, he wants to come along. I think there will be quite a crowd.'

'What are you going to wear? Do you need to buy yourself a dress?'

'Yeah, I was going to buy something tomorrow, and maybe something for Hansi.'

'Oh please don't dress him in black. Dad would have hated that. But a new outfit for him would be nice. We should go shopping together. I'll buy you something.'

30

On Monday morning, while Lisa had been sorting out funeral arrangements, Joakim sat in a meeting with his new boss talking about their plans on how to launch the new coaching season. Joakim glanced at his watch. He needed to leave for the airport in less than an hour.

'You seem distracted Joakim, are you OK?'

'Yeah, I'm fine, but I left my mobile phone at home and I need to contact someone and don't know their number.'

'Google it, here, use my computer and I'll fetch us a sandwich and some coffee before you go.'

'Thanks.'

Joakim logged on to Facebook, since it was likely the manager's PC did not have the same blocks. He quickly realised Lisa had unfriended him and he was about to give up when he decided to look up her landline number. He couldn't find a listing for Lisa Balfour but then he remembered it would probably be listed under her grandfather's name.

He Googled "Edvard Christiansen Shetland" and stood up abruptly when the results came back, the chair he had been sitting on crashed against the filing cupboard.

'Fuck! Fuck! Fuck!' Joakim slammed his hand down on the desk as Henrik walked back into the room.

'What's happened?'

'You remember Lisa, whose grandfather was a Shetland Bus man? Well he's just died; I need to get to Shetland as soon as possible.'

'Ah yes, I saw something on the news. I didn't make the connection, sorry.'

'I need to get to the airport now.'

Henrik sat down at his desk and clicked on one of the news items about Edvard. 'You've got plenty of time, the funeral's not until Friday.'

'Thank God, I know there's a direct flight on Wednesdays from Bergen I will try and get on that.'

'Book it online. Sit down man, relax. Book the ticket here. It will be fine.'

Joakim logged onto the website but all flights to Shetland were fully booked that week. He accepted the coffee Henrik handed him, muttering an obscenity under his breath.

'Couldn't you go via another airport?'

Joakim managed to book a flight to Shetland via Aberdeen leaving first thing on Wednesday morning.

He decided not to bother going back home first although he was tempted simply to pick up his phone.

He had another look to see if he could find Edvard's home phone number but it wasn't listed. He would have to be patient until he saw Lisa. No wonder she was pissed off with him and had deleted him a friend on Facebook. He hoped she would give him a chance to explain. In the meantime he needed to buy something suitable to wear to a funeral so he decided to go into Bergen.

31

Lisa woke up early on Friday morning, the day of Moffa's funeral. The first thing she noticed was the sunshine, which was a welcome relief from the three days of unrelenting thick fog. She got out of bed and looked out of the window at the garden and over to the distant view of the sea which had the faintest tinge of mist hovering over the water. In the other direction a heat haze shimmered over the valley. It was going to be a beautiful day, although the sunshine did little to lift her mood.

Hansi was still sleeping in his cot next to her bed, so Lisa slipped downstairs as silently as possible to make herself a cup of tea. The carriage clock on the hall table ticked loudly as she passed by on the way to the kitchen. Lisa could not get used to the quiet. She hadn't realised until he had gone how noisy Moffa was. He was always up early in the morning and would be humming or singing to himself if he was on his own, or would engage in conversation with her when she came downstairs, never caring for a moment that Lisa was not much of a morning person.

Lisa was glad she would be moving out of the house soon. Her mother, or her aunt, or whoever ended up owning it was welcome to it. It was horrible without Moffa. She put the radio on quietly as she waited for the kettle to boil. There was a piece of paper caught behind the radio and she picked it up. It was a shopping list in Moffa's distinctly foreign handwriting – plums, sugar, eggs, vanilla essence, potatoes and salmon.

The paper was fresh as if Moffa had only just written the list. He had obviously wanted Lisa to make his favourite plum cake. Lisa pinned the shopping list to the noticeboard in the kitchen as she was reluctant to throw it away.

'You're up too. I couldn't sleep either.'

Cecilie stood by the kitchen door, tying up the belt of her dressing gown. She pushed her jet black hair away from her face and grinned at Lisa.

'Could I get a cup of coffee please?'

'Of course! There's no need to ask; make yourself at home. I found one of Moffa's shopping lists,' Lisa replied, pointing to the piece of paper. I guess it was a hint he wanted me to make him a cake, since he never went shopping any more. I should make it for you and Karen. It was his favourite.'

Cecilie peered at the list, 'his handwriting is just like my mother's, isn't that strange?'

'Is your mum OK? Did she manage to sleep last night?'

Cecilie and her mother had shared the spare room as nobody was keen on sleeping in Moffa's room, despite the offer from Lisa to put new bedding in the room. The room had not been touched since the day he had died; not even Hansi ventured far inside the door. An imperceptible veil of sadness lingered in the room.

'She's still sleeping. It's all a bit strange isn't it; if this had happened a few weeks ago we would be none the wiser. Now after having spent just a week with her father she is broken hearted. I wish I had come over to meet him when they did.'

'Me too! He was lovely. Everyone should have a grandfather like him.'

'What are you going to do now you don't to take care of him?'

'I don't know. I expect I will need to move out of this house soon. I also want to finish writing up the notes of Moffa's biography and maybe even think about getting it published. A friend of mine in Bergen is an editor and she's interested in seeing it.'

'I would love to read it too, if you wouldn't mind. You should come over to Norway again soon; come and meet more of the family. We would love to get to know you properly.'

'That would be lovely. I promised Moffa I would try and learn Norwegian, and Hansi definitely will.'

'Moffa? I love that you still call him that. He was my Moffa too. Did you ever think about journalism or writing as a career? When you were talking last night about your degree courses, it occurred to me you have a very wide knowledge of history and culture.'

'I've never thought about it before. I always imagined I would end up as an archaeologist, or even teaching. I don't think I would like an office job.'

'Well, as a journalist, I can tell you writing for a magazine or a newspaper is so much better than an office job. Maybe you should come over to Norway and see about doing some freelance articles for us.'

'But I barely speak a word of Norwegian.'

'But our international section has a lot of it written in English. So many readers are bilingual, or are reading the paper online from the States or Australia. They might never have lived in Norway, but if they have Scandinavian heritage they like to stay in touch. Our travel and history sections are very popular overseas.'

'That sounds interesting. I will think about it.'

Lisa was intrigued by the idea of writing for a Norwegian paper; Moffa would have been thrilled. She thought of Joakim and her disappointment that he had not even sent her a text reply in nearly a week made her feel stupid for having fallen for him.

'What's up?' Cecilie asked, as Lisa passed her a mug of coffee.

'Man trouble.' Lisa smiled at her cousin. 'Nothing I should be bothering to think about today.'

'Oh, is this the man who helped you track down my mum and grandmother?'

'Yes; I haven't spoken to him in weeks. I kind of wish he could be here today, but he hasn't replied to my messages.'

'Then he isn't worth your time.'

'I know.'

32

Lisa stood at the pulpit of Lunna Kirk to deliver the eulogy. Her fingers trembled as she lifted her notes. The coffin, draped in a heavy Norwegian flag and topped with a display of red and white roses and blue cornflowers was below her. Her mother, her aunt and her new cousin sat in the front row. Hansi sat on Cecilie's lap and did not look happy. What Lisa was about to do required dignity and courage, but her hands were shaking. She glanced to the side and saw the Norwegian Minister sitting next to some local council officials. Behind them was an assortment of Moffa's friends and colleagues from his fishing days.

Lisa put down her notes and gripped the edge of the wooden pulpit. She was in the centre of the little kirk, surrounded on three sides by sombre faces. Lisa cleared her throat and then, abandoning her prepared speech, began the eulogy.

'First of all, I would like to thank you all for coming here today to say goodbye to my grandfather, Edvard Christiansen. I know some of you have had terrible journeys to Shetland because of the fog, and have been stranded in Aberdeen and Orkney, so we appreciate the effort you made to get here.'

The Norwegian Minister nodded and smiled at her.

'Edvard spent the early part of his life feeling guilty; for surviving the war when his parents and brother didn't; for taking the life of a German soldier, a young man named Frederik Kuntz, he never forgot him, and despite what had happened to his parents he never felt good about killing another man. He felt guilty for leaving Norway after the war, even though it was clear with hindsight he was suffering from what we would now call post-traumatic stress disorder; he regretted leaving his fiancé Lisbet behind when he ran away to Shetland. Many years later he discovered Lisbet had had his child, a daughter called Karen, Edvard felt guiltier still.

'There are still people alive today because of the courageous things he did during the war. Let's be honest, he was a hero – but Edvard never saw it like that. He didn't think he had any choice but to help other people escape from the kinds of things that had happened to his parents.'

Lisa paused for breath, distracted by the door of the kirk opening. A uniformed policeman stood to attention by the entrance, shielding her view of the new arrival.

'When I was growing up, Edvard was simply my grandfather. He was a fisherman; he took me out on his boat and taught me to fish, and how to cook. He taught me songs and nursery rhymes in Norwegian. He taught me to count, both in English and in Norwegian. He taught me to take an interest in the world. We watched the news together. We laughed and we had so much fun. Years later I found out a little of what he had done during the war and I demanded to know more, but he wouldn't tell me. I didn't realise it was because he *couldn't* tell me. Even sixty years after the war he couldn't speak about what he had seen, it hurt too much.

'Later, when I was at university, I decided I wanted to capture his story and I tried to persuade him to tell me. He still couldn't. But then something amazing happened. I found out Edvard had a daughter in Norway; one he had only recently found out about. He was desperate to meet her, so I went over to Norway, and with the help of a dear friend I tracked down my Aunt Karen – and her mother.'

Lisa smiled at Karen and Cecilie.

'Just a few weeks ago, Karen and Lisbet came over to Shetland and stayed with Edvard for a week. It was a special time for Edvard. He managed to set aside all of the ghosts from the war. He finally forgave himself for surviving, and for leaving. Since then he has shared with me most of his life story which he wanted me to record, either as a book or a PhD thesis. And I can tell you, it's an interesting story.'

Lisa looked down to see Hansi squirming out of Cecilie's arms. Lisa nodded to indicate her cousin could let him go. It was not as if he could go far. Hansi walked over to the coffin and stared at it for a moment, patted it then sped off towards the policeman.

'Edvard was eighty seven. Sometimes he considered himself to be an old man, but I can tell you, in the last few weeks he was like a teenager. You see, Edvard was in love again. I know that might upset anyone who knew my grandmother, but it was so lovely to see him happy again. On the morning of the day he died I heard him singing in the kitchen as he made breakfast. He had abandoned his walking stick as if he had found new strength. This was due entirely to being reunited with his first sweetheart and his oldest daughter.

'He had booked his flights to go back to Norway to see them again. It seems like a great tragedy to die just before he went home, but then again, it would have been so much more tragic if he had never met them. We should be grateful that in his final weeks he was as happy as he was when he was married to my grandmother, Mabel. My grandfather was a great man. He was a hero to me, and not because of what he did during the war, but because of who he was – funny, kind, generous, a family man, and with a great interest in the world. That is how he would like to be remembered. That is how I will remember him. God bless you, Moffa.'

Lisa stepped down from the pulpit, squeezing past the Norwegian Minister who had got up to speak next. He put his hand on her shoulder. Lisa walked past the coffin and brushed her fingertips over the flag. She sat down next to her mother, who hugged her. Karen reached over and squeezed her hand.

Lisa shut her eyes for a moment, feeling shattered now her part in the proceedings was over. Then she remembered Hansi and got up to fetch him.

She smiled apologetically at the Minister who was now speaking on behalf of the Norwegian government as she tiptoed past the coffin towards the door.

Lisa couldn't see Hansi. She looked at the police officer who indicated with a slight inclination of the head that Hansi was behind him. Lisa hurried forward and stopped abruptly when she realised Hansi was being held by Joakim.

She froze, not knowing whether to go back to her seat now Hansi was happy and safe, or whether to speak to Joakim. Since speaking was not appropriate, she half-smiled at him and scurried back to her seat and sat down, breathing hard, trying to regain her composure and concentrate on what the Minister was saying.

'... our gratitude can never be conveyed adequately, and it saddens me it is often only at funerals we truly acknowledge the burden the Shetland Bus men carried. However, on behalf of my country, my government and our Royal Family, I would like to thank the people of Shetland for welcoming Edvard so warmly into the community. I'm glad he enjoyed a good life here and raised a family; a daughter, a granddaughter and a lovely little great-grandson. I'm also glad he found happiness in his last few weeks, and found his Norwegian family again.'

He continued to speak, but this time in Norwegian, as if he was speaking directly to Edvard.

When the Minister sat down, the pastor said a final prayer and then the service was over. Grieg's *Morning Mood* from Peer Gynt played as people got up and left the kirk.

Lisa hurried outside without speaking to anyone. She found Joakim outside, still holding Hansi.

'I'm sorry I nearly missed it. I tried to fly in on Wednesday but I got stuck in Aberdeen because of the fog. I couldn't call you back as I left my phone at my house and I didn't know your number.' Lisa nodded, looking up at Joakim as he dodged his face away from Hansi who was patting him on the head. 'I'm sorry about Edvard. Are you OK?'

Lisa nodded again. Karen appeared at her side.

'Joakim, lovely to see you again. How are you?'

'Well I'm glad to finally be here, I've been stuck at Aberdeen airport for two days.'

'Yes, thankfully we landed about an hour before the fog descended. Lisa, that was a lovely eulogy; well done, Edvard would have been so proud of you. Well I know he was proud of you.'

Lisa reached up to take Hansi from Joakim. Now the eulogy had been delivered she was exhausted. The burial was due to take place in a few minutes but she did not want to witness it.

'Thank you. I think I might take Hansi for a little walk. I don't think he needs to see the committal. I'm sure he knows his Pop Pop is inside the coffin.'

'No, of course; he's been such a good little boy today, and it would be a shame to upset him now.' Karen rested her hand on Lisa's arm. 'I shall go and keep your mother company. I think she's a little lost, poor thing.'

Lisa watched Karen walk across the grass towards Ingrid. The pallbearers were preparing to bring the coffin out. Lisa blinked back tears. She held Hansi on her hip and took Joakim's arm.

'Can we go please?'

'Of course. I hired a car; do you want me to drive you somewhere?'

Lisa nodded, striding ahead of him, feeling a deluge of tears building up.

Joakim caught up with her and led her towards his car. As he clicked the door open Lisa stopped and pushed Hansi into his arms, and turned her back on them, her shoulders shaking with grief and her attempt to control her tears in front of her son.

She walked away; from Joakim and Hansi and from the swell of people who were standing around in the churchyard and the car-park, waiting for the final part of the funeral service to begin.

She heard the car door shut and a moment later Joakim had caught up with her.

'Lisa, I'm so sorry.' Joakim pulled her into his arms and stroked her hair.

She wasn't sure whether he was apologising or sympathising, but the warmth of his hug was just what she needed. She sobbed for a few moments, as he held her, and then she reached into her pocket for tissues and dried her eyes and blew her nose.

'I left Hansi in the car, we'd better go? Shall we go and get a cup of tea somewhere?'

'Yes please, thank you.'

Joakim drove them back to town. The funeral tea had been arranged to take place at Fjara. The few times Lisa had taken Moffa to the cafe he had loved sitting by the window and watching the seals on the rocks nearby. Arriving earlier than the rest of the funeral party allowed them a chance to sit down and catch up.

'I had a message from Astrid the other day. She told me I should forgive you; that nothing happened.'

'She contacted you? I asked her not to.'

'You talked about me?'

'Yes; I was upset when you didn't want to speak to me. I was kind of mad at her for ruining things for me with you.'

'Well, it doesn't matter now.' Lisa passed a biscuit to Hansi who was sitting in a highchair. The tables were decorated with red, white and blue flowers. Norwegian and Shetland flags hung as bunting around the café, fluttering in the breeze from the open French doors. A trolley of drinks had been set up, in preparation for the other guests, and the staff were busy plating up cakes and sandwiches.

'It does matter Lisa; you had every right to be upset with me.'

'Why, it's not like we were in a relationship?'

'Don't you consider this is a relationship? Because I know I do.'

Lisa shrugged as she refilled her cup with tea. 'It's a strange kind of relationship isn't it? You live in Norway; I live here. You have a new career set up and mine hasn't even begun. I still don't know what I'm going to do, other than finish the book for Moffa. But it's not like it's going to be a bestseller, even if I got it published. It has limited appeal.'

'This is the 21st century – it's the time for strange, long distance relationships. I will have lots of time off in the summer. I was planning to come back over in a few weeks to see you.'

Lisa reached for his hand. 'That's lovely, but that's not a relationship.'

Joakim didn't get a chance to reply as Karen, Ingrid and Cecilie entered the café and came over to the table.

'There you are. I was worried about you,' Ingrid said to Lisa.

'Sorry; I couldn't bear to watch and I didn't think it would be a good idea for Hansi to see where the coffin was going to end up.'

'You're right. It doesn't bear thinking about.' Ingrid looked around at the café. 'They've done a good job in here. It's lovely. Well done for arranging this, Lisa.'

Margaret came in next with some of Edvard's other neighbours and before long the café was filled with people talking in English and Norwegian. Soon there was laughter, which thrilled Lisa, knowing it was what Moffa would have wanted. His favourite music played in the background and there was a curiously festive atmosphere in the room.

Ingrid was talking to the Norwegian Minister. She was showing him Moffa's medals and some photographs she had brought with her. Karen and Cecilie were talking to Joakim. Hansi was sitting on Margaret's lap as she chatted to some of Moffa's old fishing buddies. Lisa slipped out of the café and walked a few yards along the road and sat down on the sea wall. Seven fat grey seals slumbered on the rocks a few feet away. They watched her and then settled down again when they were sure she wasn't going to disturb the peace. An oystercatcher strutted around, searching for food in the shallow rock-pools.

Lisa thought of Moffa and wished he was sitting here with her, where they had sat on many an occasion since she was Hansi's age. They had counted seals, identified the birds, watched boats and on one memorable occasion watched a pod of dolphins playing in the bay.

All of Lisa's happiest childhood memories involved Moffa. He had stepped in when her father had stepped out. He had been her funny, dependable, wise and generous best friend and grandfather rolled into one. He was the only man who had truly loved her, unconditionally.

Now as she sat on the wall watching the seals she wondered what she was going to do. Despite the fact her relationship with her mother had changed beyond recognition, and very much for the better, Lisa knew her mother wanted to live in her parent's old house and so Lisa would have to move out.

She heard footsteps and saw Cecilie walking towards her.

'I thought I might find you out here. Isn't this a lovely spot?'

'It was Edvard's favourite place to sit when the sun shone. Sometimes he would sit here while I went to the supermarket over there. He was so pleased when they built this café here, but he only managed to come in here a few times.'

'I can see why he liked it here. It seems to be a bit of a party in there now.'

'I'm glad they're having a good time,' Lisa said in earnest. 'Edvard would like that. But I needed some fresh air. I feel a bit drained. It's kind of sinking in now.'

Cecilie sat down on the wall next to Lisa and put her arm around her.

'Come on my little cousin, don't be too sad. That man of yours is sexy. I like a man who's good with children. He was teaching Hansi how to sing the Norwegian national anthem. It was so funny.'

'Hansi adores Joakim. He always seems to prefer hanging out with men.'

'I noticed. I couldn't get him to smile at me even. Why don't you come back in with me? It will be all over soon enough and we can go home and relax and I will pour us both a big glass of wine, and we can eat that plum cake you made. I want to hear all your stories about our Moffa.'

Lisa nodded and took Cecilie's arm as they walked back to the café. Joakim grinned at them when they opened the door and indicated for them to join him.

A few minutes later they were sitting in the presence of the Norwegian Minister, whose name Lisa still hadn't managed to grasp. He was entertaining them with stories from places he had visited, and important but silly people he had met during his years as a politician. When the Minister stood up to go, he shook hands with a few people and when he got to Lisa he said, 'I can't wait to read your book. I think it ought to be translated into Norwegian too, don't you think?'

33

Later that evening Lisa sat in the lounge with Karen, Cecilie and Joakim drinking red wine and eating cake. Hansi had gone to bed.

'When are you going back to Norway?' Joakim asked Cecilie.

'Not until Wednesday; we wanted to spend a little more time here with Lisa. What about you?'

'I only booked a one-way ticket as I didn't know when I would go back.'

Lisa put down her wine glass.

'I haven't asked where you're staying, but you could have Moffa's room. He wouldn't have minded.'

'Thank you. I was happy to sleep on the sofa again though. I couldn't find a hotel room, they were all full.'

'It gets busy here in the summer season.'

'Your mother said we needed to go with her to see the lawyer on Monday to talk about the will.' Karen said. 'This won't cause any trouble will it? We weren't expecting to inherit anything.'

Lisa shrugged.

'I don't know what's in his will but I do know he only changed it recently.'

Karen pulled a face and shook her head.

'Don't worry about what people think,' Lisa continued. 'Edvard did what he wanted to do and we should respect that.'

'You're right, but I would hate for your mother to feel as if we are trying to take anything from her. This was her mother's house too.'

'If it happens, it happens, it doesn't mean we have to accept it.' Cecilie said to her mother. 'But I would love to get some photographs of my grandfather, and if he had any Norwegian books nobody else wants I would love those. It would be nice to read something he enjoyed.'

'Well, I can get you some photos, even if I have to scan them and email them to you. And there are loads of books over there.' Lisa stood up and walked over to the glass-fronted bookcase. 'Most of them are in Norwegian and since neither my mother nor I can read them, then of course you should have them.'

Cecilie opened the bookcase and with a happy smile pulled over a chair and sat down as she examined the shelves. She laughed as she pulled out a worn paperback.

'I have this book at home. To think we shared the same taste!'

She read out some of the titles to Karen who nodded and smiled.

Lisa left them going through Moffa's books and went to the kitchen to fetch more wine. Joakim followed her and took the wine bottle out her hand and set it down on the counter.

'I've missed you. I haven't said that to you yet.'

'I missed you too. Especially this last week; I was desperate to speak to you. I knew you would be the one person who would understand.'

Joakim reached for her hand and pulled her towards him.

'I understand. I feel so angry now. Things were going so well for him weren't they? It isn't fair.'

Lisa touched Joakim's face.

'He liked you. He was disappointed when things seemed to go wrong. I wish I could tell him you were still perfect.'

'Perfect? No, don't tell him that. I'm not perfect.'

Lisa grinned. 'OK, so maybe that's the red wine talking. Nobody's perfect, right?'

'Well, I wouldn't say that. I think you are pretty perfect. Or is that perfectly pretty? I'm not sure. My English is not so good.'

Lisa laughed. 'You're English is fine, you're flirting with me.'

'Flirting? What is this flirting you speak of?'

Lisa giggled and put her arms around him and leaned her head against his chest. It felt so good; and even better when he closed his arms and held her tight.

'Sleep with me tonight,' Joakim whispered.

'What? Tonight? Seriously?' Lisa said, stepping back and letting go of him.

'No, I don't mean like that. I don't think you should be alone tonight.'

'I won't be alone. I will have a little monster in my bed most likely. And Karen and

Cecilie are sleeping in the guest room upstairs, just along the hall from me.'

Joakim pulled an exaggeratedly disappointed face. 'That boy will have to get used to his mother having a boyfriend sometime.'

'Boyfriend? We haven't even been on a date yet?'

'What was that week in Stranda, if not a date? I took you out to dinner at the hotel. We danced to that band. Well, you danced; I kind of wobbled around the dance-floor.'

Lisa giggled.

'OK, so we may have been on a date.'

'For a week; with lots of kissing remember? So I think I can call you my girlfriend.'

'There hasn't been enough kissing for my liking.'

'Well, that's your son's fault. In fact, I bet if I was to kiss you now we would hear him sit up in bed and start shouting.'

Lisa studied Joakim for a moment. He was elegant in his black trousers and black shirt. He had taken off the tie he had worn to the funeral and undone the top button of his shirt. There was a horizontal crease in the shirt; brand new, straight from the packaging. He smelt divine, the consequence of having tried out various colognes and aftershaves while idling the time away at the airport duty-free.

Lisa put her hand on his chest and felt both the warmth and the comforting beat of his heart which she perceived was quickening in response to her touch. Joakim placed his hand over hers.

She set aside the thought that today of all days she shouldn't be thinking about her own desires, but she had a feeling her grandfather would approve. She stepped back into Joakim's arms and lifted her face to his. Joakim responded by brushing her cheek with his thumb then bending his head and kissing her lips. The heat from his lips flooded through the rest of her body.

When Lisa pulled away, breathless, Joakim cocked his head to one side and listened.

'Silence. I shall take this as a good omen.'

'Lisa, oh, sorry!' Karen appeared at the kitchen door.

'That's OK, we were just catching up.'

'Is that what you call it?' Karen smirked. 'Listen, I'm sorry to disturb you, but I found an old photograph album in the bookcase and I wanted to know who these people were.'

'Let me get some more wine and I will show you some of the old family photos.' Lisa picked up the wine bottle and took Joakim's hand and followed her aunt back to the lounge. Joakim sat down on the sofa and Lisa sat on the floor, leaning against his legs.

Lisa turned the pages of the old leather album and talked about the photos. There was a black and white wedding photo. Edvard and Mabel stood in an unnaturally formal pose for the camera, side by side, holding hands. There was a cheeky glint in his eye; he had been truly happy when he got married.

'I haven't seen this photograph for years. That was when I didn't know about Lisbet and you guys. Wow, how strange to think Edvard wouldn't have got married if he had known. How different things would have been.'

'It was meant to be.' Karen said, fiddling with her glasses. 'She was pretty, your grandmother. You take after her. I guess you would have been about the same age as her in this photo.'

'No, she was much younger than me when she got married. But Edvard was a few years older, although he seems so young in these pictures. I wish this photo was in colour. He was good looking wasn't he?'

'Yes. He didn't show us many photos of him when we were here before. I think maybe he didn't feel comfortable showing us photographs of his wife. But you know, I wouldn't have minded. You were right, when you said in the eulogy he always felt guilty. It makes me sad, as he had no reason to be.'

Lisa continued showing them the photos and explaining who everyone was. After a while Karen yawned and said she needed to go to bed.

'It's been a strange day,' she said, as she stood up. 'Happy and sad, but mostly sad.'

Cecilie got up too and said goodnight. She winked at Lisa as she shut the door to the lounge.

'I need some water. I have drunk far too much wine today. Isn't it strange about funerals, you end up eating and drinking too much? It seems a little undignified, don't you think?'

'Not really. Food and drink are part of the ritual of saying goodbye, or saying hello. Births, deaths and marriages all involve a party. I think it is a good thing,' Joakim replied.

Lisa smiled. 'Can I get you anything?'

'No, I'm fine thanks. I think maybe I should go to bed soon though. You're right; this is not the time or place to get together.'

Lisa kissed him goodnight at the door to Moffa's bedroom. Then she opened the door and turned on the light for him.

'I changed all the bedding and tidied up in here.'

'Is this where he died?' Joakim asked, hesitating as he stared at the bed.

'Um, well yes, but he didn't die in the bed. I found him on the floor where you're standing.'

Joakim stepped away and stared down at the floor as if he was expecting to see some kind of evidence that a body had lain there.

'Moffa wasn't the kind of person to haunt you,' Lisa said, touching Joakim's arm.

'I know; but it feels kind of strange all the same. Do you mind if I sleep on the sofa?'

'Of course not. But I have a better idea. Why don't you come up to my room?'

'Really?'

'Yes, really. You're right; I don't feel like being alone. But we will have a giant contraceptive in the room, so you won't be able to get up to mischief.'

'Mischief?'

'Don't play all innocent, "*I can't speak English very well*," you know exactly what I mean.' Lisa smirked at Joakim and led him out of Moffa's room and shut the door.

34

The following morning the first thing Lisa saw was Hansi standing up in his cot, gnawing the rail as he peered over at the bed. He was curiously silent. Normally he would vocalise his awake state and demand to be released from the cot. Joakim was still sleeping beside her. She wondered if Hansi was stressed out about Joakim's presence, but he seemed content.

She got out of bed and picked up her son who clung to her sleepily. She got back into bed with Hansi in the middle and stroked his hair hoping it might send him back to sleep. It was a little too early in the morning to get up.

An hour later Lisa woke up again, when she heard a giggle from Hansi. He had woken up again and was climbing on top of Joakim, who was pretending to protest.

'Oh no, the scary monster is awake, help me Lisa, help me!'

Hansi giggled even more. Joakim lay on his back and held Hansi above his head, his little arms and legs flailing around in excitement. Joakim raised him up and down. 'En, to, tre, fire, fem, seks...' Joakim counted, as he bench-pressed Hansi. 'Who needs to go to the gym when you have a small child to use as a free-weight?'

Lisa regarded Joakim's arms as he held Hansi aloft. It was obvious he was no stranger to the gym. She slipped out of bed and put her dressing gown on over her pyjamas.

'I think I had better get this little man dressed and fed,' she said, even though Hansi had shown no indication he was hungry.

'Yes, I had better get up too. It's a lovely day; I think we should go out for a walk.'

When Lisa had showered and dressed and given Hansi his breakfast, Karen and Cecilie came downstairs. Cecilie put the kettle on to make some coffee as her mother sat down at the kitchen table.

'We were wondering whether it might be alright if we went back to Lunna Kirk to take some photographs for my grandmother. It didn't seem appropriate to take them yesterday, but I know she would like to know where Edvard's grave is. There were so many lovely flowers there too, including the wreath she sent. Would that be OK?'

'Of course I'll drive you there if you like; unless you wanted to borrow my car and go by yourselves. You know the way don't you?'

'That would be nice, thank you. I would love to explore more of Shetland. You wouldn't mind lending me the car then?'

'Of course not, Joakim has hired a car, so we won't need mine. I'll ring my insurance company and get you added to my policy. It will take five minutes.'

'And when we are out we will go to the shops and buy things for dinner tonight. I will cook, you can have a day off from taking care of us,' Karen said.

After Karen and Cecilie had gone out, Lisa cleared up the kitchen and went to find Joakim and Hansi who were sitting in the lounge watching a cartoon.

'It's too nice to be indoors, where would you like to go?'

'Well there is still a lot of Shetland I would like to see, but since it is so sunny, why don't we pack up a picnic and go to the beach?'

'Good idea.'

They spent the morning on Levenwick beach. The sun had warmed the sand and Hansi pottered around picking up shells and paddling in the icy shallows, before falling asleep on the blanket in the shade of his pushchair.

Lisa stood up and walked to the water's edge where Joakim was skimming stones into the water. She bent down and picked up a smooth flat stone and bent to one side and launched the stone into the sea, watching in triumph as it bounced seven times before disappearing into the water, easily beating Joakim's best attempt.

He grinned at her in admiration and then his competitive streak kicked in. He picked up another stone and with a determined effort skimmed it into the sea. It bounced five times. He tried another few attempts but gave up in defeat.

Lisa watched with a big grin on her face. 'Guess who taught me how to do that?'

'You've clearly had years of experience.'

Joakim glanced at Hansi to check whether he was still sleeping. Then he grabbed hold of Lisa and picked her up. She shrieked as he lowered her head back until it almost touched the water.

'No, no, don't!'

Joakim put her down again, as a small wave lapped onto the shore and washed over their feet. Lisa had taken her sandals off and her feet were bare. Joakim still wore his trainers.

'Serves you right,' Lisa said, as Joakim looked down at his sopping wet feet.

'Well at least only one of my feet is cold.'

Lisa laughed and walked over to where they had been sitting and picked up a towel for him.

'Tak!'

'Du er velkommen,' Lisa replied.

'Your accent is good; you should learn to speak the language.'

'Yeah, it won't be so easy now without Moffa. He had been teaching me a few more words recently.'

Joakim sat down on the blanket and took off his trainers and squeezed out the excess water and then dried his feet.

'I don't suppose salt water is good for your prosthesis.'

'No, I will have to take it off and clean it up properly when we go home. I don't want it to get rusty.'

'No indeed, you might start to creak when you walk.'

Joakim laughed. 'I love that about you. This doesn't bother you at all does it?'

'Why would it? I'm fascinated by it. An impressive amount of work has gone into designing it, a real feat of engineering. Did you know humans first created false limbs hundreds of years ago?'

Joakim nodded. 'I'm glad I didn't live in those times. Well I would have died from gangrene or something first.'

'And I wouldn't have survived giving birth to this little beast. I ended up having an emergency caesarean. We both have reason to be grateful for modern medicine.'

'And new technology.'

Lisa raised an eyebrow.

'Facebook? I wouldn't be sitting here with you now without the wonders of the internet.'

'True. Although, like I said in the beginning, you were the wrong Joakim Haaland, and out there somewhere is the real one, waiting for someone to reply to his message.'

'Yeah, poor guy, I feel like such a fraud.'

'He has no idea what chain of events his message started.'

Joakim pulled Lisa closer to him.

'You should write to him and tell him.'

'But suppose he writes back to me and then we correspond for a while and then I fall in love with him.'

'Ah, yes, that might be a problem. I think there's a law against falling in love with more than one Joakim Haaland at a time.'

'You're so cheeky. I'm not in love with you.'

'Why not? I'm adorable.'

'You are sometimes, but not when you're being arrogant.'

'I have lots to be arrogant about.'

'Really? Tell me.'

'Well first of all, I'm sitting here with the most beautiful woman on the beach.'

'I'm the only woman on the beach!'

'Ah, my mistake, I'm sitting here on the beach with the most beautiful woman in the world.'

'That's better.'

'Now, who's arrogant?'

'Keep going, what else?'

'That's it, that's all I've got.'

Lisa turned towards him and pushed him back onto the blanket and snuggled up next to him.

'How long are you staying in Shetland for?'

'I don't know. How long do you want me to stay for?'

Lisa bit back the temptation to say "forever." 'Don't you have to get back for your training?'

'Eventually, yes. But I don't have to be in Norway again until two weeks. I have a meeting at the resort with some potential clients. One of whom is tipped to get selected for the Paralympics.'

'Doesn't it bother you? That someone else is going to the Olympics and not you?'

'There is nothing stopping me from trying out for selection. I might think about it if I get fit enough in time for the trials.'

'Really?' Lisa sat up straight.

'Yes, maybe, if I want to.'

'Wow, that would be great wouldn't it?'

'I'm not sure. I would need to think about it.'

'What's there to think about?'

Joakim sat up and ran his hand through the sand picking up handfuls of it and letting it trail through his fingers.

'I'm not as competitive as I once was. I don't need to prove myself anymore, like I did when I was younger. I want to enjoy skiing for its own sake, and when you're training to win, sometimes you forget to enjoy it. The only incentive I have for competing is to show you can recover from such a trauma.'

'Isn't that enough?'

'Frankly, no; I would be happier helping other people by being their coach. I don't want to compete and have people feeling sorry for me that I couldn't do it in the Olympics.'

'So, it's a pride thing.'

'Yes and no.'

35

On Monday morning Lisa drove Cecilie and Karen to the lawyer's office. Joakim had offered to stay home with Hansi and since it was raining it would mean a morning in front of the television watching cartoons.

'It's a tough life, but someone's got to do it,' he said, as he waved them off.

They met Ingrid in the reception and a moment later they were called through to the office to see Mr Jamieson.

An hour later they left the meeting. Lisa was still speechless as she walked down the steps towards the car park.

'Were you expecting this?' Ingrid asked her.

'No, of course not. I had no idea.'

'But he talked to you about his parent's house in Haugesund, you must have known.'

'No, I didn't. He never went into any detail about the house. I assumed he had either abandoned his claim on it or maybe sold it decades ago. I never imagined he still owned anything in Norway.'

'He said something to my mother about it,' Karen said. 'I overheard them when we were over here before. She asked him whether he had ever gone back there. He said he had never returned but that he deals with the property and tenants through the law firm his father used to own. I remember thinking it odd he talked about it in the present tense. But it's a nice surprise for you isn't it, Lisa?'

Lisa nodded. They stood by Lisa's car while she fumbled in her bag for the keys.

'Ingrid, why don't you come back with us for some lunch? We haven't had a chance to get to know you properly. We are leaving on Wednesday,' Karen said.'

'Sure, why not. Is that OK with you, Lisa?'

'Of course!'

They arrived back at the house to find Joakim and Hansi sitting in the lounge playing with Lego bricks.

Joakim got up and walked into the kitchen where Lisa had gone, leaving Hansi in the care of his grandmother who had ushered Karen and Cecilie into the lounge.

'Is everything OK, you look a bit shocked?'

'I am. Moffa left me a house in his will; his house in Haugesund. Can you believe that?'

'It doesn't surprise me actually; I presume your mother inherited this house.'

Lisa nodded, and smiled with relief.

'But what about Karen?' Joakim said, almost whispering.

'He left them some money, some paintings, his medals and his books. Apparently he was going to leave them the house in Haugesund, but he changed his will to leave it to me, on Lisbet's instructions. She told him they didn't need a house, but I did.'

'What are you going to do with it?'

'I don't know. I have some paperwork in my bag. It has some plans and photos of the house. Apparently it has been let out for rent for years, but a few weeks ago Moffa gave notice to his tenants and they have moved out. I think he was going to go and stay there himself, or at least visit it while he was there. Apparently it's been done up and modernised in the last few years. He was using the rental income as a kind of pension, but he had loads of savings too.'

'And you didn't know anything about this.'

'No; he was always secretive about money, well, obviously he was secretive about lots of things as we found out this summer. He was always generous but he never spent a lot on himself. I have no idea how he managed to save so much.'

'Well, I imagine he had everything he needed already. I think the generation that lived through the war had a tendency to save more; what is it you say in English, saving for a rainy day.'

'That's true, and after what Moffa went through I think it must have been ingrained in him to be prepared for anything.'

'You should back with me and look at the house. Wouldn't it be good to see where he grew up? Now I have heard his story I would like to see it too.'

'You know, I think I might. He left me a little bit of money too, so I can afford to buy my own ticket now, and pay you back.'

'You don't need to pay me back. I told you before.'

'Oh Lord, this is so strange. It is going to take a lot of getting used to. I never imagined I would own a house for years and years, and now I own one in Norway of all places. That's crazy.'

Lisa laughed, and then a moment later started to cry. 'Why didn't he tell me though? I could have thanked him.'

Ingrid walked into the kitchen.

'What's up love?'

'I wish I could say thank you to Moffa,' Lisa said, between sobs.

'Oh he knew how grateful you would be. He knew what he was doing. How bad would you have felt when he died knowing you were going to profit from it. My father was the master of feeling guilty about everything. He was trying to protect you.'

Lisa brushed the tears away with the sleeve of her shirt. 'Then how come I still feel guilty.'

'It must be genetic,' Ingrid said, smiling at her. 'So what are you going to do with it? You'll sell it of course, and buy something over here.'

'I don't know. I'm going to fly back with Joakim and go and see the place. I feel like I need to see where he grew up. I know Moffa couldn't face going back to the house after the war, but there's a reason he didn't sell it. So I'm going to go and take a look.'

'OK.' Ingrid switched the kettle on. 'You are going to come back though aren't you?'

'Um, yes of course I am. I can't up-sticks and move to Haugesund, I don't have a job, or speak the language.'

'Well if you're only going for a few days, I would be happy to look after Hansi for you. I'll stay here while you're away. It would give me a chance to sort out Dad's things.'

'You wouldn't mind?'

'Of course not. I've taken a couple of weeks off work. I could do with some time to get my head around everything, and Hansi would be good company for me. And I can always take him to nursery during the day so he can play with his pals.'

36

Lisa stood in the kitchen of her newly inherited house. There wasn't a scrap of evidence to show her grandfather had ever lived in it, which after seventy years wasn't unexpected. However, Lisa was surprised at how little emotion the house stirred in her. She was almost glad Moffa was not here to see it. She couldn't imagine him recognising any aspect of the neighbourhood. The street, being so close to the centre of town, was full of modern apartment blocks, a small parade of shops, a petrol station, a couple of restaurants and a car-park. Moffa's house was one of the few old properties left.

Lisa had half expected to fall in love with the house, and possibly even want to live in it, but although it was a large attractive house in good structural order, it did nothing for her.

'I'm going to sell it. I don't think I would ever want to come here again. It feels cold and empty.'

'I know what you mean. I don't believe in ghosts, but it doesn't have a happy atmosphere does it?' Joakim said, as he opened a door to a dark cellar and immediately closed it again.

'No, let's go, shall we?'

They left the property and stood outside on the pavement in the sunshine. Lisa took some photos of the garden and the house, as she had promised her mother she would do. She remembered Moffa telling her how he had watched the German soldiers dragging his family away.

'Moffa said he hid in a neighbour's garden when he watched his family being arrested. I wonder which house it was. He mentioned something about leaving his bike in a cemetery first.'

Joakim tapped on his phone and brought up a map of the area and showed it to Lisa.

'The cemetery is about a mile in that direction.'

Lisa looked along the street where Joakim was pointing. There was one other old house surrounded by mature trees and hedging.

'Could we just go and have a look?'

Joakim nodded and took her hand. The sun was shining, but the streets were wet where it had rained earlier. It looked like clouds were gathering for another shower. They stopped outside the house and Lisa stepped just inside the gate and looked back to Moffa's old house. She tried to imagine the street at night. There was no doubt that Moffa would have been able to stay out of sight behind the hedge, if it had been here all those years ago. He would have had a good view of what was happening outside his house. She pictured him standing where she was, shaking in fear, as he heard his mother's screams, wondering whether he should have gone to her.

'He was so brave, wasn't he? I'm not sure I could have stood here and watched my family be taken away. I would have been a wreck.'

'You never know what you're capable of doing under pressure. But it's true; he was a very brave man. And he did the right thing by hiding.'

'I just want to hug him right now. I would give anything to be able to talk to him.'

Lisa wrapped her arms around Joakim and buried her face in his chest.

'I'm sorry; I'm not much of a consolation.'

Lisa let go of Joakim and smiled. 'I'm glad you're here. Thank you.'

Joakim put his arm around Lisa and kissed her cheek. 'Where would you like to go now?'

'Take me home. I don't want to stay in this town. As pretty as it is, all I can think of is what happened to Moffa's family.'

They walked back towards the car. Lisa paused outside Moffa's house and stared up at the house for a moment. She turned and almost bumped into an old wooden bench next to the bus stop. She stepped around the bench and glanced down at a brass plaque and saw it had a message engraved on it.

'Hey look at this, it has the name Christiansen on it, what does it say?'

Joakim sat down on the bench and rubbed the raindrops away.

'It says, *in memory of the family Christiansen, with grateful thanks, from the family Rosenbaum. We will never forget your sacrifice. Samuel Rosenbaum.'*

Lisa stood open-mouthed with surprise. 'Oh, that's lovely! I wonder who Samuel Rosenbaum is. Do you think he is still alive?' Joakim didn't reply, but started tapping on his phone.

'There's a Samuel Rosenbaum listed as Professor of Linguistics at the University of Bergen.'

'That can't be him. He would be too old to be a professor if he had been alive during the war.'

'True, but there is a small possibility that he might know how you could trace the Rosenbaum's who lived in Haugesund during the war. They might be related. Maybe he is one of their descendants.'

Lisa sat down on the bench and traced her fingers over the plaque. It was a little comforting to know that Moffa's family had been appreciated and remembered. The plaque and the bench were showing signs of weathering, but they could only have been put here a few years ago. Somebody somewhere had been told the story of the Christiansen family. She wished Moffa could have seen this.

'Edvard told me he used to play in the street outside his house with his friends. They used to walk down to the harbour and swim in the sea in the summer,' Joakim said, as he put his phone back in his pocket.

Lisa smiled and looked along the street and tried to picture her grandfather as a boy, before the war. There would have been fewer houses, perhaps, but even now it seemed like a nice place to live.

'He did have some happiness here, although I can see why he hadn't wanted to come back to this house. But, the fact that he never sold it shows that his heart belonged to Norway.'

'Are you changing your mind about keeping this house then?'

'No, but I am thinking of spending more time in Norway.'

'Really? Awesome!' Joakim pulled her along the bench towards him and kissed her.

Lisa broke away from him and stared into his eyes. Joakim grinned, and kissed her cheek, before looking at his watch.

'What would you say if I told you I was thinking of selling this house and buying or renting somewhere to live in Bergen?'

Joakim hugged her. 'That would be brilliant. But are you sure? What about your family and friends in Shetland?'

'But I have family and friends over here now, don't I? It doesn't matter where I live while I do my PhD. I want to get to know Norway better and this is the perfect opportunity. By the time I finish Hansi will be starting school, and I could move back to the UK if it didn't work out here.'

'It will work out. Trust me, Lisa, it will work out.'

'Do you think so? You don't feel...um, well, a bit suffocated?'

'Suffocated? Are you mad? You're the best thing to happen to me in years. No, I was just wondering whether to ask you and Hansi to come and live with me, and thinking that *you* might feel it was too soon.'

Lisa touched his cheek, not quite able to believe what he was saying. Was it too soon? In theory, it probably was. But her heart was telling her to throw caution overboard.

'We would love that. But only if you promise to teach us to ski.'

'That would be my pleasure.' Joakim squeezed Lisa's hand and they stood up to walk back to the car.

Lisa stared up at the sky and smiled when she saw a rainbow overhead. 'I think we have Moffa's blessing.'

Joakim looked up and laughed.

'I'm sure we do.'

The End

Dreaming in Norwegian

ABOUT THE AUTHOR

Frankie Valente lives in Shetland and works full time for a civil engineering company in Lerwick. She writes a column for Shetland Life magazine and writes fiction in her spare time. She has considerably more spare time than most people as she really doesn't enjoy watching television. She lives with her teenage son and stalks her eldest son via Facebook as he is currently living in New Zealand.

This is her fourth novel. The others are: Dancing with the Ferryman; Chasing an Irish Dream and Learning to Dance Again.

Twitter @frankievalente
Email frances.valente@hotmail.co.uk

Made in the USA
Monee, IL
24 July 2023